PATRICK BRIGHAM

JUDAS GOAT

THE KENNET NARROW BOAT MYSTERY

PATRICK BRIGHAM

JUDAS GOAT

THE KENNET NARROW BOAT MYSTERY

MEREO
Cirencester

Also by Patrick Brigham:

Herodotus: The Gnome of Sofia
Memoirs Publishing, 2013.

Also in eBook including Kindle.

Published by Mereo

Mereo is an imprint of Memoirs Publishing

25 Market Place, Cirencester, Gloucestershire GL7 2NX
Tel: 01285 640485, Email: info@mereobooks.com
www.memoirspublishing.com, www.mereobooks.com

JUDAS GOAT:
The Kennet Narrow Boat Mystery

ISBN: 9781861510006

Book jacket design Ray Lipscombe

Printed in England

For Matt and Louisa
'to remember me by'

"A rich man's war in poor man's blood
Silent their cries, the lost and loved
Led to the slaughter, led by false hope
Follow behind the Judas Goat."

Hosannas from the Basements of Hell Album Lyrics

CHAPTER ONE

THE KENNET AND AVON canal meanders from the River Thames just above Caversham lock in Reading, past the old Huntley and Palmers biscuit factory, through Highbridge wharf under London Street bridge, behind the old Simmond's brewery and on into the Berkshire countryside. From there on there is lock after lock, until you get to old Burghfield Bridge close to the Cunning Man public house and then on towards Old Aldermaston lock itself.

On the Reading side of the bridge there are many little dilapidated cruisers moored around a virtual island amongst which are a variety of colourful narrow boats. Ranging from twenty to seventy feet in length, the larger ones are occasionally used as homes or they make a good weekend retreat.

Painted in bright reds, blues and greens and other decorations of roses and castles, they are peculiarly English. Their history goes back to the 1830s and the Industrial Revolution. Then the digging of the canals across England was by the navigators, or navvies, as they were better known.

On the Kennet and Avon canal in those days, a

'barge and butty' could travel from Reading or London all the way to Bristol and the Severn estuary. They carried anything from bricks, beer, seeds, processed tobacco or biscuits, to heavy machinery and even livestock. On the way back they might carry Bristol glass or ceramics and wool or cotton from the colonies.

In the early days they were pulled by horses, or pulled and pushed by men. Sometimes they would even walk the narrow boats through tunnels by lying on the top of the boat and relentlessly pushing them through the darkness, scuffing with their hobnailed boots on the roof of the tunnel.

Working in all weathers and through long arduous days and weeks, the boats were often operated by whole families who needed to be tough to survive. Strong arms and legs were required to clamber on and off the many locks; to wind the paddles up and down with their windlasses, and strong backs were required to push open the lock gates.

Nowadays these boats have powerful diesel engines and are deceptively easy to manoeuvre due to their heavy weight and their shallow draft. But you still need to be agile and strong to manage the manually operated locks, with someone else to keep a firm hand on the tiller.

It was a midsummer's day in 2001 and although the morning had been hot, the afternoon was deliciously cool especially in the shade of a willow tree, or amongst the rushes and reeds that inhabit the bank. The water hardly moved. And apart from the splash of a Mallard duck, or the tweet of a red beaked Moorhen, the only other sound was the cough of a distant angler hidden somewhere amongst the reeds. Sometimes it was the plop of a pike or perch, as they jumped in the old millpond which now formed a part of the weir that ran into the canal that flowed from Old Aldermaston lock.

If you sat very still you could hear the crunch of a cow chewing the tall hedgerow grass in a nearby field, the chirp of a Pewit or Curlew, and maybe the distant sound of a haymaking tractor. Within this noisy silence, if you concentrated very intently, you might also hear the sound of the number nine Thames Valley bus honking its horn, crossing the narrow Burghfield Bridge; stopping by the Cunning Man public house, then on to the Mearings and the hamlet of Burghfield. But it was also the sound of nothing, and that is why people liked it so much.

In the shadow of a weeping willow tree, *Fienna* was moored next to a dilapidated metal shed which also served as the garage for an old Morris 1000 Traveller. *Fienna* was a seventy-two foot metal-hulled boat with a wooden superstructure housing a big open planned cabin at the front, an integral kitchen—with a smaller cabin next to it—and a separate bathroom. The rear cabin was partly made of metal, and contained the big Perkins diesel engine which propelled the boat through the canals.

Fienna was mainly painted in red, but the rear cabin housing the mechanical parts had an oblong green decorated sign on its side. It said *Fienna—Bristol*. But if you looked closely under the bright paint you could just read the name of the original owners, in relief, of this once working boat. It said *Willow-Wren Braunston*.

The boat was spotless. All the windows and portholes had recently been cleaned and polished, and on the roof, apart from the decorated chimney for the wood-burning stove, there was also a hand-painted watering can which stood next to a plastic trough of trailing flowers. Further up on the roof by the brass running rail was a painted water bucket and a mop. The owner had obviously been busy.

Running from the side of the boat was an electrical cable and a telephone line. Inside one could hear the sound of music and see the glow from the screen of a computer. The music came from two speakers next to the screen and was the unmistakable sound of *Art Tatum*. All the beds had been made and the carpets vacuumed. The kitchen gleamed and the pots and pans shone from the streaks of sunlight that passed through the window opposite. The phone was ringing.

A man sat in a Lloyd Loom cane chair at the front of the boat, seemingly deaf to the sound of the beckoning telephone whilst serenely content to gaze ahead at the peaceful setting—perhaps at the shafts of sunlight that shone through the willow tree, which played on the water between the little ripples of a feeding fish and the travelling water boatman. Or was he looking at the old oak tree in the small field opposite and the horse that stood beneath? It was swishing the flies away with its tale, its skin quivering from the irritating mosquitoes which had landed on its neck hoping for a late summer's day feed.

The man, in his fifties, looked quite hefty. His narrow features were almost Levantine, his eyes set wide apart and brown, his greying hair closely cropped and curly and his nose thin and sharp. He was grasping the *Sunday Telegraph* in his strong hands although it was Monday.

Dressed in a white and red striped shirt, he was wearing slightly dated narrow cavalry twill trousers and there was a double-breasted blazer draped over the back of the cane chair in which he sat. His brown, half brogue shoes were highly polished and he wore some obscure military or club tie. He was still sitting in the same position at 10.30 a.m., the following day, just as Art Tatum started to play 'Begin the Beguine' for the umpteenth time. A passing jazz-loving all-night fisherman stopped to ask him if he owned any other Art Tatum records, but he received no reply.

Rushing down the towpath, Henry Stillman ran into the Cunning Man public house and called the Police. Within ten minutes two uniformed Policemen arrived on the scene, closely followed by a Paramedic Ambulance. When they arrived at the boat they could clearly see that the man was staring into oblivion. Sergeant Wally Park had never seen anything like it before and Constable Adams was confused and somewhat ashen faced. He had only been on the force for three months and this was his first dead body.

'He's brown bread Sergeant, I'm afraid, he snuffed

it.' Paramedic Stuart Knowles had seen a lot of dead people in his time as a soldier in Iraq and later in Bosnia. 'I think he's been murdered, he's got a wound in his head! Who is he; does anybody know who he is?'

Henry Stillman was shocked and understandably agitated. 'Calm down Mr Stillman, there is nothing you can do for him now.' Sergeant Park knew his way around in this peculiarly provincial setting, although he was aware that nothing like this had happened in Burghfield for many years; well, not since the Second World War anyway.

'Take it slowly, take your time and tell me what you know.'

Stillman told him all he knew in his broad Reading accent. 'Well, it was like I said anat; no-one seems to know much about him... Alf the landlord at the Cunning Man said he didn't go to the pub much and kept hisself to hisself... Like I said, he's been staying here on his own for about a mumph, and no one knows who he is.'

The Sergeant seemed perplexed. 'Doesn't anyone know his name?'

Stillman's large shiny face seemed to show every process of thought by the way he frequently changed his facial expressions. 'Like I say, you will have to ask Alf at the pub anat, but he said that he was called Liam. Like I say, that's all I know.'

Sergeant Park had been on the force for over twenty years, so he well knew that this was a job for a specialist murder squad and he personally didn't really want any part of it.

'Adams, I want you to call up for some reinforcements and when they arrive I want you to cordon off the area and to close the towpath in both directions for about a mile. We don't want the local papers to know anything more than they have to. If someone asks you, just say that there has been an accident. And Adams, try not to fall in the river!' The Sergeant was getting near to retirement and rather disappointed with young police recruits.

'And you, Mr Stillman, I want you to wait here and then come with me to the police station, when the others arrive, to make your statement.' It was time for a spot of lunch anyway and they had shepherd's pie on the menu in the canteen that day. So he told the Paramedics to piss off and waited for the others to arrive.

Within twenty minutes and with no explanation, six hefty policemen from a special armed unit arrived from nowhere, the large powerful Inspector having told Constable Adams to keep out of the way and to stand by the bridge to keep the traffic on the move.

On the opposite bank, a hatless thin grey haired older man walked past *Fienna*, carrying a bag in which there seemed to be some kind of weapon. Taking up his position in a copse overlooking the whole stretch of the river, he removed an MP5 sniper rifle, attached a short seven shot clip and put an extra round into the breach. He connected his scope, pointed it either way up and down the river to focus it, and then sat back, lit a cigarette and waited.

As he watched, he saw a very unusual figure approaching down the towpath. Eddie Randhawa Singh seemed very out of place as he pushed the overgrown bushes out of his way, his red Turban bobbing from side to side, his bulky form almost bursting out of the loud checked suit he wore. Behind him was a rather seedy looking and balding man, carrying a Nikon D 90 camera, a flash and tripod. When he arrived the Indian Sikh turned to the armed police commander.

'What the hell's going on Inspector Timms, are we being invaded?' he asked. 'Is there something important you need to tell me?'

Eddie Singh was the local pathologist and Carmichael the Police photographer. Approaching the narrow boat Singh put on his thick glasses and laughed.

'Got a stiff one for me today I see.' Chuckling through his bushy beard, he turned once more to the Inspector. 'Blimey, I thought you boys were only interested in spooks and bank robbers! What the hell's happened here? I got a call saying someone had drowned in the river; seems it wasn't exactly true! Eh?'

In his early fifties, Inspector Timms seemed an equally incongruous figure. Decked out in a giant sized bullet proof vest, he was tougher than his growing paunch suggested. He liked Dr Singh because he was always jolly, which is more than you could say about the photographer Carmichael who never seemed to smile.

'We were up at the Royal Ordinance Factory, Eddie, helping the MOD police out with a little security problem they have, when we heard about it over the radio. We were the nearest team to the crime scene and came to help.'

His thick Belfast accent didn't seem somehow to fit into the tranquil English setting. He and Singh were both strangers in this part of the world. His strong hands pulled the mooring rope, bringing *Fienna* nearer to the canal bank so they could see the position of the man a bit better.

Timms continued: 'Adams said on the radio that a man had taken a round in the head—that's why we came running, Eddie, and quite honestly I really don't think you want the standard plod around with these cases, do you? They might have destroyed some of the evidence already.'

Eddie Singh put on his favourite yellow Marigold rubber gloves, which made him look more like an eccentric housewife than a pathologist. With some translucent plastic shoe covers, he carefully climbed onto the boat.

'Is Chief Inspector Lambert coming? He must surely be the best man locally. I expect we shall need some serious forensic people too by the looks of things.' Singh carefully inspected the side of the dead man's head, gently moving aside some of the curly grey hair for closer inspection.

'It is a very small bullet hole, and there seems to be very little blood around.' Then looking up at Timms through his highly magnified glasses, 'This could be a professional assassination job, you know. Better not move the body until forensics get here.'

Dr Singh looked briefly around the boat and into the nearby cabin. 'I don't suppose anyone has found a gun? Although, I can't see any powder burns so I doubt if it could possibly be a suicide. What do you think, Maurice?'

Maurice Timms left his own country to get away from the sight that was before him; you could have too much excitement in your life and also far too much death. 'That looks like C.I. Lambert coming now Eddie, let's leave it to him. This one is just up his street!' A lot of people believed in Michael Lambert.

Chief Inspector Michael Lambert sauntered towards the boat; his face sunburned from playing cricket for the police team the previous Sunday at the Jacks Booth cricket ground in Sulhamstead. He didn't seem to have a care in the world and was enjoying the summer weather.

'Nice music chaps; Art Tatum isn't it?' Lambert was a very untypical policeman. Dressed in an impeccable tailor-made lightweight pinstripe, he looked more like a bank manger than a detective.

'Is that the stiff that all this fuss is about?' He looked closer at the man and then remarked, 'That's funny; he's wearing a Cavalry and Guards Club tie.'

Carmichael took numerous photos as he swiftly mooched around the parameter of the boat, taking shots from every angle and from both sides of the river. With his powerful micro-macro zoom lens, he managed to photograph every detail of the man and the boat, at the same time not touching anything at all. He loved his Nikon camera.

He sneezed occasionally from an almost permanent bout of hay fever, which only really seemed to disappear in the smoke-filled bar of the Turks Head in London Road, Reading or the Gladstone Club in Eldon Square; he did not like the countryside very much.

Finally the photographer said to Lambert, 'Well Mr Lambert, that's all I can do until forensics have done their stuff and Dr Singh has taken the body away for an autopsy. I don't want to tread on any important clues, although the plod has probably done that already or those bloody paramedics. By the way, what sort of beer do they sell at the Cunning Man? Not eurocrap I hope.' Boring and dependable, Carmichael was off to visit familiar territory.

Michael Lambert was tall, trim and athletic, and very different from his colleagues who appeared to survive on a diet of best bitter and corned beef sandwiches. In his early fifties, he had the easy grace of a man who fitted into his own space.

What kept him in England, apart from his capricious wife Arabella, was not his son Jedd who now worked for Merrill Lynch as an investment banker, or his daughter Kate who studied cooking at Prue Leith in London; it was his consummate fascination with crime.

He was a policeman by nature, viewing the conspiracy theory as a very real part of his existence. It made him a difficult man to live with at times; a matter that his wife Arabella could easily attest to, but it instinctively made him a very good detective.

Forensic science is about the minute inspection of every item at a crime scene and every particle of dust and debris. The most important thing is not to disturb anything unnecessarily, to fingerprint every flat surface inside and out, and to look carefully at all the objects surrounding a murder victim.

The objective is to try and establish who they were; what they did, and how they died. How they died was often easy to explain and why they died. But in the case of the *Kennet Narrow Boat Mystery* as it came to be named, the motive for murder was not easy to establish, nor was the identity of the victim!

The contents of the corpse's pockets, when it was time to remove the body to the local mortuary, revealed very little other than quite a lot of cash and some petrol receipts. There was no identification, no credit cards, no address book or even a cell phone.

Dr Singh was confident that he would solve the mystery his way, and oddly enough even looked forward to the autopsy. The clothes the man was wearing would also be minutely searched by forensics in their laboratory later that day. Lambert hoped that his team would not be slapdash in any way and he begged them to take their time and to be careful.

The search of *Fienna* itself revealed very little in the end and whoever it was who had spring-cleaned the boat, it was obviously not the dead man. The shed containing the Morris Minor 1000 Traveller was equally unrewarding. But the car did have a registration number and Sergeant Park, having consumed a vast portion of shepherd's pie, was able to come up with some helpful answers when he phoned Lambert on his mobile later in the day.

'The car is apparently owned by a Mrs Cynthia Walters, and the address given is Rivercourt Road in Hammersmith; it's down near the Thames in London. I asked one of the Hammersmith lads to go and see her.'

Park had given up the traffic police years before, because he had got sick of spending his life on the M4 motorway. 'It's too bloody dangerous, with too many crashes and those London Paramedics are always late,' he had told his wife Donna. 'Talk about the golden ten minutes! With them it is the golden hour and then only if you're lucky.' The traffic going to and coming out of London was horrendous.

But he knew the routine. He also had to admit that this particular case fascinated him, which was most unusual. Twenty-five years as a copper hadn't completely stifled his interest in police work, despite being confined to a Panda car with an idiot like Constable Adams.

He told his wife Donna, 'He did, he bloody well fell into the canal, didn't he? He said—something like—his mum was going to write to the Super about getting danger money. I ask you! Then he said that his uniform had shrunk and he needed a new one!'

The good thing was that Constable Adams had somehow managed to make the radio call before he fell into the canal, prior to writing off his police radio transceiver!

Lambert was at the Cunning Man and on his second half of bitter shandy when Sergeant Park appeared. It was eight o'clock at night and the tow path was getting dark outside. Forensics have removed all their spotlights, their vacuum cleaners and had locked up the narrow boat. Adams was once more on duty keeping an eye on things. The diver had found nothing except an old bicycle, and a number of used condoms. There was no sign of a shell case and no gun; there was absolutely nothing. Maybe Dr Singh was right after all.

'What did you get from the landlord Guv, was he of any help? He seems a nice bloke, but I think he drinks more than his customers!'

Lambert liked Park, because he reminded him of his company Sergeant when he was a soldier in the Falklands. McEwen had said that the Sergeants ran the British army and Lambert had not disagreed with him. As a young Captain, when things went wrong, as they often did, his men always stood behind him. Wearing jeans, the off duty Sergeant was not surprised at what he heard.

'According to the publican, what was this man like Sir?' Park ordered himself a pint of Courage best bitter.

'He was monosyllabic, nervous, talked outside on his mobile phone a lot but never talked to anyone in the pub. He drank red wine, usually a second rate Merlot and chain-smoked all the time. Nobody visited him and none of the locals except Stillman even noticed him. He was a complete enigma.'

Lambert continued, 'You see, around here there are

only fishermen and weekend boaters. His was the only permanent mooring on that stretch of the canal, so there were no cosy chats or nosy neighbours. That's probably why he liked it here. By the way, did they find a mobile phone amongst his stuff? He must have had one. Anyway, tell me about the car?'

It was the old story. 'According to Hammersmith, Mrs Walters sold the car about five weeks ago for cash to a man calling himself Adrian Goodall. He said that he had seen it advertised in *The Trader*. He also seems to fit the description of our man, but he gave her an address in Putney Bridge Road. She thought nothing of it, partly because he gave her a very good price, so she grabbed the money and that was that. She just gave him the registration document, tore the bit off at the bottom, filled in the details he gave her and sent it off to Swansea.' Park swilled the remaining beer around the pint glass he was holding. 'He didn't even want a receipt.'

He continued: 'The Hammersmith boys got in touch with Swansea, who then found the slip which she had sent, got his exact address and went there to see what was going on. When they got there nobody had heard of him or seen him, so it was obvious he didn't live there at all. There was just an old lady living there. They got a written description from Mrs Walters, confirming that it was our man and really that's all I've got to report Sir.'

It was ten o'clock when they both left the Cunning Man and while Park went home to Donna and his house in Links Drive, Tilehurst, Mike Lambert took a short walk down the canal to look at *Fienna* and to think over a few things. It was getting dark, but he could easily see Constable Adams standing there. He was inspecting the contents of a sandwich before finally biting into it and consigning it to its irredeemable demise.

'Evening Mr Lambert, I'm just having a bite to eat. Nothing's happening and no one has been down the canal. Bit boring really.' Perhaps Sergeant Park was right about Adams.

Now that the boat had been thoroughly inspected and searched, Lambert could look around at his leisure. Shining his pencil torch on the surface, he walked around the outside of the boat and then by standing on the gunnels, he was able to inspect the surface for any signs of a fight or damage, but there was none to be seen. He unlocked the hatchway with the key Park had given him, climbed down the steps into the cabin and switched on the 12-volt lighting.

He looked into the cupboards, searched the kitchen, the bathroom and toilet, but it was spotless. He sat and looked through the dead man's CDs and saw that he had quite a comprehensive jazz collection. Bobby Timmons, Errol Garner, Oscar Peterson, Keith Jarrett, and even a rare copy of Ruby Braff playing at Ronnie Scott's club. Lambert preferred pianists but he also loved Ruby who he regarded as the best trumpeter in the world.

After he had swallowed the remnants of his sandwich, Adams stuck his head around the hatchway door. 'Excuse me Sir, I don't want to interrupt you or anyfing, but I saw something unusual through the window of the boat just now and I couldn't work out what it was being dark and all. It's jammed between that locker and the bed just behind the curtain. I saw a tiny green light flashing, you can hardly see it. Do you know what it is? I thought that they had disconnected the mains electricity and the telephone just before they left, and that only leaves the boats batteries and the 12-volt supply.'

Lambert yawned; it had been a long day. It was time to face Arabella, to go home to Sonning Village and to find out about any further shortcomings with their relationship. How she hated his job.

'I don't understand you Mike, you are much too classy for your job, and they don't pay you enough for what you do and most of them are such silly berks. You could have easily gone into the City when you left the army, made some money by now and we would have been much better off. Instead you had to become a bloody policeman. It's so naff. We have got nothing to show for our life together except that rotten little hovel in France. I don't know why you like it so much? If it weren't for Daddy, we wouldn't be living anywhere decent now.' She was right; perhaps it was time to do something else and to move on.

During the summer he would sometimes spend his leave at the little house in Normandy, surrounded by books and his stamp collection. Whilst most of his police contemporaries took a package tour to Benidorm or to Tenerife, it was where he could escape from Arabella.

She never came with him, although, just occasionally the children came for a few days.

'There it is Sir, forensics must have missed it in the daylight; look, you can just see it. I think it's a very small mobile phone.'

Perhaps Adams wasn't so useless after all. Lambert somehow moved it out of its hiding place with his penknife and onto the floor. Picking it up and depositing it into a small plastic bag, he slipped the tiny cell-phone into his pocket. It was time to face yet another lonely night in the spare bedroom.

It was six o'clock in the morning when he was woken by the shrill ringing of the mobile. He had not switched off the cell-phone and quite sensibly he didn't answer it. Lambert quietly pattered down the stairs to the kitchen, past the portraits of Arabella's recently acquired ancestors and the bric-à-brac of twenty-five years of accumulated family possessions. He let their white Labrador Samanda out into the garden and she bolted off at great speed.

It was a dull day and the garden was looking tired after the long hot summer. There was a hose ban in the area and their nosy neighbours made sure that the lawns and flowerbeds were not watered. The garden was Arabella's job. Hopefully today it would rain. Under the water regime they could only use a watering can which was cause for further criticism due to his protracted absences.

Samanda bounced around on the thinning lawn for a bit and then disappeared into the shrubbery. The roses were shedding their petals and the flowering cherry tree stood gauntly overlooking the swimming pool which was hardly used these days. The dog sniffed loudly at the undergrowth, where Lambert grew tarragon, basil and fresh horseradish. Growing herbs was one of the few passions which he and Arabella still shared.

Whatever one said about Arabella she was a very good cook, as was their daughter Kate. Suddenly the hiss and gurgle of the Braun coffeemaker intruded into his thoughts, and he turned away from the garden door back to the kitchen. A strong mug of black coffee and a Marlboro cigarette would start the day. He would go to his office early and get on with the case. Murders needed to be solved quickly before the press became too involved with speculation, criticism and intrusion.

In the driveway and parked next to Arabella's Citroen *Deux Chevaux*, Lambert's dark red Alvis TF21 was about the only stylish car left in the village. Sonning had always been the nouveau riche area of Reading, although remarkably, the inhabitants still possessed a very pronounced provincial attitude. Now, everyone had to buy more and more expensive cars in order to display their wealth.

At one time Sonning had been a place for slightly dotty artists, writers and show business personalities. These days it was mainly businessmen and footballers, garishly and ostentatiously spending their money; jabbering about their successful investments, whilst guzzling expensive cocktails at the White Hart Hotel.

Lambert couldn't stand them anymore and preferred the little pubs and restaurants in Henley, because at least they still retained a certain character and old world charm.

The thick paint gleamed on the original Park Ward bodywork although the morning was dull and the 153 BHP three-litre engine rumbled into action at the first touch of the starter button. With the chrome plated spoked wheels and the knock on hubs twirling in a sudden ray of morning sunshine, Lambert made his way to his office in Castle Hill and a world that Arabella totally despised.

The only real change to his totally authentic Alvis was a new CD player. Driving down the Henley Road towards Reading, it was the sound of Jimmy Smith that filled the car. Grady Tate was singing 'She's out of my life,' which seemed very apt to Lambert under his present circumstances. As he drove into the police parking area he was still listening to 'We Can Make it Work' when he came to a stop with a final rev of the powerful engine.

The first thing he did was to hand over the cell phone to the duty Sergeant and to tell him to get the CID specialist to dust it and then to get the contents analysed. It was an important piece of evidence because it had a direct connection to the dead man.

'Ask them to get me a printout of any stored telephone numbers, and the last phone calls he might have made. Also, tell them that I want to know the contents of the computer on the narrow boat and any emails that might have been sent or received.'

When he got to his office there was a pile of paperwork, some magazines and a number of photographs for him to look at. It seemed that things had moved along quite a bit, despite the short time that had elapsed since the original phone call from Stillman. *Fienna* was a pretty boat and Carmichael's coloured pictures were excellent.

Shots of the dead man were more like portraits than police photos, thanks to the rather dull Carmichael, all of which he studied carefully. The victim appeared totally at ease, his face in repose seeming quite normal. It was almost as though he had just quietly died one sunny afternoon. But Eddie Panisar Singh's interim report told another story.

To Chief Inspector Lambert

Case Officer Thames Valley Serious Crime Division.

Dear Mike,

We have carried out a full autopsy on the victim, and briefly we have found that although the bullet which might have finally killed him was from some sort of .22 target pistol, he had been heavily drugged beforehand. He had also received an injection of Potassium Chloride directly into his heart. This would account for the small amount of blood found from the head wound. The shooting was a sort of coup de gras, but the injection stopped his heart. Perhaps the bullet was a final statement by someone. Therefore he was unquestionably murdered.

Because we found evidence of large amounts of Thiopentone Sodium or Sodium Pentothal in his bloodstream, it would account for the fact that he was so easily killed. Other than a number of injection punctures in his left and right arms and a little bruising, he seems not to have put up any kind of fight at all. They must have lightly held him down because he was heavily drugged.

Whoever killed him must have placed him in his Lloyd Loom chair and just shot him, perhaps from a distance of about ten feet or so, because there were no powder burns or discharges that I could see. It was a low velocity .22 shell, much as you can find anywhere in the UK, which is why there is no exit wound.

Paramedic Stuart Knowles knew what he was talking about. Also, what was strange; although I am waiting for a complete analysis from a specialist laboratory, was that the victim was dying anyway. His stomach, when we inspected him, was full of cancerous growth and I don't suppose he had much time left to live anyway. What is also very odd are the contents of his stomach. There was only a little bread, some potatoes and a little water, as you might expect with a man in his condition. How he could go to a pub and drink red-wine simply baffles me; he should have been in a hospice.

Other than that, there were no noticeable scars; he had received no operations, other than an appendix removal; probably when he was very young. There appears to be a puncture mark in his side—maybe from a bullet wound—but that too was very old and hardly noticeable. However, he appears to have had some plastic surgery in the past ten years and his teeth were capped. This was all top class work and probably carried out in Germany or the States.

I would put his age at about early fifties and although he seemed reasonably fit from the outside it is clear that he was obviously not. At a guess, I would say from his general appearance that he had been an athlete, a soldier or perhaps a policeman. His muscle tissue had not deteriorated too much, and so he must have been quite active in the recent past. We are having a nuclear DNA test done today and sometime this week, a mitochondrial DNA test as well. Also, we will have a detailed blood grouping and analysis later on too.

From his general deterioration, I would put the time of death at about twenty-four hours, prior to his discovery by Mr Stillman. Because he'd been sitting in the sun and therefore quite warm, rigor mortis had practically dissipated.

That is all I can tell you for now, and I will contact you later on, and give you my full report as soon as I can.

All the best,

Eddie Singh.

CHAPTER TWO

LOOKING THROUGH the thick security window in his first floor office, the day was becoming even duller. Lambert went down to the parking lot and put up the hood of his beloved Alvis which he then drove into the underground section of the police car park. Whoever the love of his life might have been in the past, they now had chrome wire wheels and a very long bonnet. Lambert looked at his watch, considered phoning Arabella but didn't, and then thoughtfully walked back to his office.

Arabella Lambert lived in a world of clichés and stereotypes. Belying her background, she seemed to have given up her obsession with social standards, loyalty and the slightly dated set of values she and her family had once held so dear.

Although it was not that unusual for wealthy middle class parents like hers to pamper their children or to offload some of their assets—perhaps to help their grandchildren by paying for a private education—Arabella always complained about her husband's inability to provide enough from his income.

Their daughter, Kate, went to Roedean as had

Arabella before her. But, mainly due to his dyslexia, Jebb had chosen to go as a dayboy to Summerlake College. It was not far from their home in Sonning and near enough for him to cycle to school each day. Private education was not usually on the cards for a policeman's children and so the bill was paid by his father-in-law, George Mostyn.

When he was free from police work, Lambert enjoyed teaching Jebb how to play cricket and Jebb in turn introduced his father to the river. Summerlake is a Thameside rowing school and by the time he was sixteen, Jebb was rowing in one of the school's eights at stroke. Lambert always thought that it was part of normal family life and felt content with the way things were.

Arabella's father had served in the army during the Second World War, so he had a strong empathy with his son-in-law—who had served in the cavalry—and enjoyed his company as much as he did his daughter's. He visited them frequently, especially after the death of his wife Dorothy, and when Lambert's time came as a young Major to finally leave the army, Arabella's father George Mostyn offered him a job in his successful public relations firm in London. Mike had refused the offer, but this was mainly because he didn't really know what he wanted to do.

The army was easy and cosseting. In the beginning, Arabella seemed to enjoy the usual upheaval when various new postings occurred and they had to move house. But after Abu Dhabi she seemed anxious to have a permanent home. Lambert's secondment to the Army of Abu Dhabi had been fun for her in the beginning and she had thoroughly enjoyed the expatriate social life and the famous "Club." Of course she enjoyed the money too, and with frequent trips home to visit family and friends, it seemed an ideal life for a young tank commander and his family. Enjoying the largess of this tiny Emirate in the Middle East was especially true for their two young children who made many friends during their school holidays.

The reality of civilian life was considerably different. George Mostyn realised that his son-in-law was not destined for the PR business, and so he bought them a pretty house at the end of Sonning Lane in the Berkshire Thameside village. It was the final gesture of his acceptance.

A six-month course at Hendon Police College, followed by three stressful years with the Metropolitan police as a uniformed policeman in Notting Hill, and Lambert was quickly promoted to Sergeant. As part of a rapid promotion leadership scheme for officers, it was not long before he was promoted to the rank of Inspector. Deciding to move to the less challenging environment of Reading, and to be closer to his family, he had finally transferred to Reading as a senior detective in the Thames Valley Serious Crime Division. He had been there ever since.

Lambert's mother and father were tenant farmers in Staffordshire and he had therefore come from quite a down-to-earth background. With only three hundred acres, although they were considered wealthy by local standards, they could not afford to pamper Lambert or his brother Tom. Jebb and Kate would often stay when young with their grandparents for a month in the summer, helping to milk the dairy herd, and enjoying a ride on the tractor. Then things began to change.

Twenty years on and Arabella was almost completely preoccupied with money and possessions. She had become envious, grouchy and uncharacteristically snobby. When their children were young, family life had always been so much fun. Now, with the encroaching lines of middle age serving to challenge her all-consuming self-approval, she had lost any interest in Lambert and their once redeeming lust for one another.

These days she expected far more from life than her snobby friends, her extensive collection of Meissen porcelain, her array of Czechoslovakian glass paperweights; the dolls and the dollhouses, because these days she also wanted some adventure too.

Quite recently she had discovered new life in the pseudo art world of the Maidenhead Chamber of Artists. In so doing, it was amongst their number that she had also found consolation in the arms of an equally unknown local artist called Marcus Smith. He instinctively knew how to flatter Arabella and her mediocre paintings, as she also did with his random daubings; his blobs and his splobs.

Away from her middle class existence, she now chose to share Marcus Smith's menopausal world; the complete opposite to everything she had claimed to represent in the past. Capitalising on their two children's newly realised independence, she instinctively believed that it was the right time to part from Lambert. His practical nature also told him that it was the end; the only question remaining was who would take the first step?

It was a strange collection of magazines, presumably dumped on his desk by one of the forensic boys, which to him seemed of little interest. Scientists are only concerned with microscopes, electronic gadgets, test tubes and solvents. Lambert casually looked through the pile, in order to understand what the murder victim's interests might have been. There were some old copies of the *Shooting Times*, some light porn, the glossy sections from the *Sunday Times* and *Independent*, together with a holiday brochure about Havana.

But there was one odd one out. It was called the *Balkan Western News* and it was published in English. An old edition, it had become dog-eared since its original publication in a country called Bulgaria. On the front cover there was a cartoon of some unknown foreign politician or businessman. On the front inside page there was an announcement about The Queen's Birthday Celebrations at the British Embassy in the capital called Sofia, together with a photograph of a wedding couple and reports on various local events. There was also an article called 'The Field of Blackbirds' concerning NATO and in particular Kosovo, headed by a black and white photograph of General Wesley Clark waving a silver plated rifle in the air. It was a report from Pristina on the ongoing disturbance.

As he leafed through the pages he abruptly stopped. It was then that he saw him. Very much like the murder victim from the narrow boat, he was smiling from a page called 'The Editor Rambles On'. Not a very good photo, but it was unquestionably like him. Underneath the photo, he was named as being Liam Side and Lambert couldn't believe his luck. Suddenly the case was beginning to fit together, or so he believed!

The fingerprint report was a little more disappointing and other than the fact that they were able to take the fingerprints from the corpse, the boat and the car had been completely wiped clean. Apart from those of Sergeant Park, Stuart Knowles and of course Constable Adams, there were no other prints to be found. They had run the victim's prints through the police computer twice, but to no avail and so on this account, his identity remained a mystery.

Stillman, who had lent over to touch the victim by holding on to the roof of the front cabin, had left a palm print. Although he had been the first person to find the dead man, his statement and that of Alf at the Cunning Man was virtually useless. Perhaps Stillman was an all-night fisherman because he was thick. But as far as the man Liam Side was concerned, there were no clues to why he had been killed or by whom.

The press then started to become a nuisance. At a press conference, Lambert found himself quoting the usual police platitudes. 'Detective Chief Inspector

Lambert, can you tell us anything about the dead man, who he was and if you expect to determine the cause of death shortly?' It was a journalist from the local television station, plus the usual bunch of newspaper reporters and some stringers from the nationals.

'We have presently been unable to identify the victim, but I am able to tell you that he was a male and probably died sometime early on Sunday morning.' He couldn't believe the banality of this statement, but it was recommended by the police so called public relations department for all such occasions.

'Was he murdered or did he die under mysterious circumstances?' Fred Dodd of the *Post* was only able to ask this one question because of his terrible hangover. It was ten o'clock on Tuesday morning and the pubs were not open until eleven.

'All I can say is that he died under very questionable circumstances and that we are continuing with our inquiries; however, I can say that we are presently treating it as an unlawful killing. And that is all I can tell you at the moment.' Lambert thought that it was almost time for the police to employ an imaginative speechwriter, if nothing else than to convince the public that all policemen were not a bunch of mindless idiots. 'We will be releasing a statement to the press later on today. Thank you Ladies and Gentlemen, I'm afraid that is all I can say for the time being.'

Thirty minutes later his mobile phone rang. 'I've just seen you on the news Dad, you looked very posh! I hope mummy doesn't hate you for it. How are things at the moment?' Kate loved them both, but now found herself far too often in the middle of a battle and so she stayed put in London. It also proved that the murder case was irredeemably in the public eye.

Lambert was more interested in his daughter. 'How is that new flat of yours in Wandsworth? Have you got all the things you need, and when can mummy and I come and see it?' He knew she didn't want them to come, that she had her own friends and wanted to keep her independence.

'I'm coming down to Sonning soon Dad and I will tell you all about it then if you like. Anyway, good luck with the case, I love you.' It was always the same, one mystery after another. Children were suddenly none of your business, but if you were lucky, one day they might simply become friends.

'George, do you know anybody who can bring that narrow boat up to the police wharf on the Thames?' It was time for the scene of the crime to be moved. They had done everything that needed to be done in Burghfield. George Durant was his most trusted Detective Sergeant who had been Lambert's assistant for almost ten years. Never taking promotion, Lambert suspected it was because of his loyalty to him. All he knew was that he couldn't do without him.

'The Missis and I did a trip on the Norfolk Broads once Boss, so I reckon I could bring it down to the Thames police boatyard with the help one of the guys from the River Police, I'd enjoy that.' Lambert gave him the thumbs up as he bit into a bacon sandwich from the Police canteen. 'Will this afternoon be all right with you, Boss? I assume you will need me later on?' The thought of George running across the lock gates made Lambert chuckle, for he was becoming more than a little overweight.

'If you like George, but don't do yourself an injury, because I am going to need your undivided attention in the next few days. Oh! And take that idiot Adams with you, he knows all about canals. I hear he fell in the drink the other day, so he should be a bit of an expert by now!'

Spending so much time on police work generally meant that colleagues became your family after a while, and despite the many tragic circumstances they might have to share, there could be happy times as well.

Most killings were domestic, easy to establish and were not very compelling. The racially motivated deaths were the most confusing, together with the odd street fight or stabbing. As it was with alcohol, so it was with drugs and there was very little premeditation involved. Despite a few plausible stories and ridiculous alibis, very few cases took more than a few days to button up.

After that there were the predictable feelings of guilt, admissions, statements and finally a formal arrest. Holding people on suspicion for twenty-four hours usually achieved a run-of-the-mill detective's job for them. If people became tired; that was when they broke down emotionally during an interrogation. When faced with often basic evidence, other people's statements and the usual contradictions, offenders generally gave up quite easily. This was followed by a trip to the Crown Prosecutor's Office, a visit to a magistrate's court and finally, to the Assizes to give police evidence. To some extent, Lambert also lived a predictable existence.

But the *Kennet Narrow Boat Mystery* was very different, because it had a definite international flavour to it. Chief Superintendent Ken Burrows spoke to Lambert at his office that afternoon. 'Listen Lambert, I know things are a bit tricky for you at home but you have really got to stay on the ball with this one. MI5 is poking around and when I spoke to the Home Office yesterday, that git Kranz said Side might be on an old list of Irish volunteers. He thought that our man might be one of the boys from the Ardoyne although I know all that stuff is supposed to be over by now. Anyway it's surely worth considering unless you want the sodding spooks crawling around all over the place.'

Lambert also didn't want Scotland Yard involved at this stage, although they knew him well enough and had always trusted him in the past. 'I understand Sir, but we still haven't got the full forensic report and I am also waiting for the run down on the computer. Then there are the contents of a cell phone which the unremarkable Constable Adams found late last night!'

Back in his office he listened to the cell phone and IT report with interest. 'It's a mixture of some English, what looks like Russian and a bit of Spanish. I know it's a GSM, but it operates with one of those Swiss call back cards, so there is no detailed account of the incoming calls and it operates with a pre-pay card which could have been bought almost anywhere in the world. I'll have to contact someone in Zurich to get some answers and to discover when and where the phone card was originally purchased.'

Marty Collyer was an Australian who had recently discovered that the web boom was starting to decline in the UK, despite all the optimistic financial reports in the FT. He believed that it was better to get a reliable job rather than hanging around wine bars hoping that he would be paid by some wunderkind at the end of the month. Reading Police were lucky to get him and not some 'also ran' which was the usual case these days. Anyway, it was much easier to get on with an Aussie than some locally grown and spoilt techno-brat.

Lambert's interest in the pre-paid phone card was now increasing dramatically. 'I don't suppose we have got any Russian speakers on the force, have we? If not I'm afraid it looks like we will have to go to the Met whether we like it or not.'

Gloria Hislop was an exception to the rule. She had studied Russian and Slavic languages at Leeds University in order to become a translator, but sitting in her ground floor apartment in Southcote, she was well aware that life had not quite worked out as she had originally planned, especially when she passed her MA Dip with honours. After a visit to Yellow Pages, Lambert had found her quite easily and it was all because of an ill-fated student car crash.

Confined to her wheel chair, at first Gloria Hislop had wallowed in self-pity. Then came a visit from a shady government official, who wondered if she might like to become a translator in some forlorn underdeveloped godforsaken part of Eastern Europe?

'It would be to help the local British Embassy glean information from the newspapers and the local community.' The pseudo upper-class accent was far too nasal and tinny to be real, making him sound rather more like a pompous West London estate agent. She had been warned about these clowns and had expected a visit all along.

But they had obviously not known about her wheelchair, because by then it hadn't appeared in her university records. It had all sounded so sleazy to her, as was the little weasel of a man who had come to see her. But how was she to make a living? That was the question that confronted her for a very long time.

The answer came quite unexpectedly with a changing world order, and after the Berlin wall was so successfully dismantled, she found her language skills in great demand. It was a time when many British businessmen decided to go to Eastern Europe and try their hand at investing in the flourishing embryonic bond markets. In the end and carried along by the prevailing vogue, she became a translator and editor of Russian and Eastern European literature. A short course in computer studies at Reading Technical College and the world came alive for her once more.

Now, in her comfortable and semi-automated

environment—or as much as her well organised but immobile condition would allow—she had established her independence. Possessing almost everything that her disability required, and brandishing a highly sophisticated handheld programmer—with a lot of her own inspiration and imagination—it seemed to accomplish all the things which she had previously been unable to do without assistance.

Not only did it operate her TV and combined computer screen, but it also opened and closed the curtains, switched the electric kettle on and off, operated all the security video cameras and controlled the security door. In her self-created thoroughly independent world she no longer needed the aid of any social workers, just a little domestic help once a week. Also, she most especially did not need the assistance of any sordid little spooks from Battersea. Her resolve did weaken however, when C. I. Lambert strolled down the garden path and rang her doorbell.

To Lambert she seemed such a cheerful character and he didn't want to leave when their business discussion was over, although he was finally forced to say, 'I am afraid you will have to sign the Official Secrets Act, Miss Hislop, if you work for the police. But don't let it worry you unduly because you would have to sign it even if you were to work as a Christmas postman!'

The mobile telephone held over thirty telephone numbers in its memory. Despite the fact that it had been locked with a pin code, Collyer had easily extracted the information, once he had spoken to the telephone manufacturer in London, the local GSM provider and to Swiss-com in Zurich. Between them, they had successfully instructed him on how to open the *magic box of tricks* which would allow him to download the information he required. Lambert faxed a copy through to Gloria Hislop at once.

'It is not Russian Mr Lambert, its Bulgarian or Serbian,' Gloria Hislop said over the phone as she viewed the list with an experienced eye. 'The alphabet is practically the same—it's called Cyrillic—but there are quite big differences particularly when it comes to people's family names. The alphabet is named after two brothers who lived in Bulgaria many hundreds of years ago, called St Cyril and St Methodius. They invented this alphabet for Slavonic languages in about 400 AD, although these days, many countries are returning to the international Latin text. Judging by the telephone prefix codes, most of these phone numbers are in the capital of Bulgaria which is called Sofia.' Gloria Hislop's enthusiasm had finally created a little continuity to the case.

'Have you been able to translate the names into Latin script for me, Miss Hislop?' Lambert wrongly believed that he might be able to telephone someone who spoke English in order to make enquiries about Side.

'Don't worry about that Mr Lambert, because I can do that for you.' Gloria Hislop literally glowed with enthusiasm as she explained her findings to him. She liked the idea that she was clever and very often had to underline the fact. 'I've been able to do more than that because I also speak a little Spanish. So I have checked the telephone codes and nearly all the Spanish sounding names are not from Spain at all, but from Peru, Columbia and Ecuador. The rest are numbers in various countries, probably for hotels, airports and taxis, and I suspect some girls as well. There may be a couple of numbers in Cuba but I'm not totally sure of its international code right now, because Cuba is a very rare telephone destination.'

It was early Wednesday evening and Gloria Hislop's email confirmation of all these facts would have to wait until the following morning. It was time for cricket practice. Driving his Alvis along the Shinfield Road, he turned left into Luton Park School where the police cricket team occasionally used the nets. Parking well away from the sports ground he stepped out and opened the trunk of his classic car, took out his whites, cricket pads and boots, and an aging cricket bat which had been signed by Brian Lara. The trunk of the Alvis closed with a beautiful metallic clunk.

The Police team was practicing in the nets, and George Durant was attempting to spin a ball past Adams. At that very moment, Lambert's respect for Adams as a cricketer improved markedly, because as he watched, Adams whacked the ball out of the nets and into the car park only missing his Alvis by inches. 'That was quite a shot Adams,' he said breathlessly, having retrieved the ball. 'I hope you can do that again next Sunday.'

The Reading Cricket League final was being played once more at the Jacks Booth cricket ground in Sulhamstead. That Sunday the police team was playing Reading first team, amongst which were two notable ex-police offenders. Both Jamaican brothers were good pace bowlers although in the past they had a tendency to become over enthusiastic when playing the police team. It was not always as amusing as it sounded, especially if you were on the receiving end of a fast ball. They were both good cricketers though, and Lambert believed that one day they would easily get into a county side; if they kept their noses clean.

It was then that Lambert had a premonition that he would not be there for the match. Something was nagging at him in the back of his mind, as George Durant came plopping towards him in his ancient white canvas gym shoes. The cricket sweater he was wearing seemed to be two sizes too small and systematically crept up over his growing stomach with each passing cricket season.

'We moved the boat up to the police wharf as you asked Boss, which was great. Nobby from the river police steered the boat; I did the ropes while Adams did all the jumping on and off at the locks, and by the way, he didn't fall in once!'

Adams started to laugh and Lambert put on his pads. Taking his place at the crease he asked Durant for middle and off. Then the balls started raining down on him from all directions which he either kneed into the net or blocked with his bat, mainly off the front leg.

'I've still got your key to the hatch if you want to go down later Boss, but the boat is the same as it was when we found it, apart from a few empty beer cans. But that's boating for you!' George Durant spun a googly past Lambert's right ear and gave him a smug look.

After an hour the light started getting bad, so they pulled up stumps and the team made their way home. Lambert took off his pads and still wearing his whites he drove out of the gates down to the Thames. His CD was playing a Mose Allison blues number.

"*If your thoughts were worth money, you wouldn't be worth a dime. Your mind is on vacation, and your mouth is working overtime…*" The chaotic piano style was the hallmark of this famously cranky musician.

When he got to the wharf it was nine thirty and practically dark. He steered the Alvis into the Thames boatyard and parked leaving the sidelights on. *Fienna* was tied up next to an old barge moored there by the Thames Water Authority. The barge was full of old pieces of timber and detritus pulled that day from the river. There were plastic bags, the remains of a sunken clinker built rowing boat, a bicycle and finally a rusty Lada motorcar. It was incredible the things that people dumped into the river just because they didn't care.

When he got onto the narrow boat he noticed that the lock on the hatch entrance was broken, and although it seemed a little odd he still entered the saloon. As his eyes became accustomed to the dark he fumbled around to find the 12-volt light switch. In the middle cabin he could just see the outline of a seated figure smoking a cigarette. He thought it might be Sergeant Nobby Jones.

'That you, Nobby? Are you going to be at the match next Sunday?' But there was no reply. Instead he felt a terrible pain in the back of his head, a blinding flash and then nothing at all. When he came to he saw that the lights were finally on with Nobby Jones standing over him.

'Are you all right Sir? There were two of them. I saw them running past your Alvis. You left the sidelights on; they must have been looking for something important.' Jones nodded his head disapprovingly. 'This bloody case gets weirder and weirder doesn't it,' and then finally, 'do you need a doctor, Sir?'

Lambert knew that he was getting too old for this game, but he said no out of pride. 'What did they look like Nobby; did you get a good look at them?' He felt the bump on the back of his head and the warm blood on his neck.

'Not really Sir, it happened so fast; but I did get a look at their car and I've got the registration number— it was a Morris Minor Traveller!'

Damn it, thought Lambert, it's that bloody car again! We must have missed something important in it; I knew we should have ripped it apart. Why did we leave it parked in that shed, how stupid can we be? But, only he knew the answer.

'Get on the radio and put out a full alert, airports and ferries, the lot. We have got to find those bastards before they cause any more problems.' Jones helped Lambert to his feet and held his arm as he got off the boat.

'Are you sure you can drive Sir?' But he didn't answer. The fresh air was starting to clear his head. As he painfully walked towards the Alvis and slumped behind the driving wheel he asked, 'Did they say anything that you can remember, Nobby?'

Nobby Jones handed Lambert some tissues, then shook his head. 'Well Sir, I don't know what they said. It sounded like Russian or Polish to me. Anyway, they were shouting at each other in some funny language so I can't really say!'

Arriving at the house in Sonning he could see that Arabella's car was in the driveway. He hoped that for once she would be capable of an unselfish act but unfortunately once more, he was due for a disappointment.

'You bloody fool. When are you going to stop this crap and be a normal husband? Why don't you stop playing little boys games and let the Neanderthals deal with it? Don't you care about anything except that silly job of yours? You're fifty years old for God's sake!'

On balance she might have been right, but tonight Lambert decided that he'd had enough of Arabella and she could finally go to hell. Perhaps it was time for a few weeks away from her or even a trip abroad? He put his head under a cold shower, which helped to make the pain go away and he then looked into the mirror to inspect his scalp. It wasn't a bad abrasion and the bleeding had almost stopped. Taking four Aspirin and a sleeping pill, he wrapped his aching head in a damp hand towel and went to bed. Arabella could wait, but those foreign bastards could not.

It might have been the cricket but he doubted it, because the following morning, he found getting out of bed to be a particularly painful process. But a long hot shower had made the difference, and leaving the house early before Arabella emerged, he carefully drove to Reading determined to consume a large greasy police breakfast in the canteen. Bill Evans was playing '*A waltz for Debby*,' causing him to remember an old 33 with Tony Bennett singing his beautiful words. 'Streuth,' he thought, 'that is going back a bit!'

George Durant believed that his day should always start with a good blow out, and he was wiping his plate with a slice of Sunblest as Lambert walked in and sat down at the same table. 'I hear you got a bit of a smacking last night Boss! All right, are you? I understand that they were some bloody foreigners. According to our Nobby, he said that the way they were jabbering away, they might have been Ruskies or Polaks.'

Two Cumberland sausages, four rashers of smoked back bacon, and a great pile of bubble and squeak helped to slow down the thinking process. Poking his fork into both fried eggs, Lambert gave Durant a resigned look. The yoke dribbled over the bacon which he then squirted with tomato sauce. 'Might have been bloody Bulgarians you mean.' Lambert wished that they served real coffee in the canteen and not watery owls' piss.

The email confirmed everything. Gloria Hislop was exact and capable and had accurately described the memory contents of the Motorola handy. It was now Thursday morning and in the email she concluded that she needed his full instructions on how to proceed and a copy of the famous Official Secrets Act. She also had a contract for Thames Valley Police to sign as well. Ten years as a translator had underlined the need for correct paperwork. Over the phone she laid out her proposals.

'I thought that I could tell the people I phone in Sofia that you are a relative of this man Liam Side, whoever he may be, and just judge their reaction. Also, you could contact the British Embassy and see if they have some information. There may be someone who knew him? Anyway, phone me later Mr Lambert.'

His head was aching like hell and not unexpectedly the greasy breakfast was beginning to react on him. Turning to his office coffee machine, he made himself some very strong black filter coffee which helped to clear his drowsy head. The report from Collyer about the computer was equally flawed. The deceased did not have an email provider, just an internet server. This had been pre-paid in the name of one Peter Jarvis, who apparently owned the boat and who paid for the telephone as well. They had tracked him down to an apartment in Oxford, where Oxford Constabulary had interviewed him the previous night.

'We believe that the victim must have used Hotmail or Yahoo for all his messages, sent or received, which means that it is practically impossible to discover his email address and password without spending a lot of time on it. It's a real drag.' Collyer had looked through his own Hotmail service directory for a Liam Side, which had listed a number of people with that name, including one in Bulgaria. Hotmail has a confidentiality agreement with all its users and they would have to ask the Americans if they wanted further information.

It turned out that Peter Jarvis was just a woolly-minded lecturer in building technology at Oxford Polytechnic, who rented his narrow boat out during the summer, and had the same story as Cynthia Walters.

'He said he met this man called Adrian Goodall, who paid the full asking price in cash—two months' rent in advance plus a month's deposit—and that he was as pleased as punch.' George Durant's intestines had been better designed than Lambert's and showed no signs of his earlier ingestion of sundry animal fats and carbohydrates. The sergeant went on, 'He was gobsmacked about what has happened. He told the interviewing coppers that he was going to sell the boat when he got it back and take up flying instead. Shame really, it's a very nice boat. Adams and I enjoyed our trip down the Kennet and Avon canal Boss, it was brilliant!'

Later that day the Morris Traveller 1000 was found in a multi-storey car park in Maidenhead and was presently being stripped down at the police garage. They had found no prints other than those of Cynthia Walters and it seemed to Lambert a shame to practically destroy it. The only news so far was that one of the tranions needed replacing and the woodwork was full of

Brummer stopping. The two men had obviously disappeared for good and with no description; other than they were foreigners talking a funny language, it was all a waste of time.

'It must have been the mobile phone they were after.' Durant agreed with his boss and Lambert's bump on the head helped to confirm the fact. After all, his attackers obviously thought that the narrow boat had been swept clean and remembered the mobile phone sometime later.

Chief Superintendent Ken Burrows was sitting in his office surrounded by a mountain of assorted paper. As he viewed the rising plethora of documents, he occasionally swallowed a teaspoonful of some mysterious pink liquid from a bottle he kept in his desk. He seemed a very harassed man and often exploded for no apparent reason. Getting close to retirement, his bulky form was often seen in the local newspaper plastically smiling at visiting royals or occasionally discussing police statistics on local TV.

The Rotary Club was his only real relaxation as was his membership of Calcot Golf Course, where he played golf occasionally with the local managers of industry from the famous Winnersh Golden Triangle. Forty years as a policeman, he had started his career as a humble copper on the beat.

According to Burrows, Lambert was '*one of them blue eyed boys from the army, who'd had a bit of a leg up.*' But although he was a resentful man, he admired Lambert because he was a good detective. He despised his arrogant wife Arabella, their posh friends and their perceived lifestyle, but that was because they came from two different worlds. However, from a police point of view, Mike Lambert was unquestionably a great asset.

'What's happening with this bloody case, Lambert? I've got that horrible woman Venetia Strang up my bottom! These damned Labour councillors think that we're a load of Muppets who can't think their way out of a paper bag! Don't know what's happening to this bloody town Lambert, perhaps it's time for me to retire?'

Even if Lambert believed that he was right, he was not particularly keen to replace him despite the helpful suggestion of the Chief Constable whom he knew quite well socially. 'Mike, police work is changing. Burrows is from the old school and he can't deal with all the middle management and technical stuff. I know Arabella hates what you do, but you would be very good in that job. All your colleagues respect you and you can't expect much more than that.' Sir Patrick Goddard knew Lambert as a family friend and had known his father-in-law, George Mostyn, for many years.

He went on, 'Burrows was a good policeman in his day, but even the police force has to change and adapt to the new Euro-bloody-ethic. Chasing villains was an important part of the job in the old days, but crime is becoming more sophisticated.' Lambert was resigned to the fact that his Chief Superintendent was getting out of touch with reality and couldn't really cope any more.

Lambert smiled at Burrows. 'Well Sir, we might have

tracked the victim down to Eastern Europe. It seems he may have lived there for some while and apparently might have been the editor of a glossy news magazine in Bulgaria. There is also some evidence to indicate that someone might have murdered him from that part of the world. And judging by the pain in my head, we believe that they are still trying to find our main piece of evidence. They must have missed it when they swept the narrow boat. We think they were looking for a very small mobile phone.'

Lambert looked at his notes and went on. 'I got well and truly thumped last night on that narrow boat, Sir. They must have been watching our police activities since last Monday and it's very clear to me that these people are not frightened of us—that's for sure.' Lambert could still feel the lump on his head and he was annoyed by his own vulnerability.

'You ought to get that looked at Lambert, we are short enough of manpower as it is and we don't want you conking out. Why don't you go and visit the quack just to be on the safe side?' Burrows' sudden concern for his health was an unusual detour from his usual views of policemen as '*a bunch of winging incompetent pansies, who all need a bloody nanny,*' which he obviously felt him to be!

Burrows looked thoughtful. 'What about the British Embassy, do they know anything about him?' Burrows had little time for diplomats in general, or the vast majority of bureaucrats. 'I know it is a bit unusual but bearing in mind that this man Side appears to have been one of us, either a Brit or possibly a Paddy from the Republic of Eire, there may be a case for someone going there and making some discreet enquiries. It can't hurt.'

'I wondered about that too Sir, but I was also concerned how you might feel about the cost of such a trip? It would only take about a week and I'm quite happy to go. I've got some leave due to me anyway, and I could do with a break.' Lambert hadn't taken any leave for some time and it seemed a wonderful excuse to get away from Arabella. His only regret was that he might miss the forthcoming cricket match which was another matter entirely.

Burrows nodded his head. Taking a further slurp of his pink unction he said, 'I agree that you can't do it all by phone Lambert and I am told that in that part of the world Interpol is about as much use as a chocolate teapot.' Then as an afterthought, 'It might also give some of those ruddy local diplomats there something to do for a change, apart from going to bloody parties!'

To Lambert's ears, Burrows' words were like manna from heaven. It was a chance to get away, to experience something different and to escape from his tedious and numbing domestic existence. What Arabella would have to say on the matter, was something else!

'So you want to go and meet some cheap little whores, do you? I've heard all about it from Jimmy Prothero's wife Fiona. She said they all go there once a year, supposedly on business and fuck themselves silly. Not much of a secret is it? Then they come back and tell everyone how horrible and boring it all is. You're pathetic, Mike! And I might add, at the British taxpayer's expense! Brilliant! You'd better take some condoms with you, or I'll never sleep with you again!' She didn't anyway, so it was all rather academic, and rather too late.

British Airways offered a special ticket price if you stayed for a week and over a weekend. Because he was on a special assignment he got a good deal and he no longer required a visa because Bulgaria had relaxed its regulations in order to encourage visitors. So with his passport in date, he decided to go to Sofia the following morning as a tourist on the early flight from Heathrow Airport.

The police administration officer Kevin O'Brian gave him a thousand pounds in cash and told him to check his credit card and to make sure it was in date. He also quite remarkably gave him a book on Bulgaria written by Peter Carney. He had visited Bulgaria on an archaeological dig, which apparently was his secret hobby.

'I don't tell many people Mr Lambert, because you know, they might think I'm a bit soft. But you'll enjoy it there and remember it gets very hot at this time of the year so take some shorts with you!' Lambert had known O'Brian for years and knew little about him other than he always seemed happy.

Gloria Hislop was also very pleased, and almost by proxy she felt a part of an important event. 'You'll have to give me your cell phone number while you are away.

I am sure to have some important information and names and addresses for you if that's okay. It's not just the money with me Mr Lambert, but from what you have told me this man Side could have been almost anything; it is all rather fascinating.'

That afternoon Sergeant Durant signed Gloria's contract and she in turn signed the Act as he called it. The thirty-five pounds an hour plus costs and telephone calls was a very good deal indeed, but the excitement she experienced from her wheelchair was worth much more. 'I can phone you as new information arrives and keep you posted.'

Lambert remembered her sunny smile, and took it with him to Bulgaria. Finally he said, 'Gloria, please call me Mike.' After all, they were colleagues now.

Michael Lambert took very little with him and expecting only one or two serious interviews, he chose to take a lightweight blazer, grey slacks, a short sleeved shirt and his Cavalry and Guards Club tie. The rest was all casual wear, but before he left for Sofia he had one important task to fulfil.

That evening Lambert drove to London and visited the Cavalry and Guards club in Piccadilly to ask a few questions. 'We have never heard of this man Liam Side, Major Lambert.' Old Sergeant Noakes had been there for years and he remembered Lambert from the Goose Green episode. The club had received an unexpected telex from Lambert via the Navy when the battle had been won.

'You get all sorts in here these days and a member might have just given him a tie as a keepsake, you never know. The officers do entertain a lot in here Sir, as you yourself might remember. Give me your number and I will let you know what I can find out.'

The rest of his clothes were tripper stuff comprising two polo shirts, a pair of shorts, some T-shirts and a pair of Adidas trainers. He also took his laptop and the travel book about Bulgaria by Peter Carney. It was easier to take one bag onto the plane as in-flight baggage, because it meant no intrusive Customs inspections or delays at the airport.

Collecting a few belongings from his office he saw a letter from Dr Eddie Singh on his desk. It was concerning the victim's blood group and the DNA testing. In his analysis Eddie Singh immediately turned some of Lambert's theories on their head.

To Chief Inspector M. Lambert
Case Officer Thames Valley Division.

Dear Mike,

As you know things have moved on in DNA analysis, and a very strange thing has occurred as a result of the mitochondrial test. It appears that the victim was of Spanish origin, and not of British or Irish origin as you might have suspected.

It is possible that if he came from somewhere like Cork he might have had some Spanish genes, because of the mixture in stock which existed at the time of the Spanish Armada. Otherwise, it could have been because of some intermarriage in the past involving a Spanish woman. These genes are traced through the female line.

But what is for sure, is that he was not a common or garden Englishman and might very well have been of Mediterranean or even South American origin. As far as his blood grouping is concerned his blood type for your information is AB.

Finally, I understand from Sergeant Durant that you will be abroad for a few days, and he has given me your mobile number if anything unusual crops up.

Eddie Singh

The trip to Heathrow was fraught with the usual delays and traffic jams, but the Alvis was a perfect refuge away from the madness which many people display on the road. Most motorists allow you the benefit of the doubt, if you drive a classic car and give you a wide berth. It was now seven o'clock on Friday morning, and leaving home had been an oddly traumatic event. Arabella put her head around the bedroom door to say goodbye. 'Don't forget to phone me when you get there, the children will both want to know that you are safe.'

Les McCann was playing *Too Close for Comfort*. He was a very special performer for Lambert, because he was the first pianist he ever really loved when he discovered jazz as a teenager. Up until then there'd only been Oscar Peterson or Achmed Jamal. As a boy, the old black upright Pohlmann piano at the farmhouse had given him the chance to imitate their style, but the funky sounds of Les McCann and Errol Garner were his real inspiration and also the very remarkable Dudley Moore. To Arabella Lambert's piano playing was simply a Christmas party piece, but to him it was a part of his very private world.

When he had discovered how to burn CDs on the home computer, with the help of Jebb he had successfully managed to re-record some of his favourite 33s—recordings which he had loved and protected all his life. Since then his driving had improved immensely. As he approached Heathrow airport on the outer ring road, Les McCann was playing *The Shampoo*, with great rising tenths in the treble cleft.

Lambert parked the Alvis in the long-term car park and explained to the man on the security gate who he was. Inspecting the Alvis the man just laughed, 'Blimey Guv! They must be paying you coppers a lot of money these days.'

Putting his Samsonite bag over his shoulder he carefully locked up the car and turned the mirrors inwards. Collecting his car parking ticket, Lambert smiled at the man. 'You can laugh as much as you like, but you're actually looking at my entire life's savings, so keep an eye on it for me please, it's all I've got in the world.'

The ticket was waiting at the BA information desk. 'If you would like to sign here Chief Inspector, the aircraft will be leaving in just over an hour and you need to check in well beforehand. Although maybe only half an hour before if all you have is some hand luggage. The flight is not very full and there are no delays, so try not to be late and have a nice journey Sir.'

The plane was practically empty and ideal for him, because he could stretch out his long and rather painful limbs, by lifting up the arms of the three empty seats he occupied.

'Would you like a newspaper Sir, we've got all the British papers on board and a copy of the *Sofia Independent*.' The steward seemed to talk without thinking, 'If this is your first trip to Sofia this might also interest you, it has all the bars and clubs advertised in it and tells you about what the expats do and where they go!'

It was going to be a long journey, but more than anything he wanted some sleep. 'Do you mind if I sleep a little after we take off?' The steward smiled, and said, 'I expect you would like a spot of breakfast later on, I'll wake you up when it is ready. And you can have as much as you like today, we're only a quarter full this trip.'

Lambert put his watch forward two hours. It was now one o'clock in the afternoon Eastern Europe time, and having eaten in some discomfort, he looked closely at a newspaper called *The Sofia Independent*.

Although the political analysis was considerably oversimplified, it seemed that the ex-King Gregory III of Bulgaria had now become the new Prime Minister, replacing the previous government which had been very corrupt. He wondered what it might have been that

Liam Side had found so interesting in a country fraught with so many problems. But while the general level of information was very weak on business and politics, as he read it seemed to be far better informed, on sex and rock and roll, because in the advertising section of the *Independent* there seemed to be nothing but Irish bars, pretentious apartments and escort agencies. Perhaps Arabella had been right, maybe that was why so many men visited Sofia? He would soon find that out, but firstly, where were the jazz clubs?

The seatbelt sign lit up and the steward walked down the aisle checking the passengers and asking them to put their bags under the seats or in a locker above before landing. Looking through the cabin window at Sofia City, all Lambert could see through the haze were the occasionally protruding concrete tower blocks.

It was a quite a gloomy sight for July. Peter Carney's book had told of beautiful cathedrals and churches, French colonial style buildings and the usual Eastern European Stalinesque monoliths, but he could see very little evidence of that. As the flight touched down and the tyres rumbled on the concrete runway, the engines went swiftly into reverse thrust and all the passengers enthusiastically clapped their hands. They had all arrived safely.

The Englishman went through the EU exit gate with no questions asked. With just a single stamp in his passport and a quizzical look, he fought his way through a gaggle of waiting relatives and friends into the bright airport lounge. It was nothing like he had imagined. It was modern and streamlined, with signs in English everywhere. He went to a change bureau and converted fifty pounds into the local currency and stuffed the Leva into his trouser pocket.

He pushed his way past the aggressive taxi drivers—which he had received warnings about from his Carney guide—and suddenly he found himself standing in bright sunshine. Sofia was humid and he began to sweat profusely. 'How much to the Radisson Hotel?' he asked. The taxi driver said thirty dollars, smilingly displaying a number of gold capped teeth, but following Carney's instructions, Lambert made for the 84 bus.

He was going to be nobody's fool on this trip, but jammed in a bus with all sorts of hot sweaty people, the journey turned out to be rather uncomfortable. The bus seemed to go in each and every direction until ultimately arriving at its final destination. Close to a tall building which looked like a Communist Party building, he grabbed his bag, crossed the road and made for the Radisson Hotel. According to his guidebook, he would find it in the Narodnie Square opposite the House of Parliament. Walking into the reception area it was cool and very Western.

'My name is Lambert; I believe you have a room booked for me?' The receptionist looked at the monitor in front of her for some while and then nodding her head as if to say yes, she immediately said "no" in English. She then made an almost silent phone call.

A polite man finally appeared wearing a dark suit who smiled at Lambert. 'I'm sorry, there has been some confusion Mr Lambert, but don't worry we have plenty of rooms available; it is very quiet here in July because everyone is on holiday. How will you be paying, Sir?'

Lambert's reply was simple and to the point, 'How much are you asking, surely that is the most important question?' and the man smiled. Lambert knew all these silly games from his past travels abroad, remembering how Italy had been the worst. But paying by cash in advance, he was given a special price for the week. Ushered into the lift he finally found himself in a large and comfortable room overlooking the square.

He stood for a while looking through the balcony window, relaxing in the cool air-conditioned atmosphere. He could see the Nevski Cathedral in the distance and he felt somehow that he was finally at the farthest point away from Arabella that he could possibly find. Now it was time for a shower and later perhaps something to eat.

Later Gloria phoned him on his handy which was quite a shock, and brought him swiftly back to reality. 'I've got some bad news for you Mike. The British Embassy is closed on Friday afternoon, so you can't see them until next Monday.'

This wasn't such a bad revelation as she might have thought, and hanging his rumpled blazer and grey slacks in the wardrobe, it was time to relax and to look around the city.

CHAPTER THREE

THE SQUARE was practically empty when Lambert surfaced at seven o'clock that evening. In the quiet and peaceful surroundings of the hotel, after a lifesaving shower and having tried the cable TV, to discover that it also had BBC World, he had simply fallen into a deep sleep.

Waking had been a slow painful process, but his head was clear and his body relaxed. The fact that the British Embassy was closed on Friday afternoon had proved a blessing after all. He had inadvertently developed a holiday feeling and his subconscious was beginning to dominate his thoughts with unconnected and random images. He no longer felt tied to his rigid and disciplined life. He was suddenly free from the inhibiting matrix of family versus job and job versus family, which had recently plagued his narrow and provincial existence.

He plugged in his mobile phone charger, sat in a comfortable club chair and looked out of the window at the passers-by, but with only minor interest. As his mobile charged up he counted his money. After paying the hotel bill in advance he now had 600 Pounds in his wallet and what seemed to be a large amount of local currency, in his money clip. The ticket to the city from the airport had cost virtually nothing, so he thought of the gold-toothed taxi driver and smiled at his obvious disappointment. When the handy rang it was only five o'clock in England. Once more it was Gloria.

'I hope I haven't caught you at a difficult time?' The familiar voice and the closeness of Reading seemed incongruous, as the pale pastiche of urban England intruded into his random thoughts; reality was back with a vengeance. 'No, it's seven o'clock here Gloria, we're two hours ahead in Bulgaria.'

'Good. Well, I've got some news for you. I've made contact with a man named Georgi Panov. It seems that he and Side were friends, but what is more interesting is that he is a local politician and has agreed to see you tomorrow morning. He speaks good English, although he said that he hadn't spoken to Side for some while. I'll give you his mobile phone number and you can make your own arrangements. I explained that you were a friend of the family, that it is all very unofficial and that you were trying to track down Side.'

It was the small lies which Lambert hated, the ones that finally broke all trust. Sometimes the bigger lies were more revealing than the truth, but that was a matter of how you thought. Georgi Panov lived with his wife on the outskirts of Sofia and told Lambert to jump into a taxi the following morning.

'It will be good to see a relative of Liam, and you can swim in the pool if you like, or we can play basketball.

Just tell the taxi driver my name and he will know where to go in Ventzia. Come around eleven.' Lambert thought that it would be good to see how real people lived in Bulgaria, to catch up with local events and to actually meet someone who had known Side when he was alive.

Putting on some summer shorts with a white polo shirt, Lambert decided to go outside for a look around and to inspect the cathedral. He put his local money clip into the small pouch attached to his belt, together with his passport and cell phone and locked his pounds and credit cards in the bedroom safe. Outside the sun was deep and low, and the heat unbearable. Wearing his Gucci sunglasses, a present from Kate who accused him of being too stuffy, he made for the square.

The cast-iron statue of Tsar Alexander II on horseback glared down at him. As he crossed the street innumerable yellow taxi cabs drove at breakneck speed in all directions continuously sounding their horns. It told of an obvious cultural difference far away from the ordered streets of Reading. To Lambert it seemed more like Barcelona, which had been one of his worse driving nightmares ever.

He watched a scruffy police Sergeant with a stop-bat waving down wary motorists for no apparent reason, whose documents he then carefully inspected. His victims all appeared to be tough looking characters, who were driving large but dated Mercedes, BMWs and Audis. What amused him was how this policeman seemed always to put his hand into his left trouser pocket after the event, and after they had driven off. At home the British police often seemed to provide the same service to mainly black drivers, who they were continuously accused of harassing, but hopefully without the financial inducements. It was where a lot of racial violence and resentment stemmed.

Old yellow Lada taxis seemed to be this particular policeman's second choice, but only if they were driven by gypsies. At the onset Lambert was able to distinguish between Bulgarians and the much publicised Roma. But it was no wonder that gypsies tried to escape to the west if they were treated like rubbish in their own country and had become so despised.

The round vaulted domes of the Cathedral were gilded and certain parts of the building were being renovated. The huge square around the cathedral was cobbled with yellow shiny bricks, as was the main road and the smaller square by the hotel. Everywhere he could see ornate and globed street lighting. Around the nearby parliament the buildings were well decorated and far more pronounced. This was due no doubt to the recent elections and the sudden appearance of the well documented King Gregory III, who was now remarkably the new Bulgarian Prime Minister.

Flannigan's was the Irish pub he had read about on the flight to Sofia in the Independent and Lambert drifted into the bar which was a part of the hotel. It seemed a little bit characterless and over spacious, but filled with recognisable junk shop memorabilia, it was much like any other so-called Irish bar he had been to. They could be found worldwide and were not particularly Irish save for the names.

It was practically empty except for a few other foreigners and the large bar staff. Sitting at the bar he looked at the corny menu describing greasy spoon food as if he was in some Michelin starred restaurant. '*What the hell is Irish shepherd's pie, or an Irish breakfast?*' Lambert's mind boggled at the absurdity of it all.

But with epicurean thoughts of Reading police canteen late on a Friday evening, he ordered some fish and chips and a pint of bitter or red beer as it was described. A bald headed little American was in full flight on the subject of mouthwash and another was holding court on the subject of the IMF and the World Bank.

Lambert's thoughts turned to the White Hart Hotel in Sonning and in his mind's eye, he could see very little difference between the respective customers within either bar. Unfortunately there were money bores everywhere one went these days—whatever happened to jazz, cricket and sex? The banker type seemed to use the word *proactive* a lot and then turning his attention to more important matters he continued his trite utterances on globalisation.

They seemed so self-important, like amateur actors in a Chekov play. With guarded sideways glances it was obvious that they perceived Lambert to be a possible audience, and by their protracted stage whispers.

'New in town?' The short bald headed man—who was obsessed with discussing mouthwash—stood next to him at the bar and ordered some more drinks for him and his companion and Lambert smiled.

'Yes, that's right! How do you do? My name is Michael Lambert; I've just arrived here.'

'Oh! You're a Brit I see. What are you doing here?' Lambert was not used to such casual impertinence, but after all the little man was an American. 'I'm here on holiday, you know, sightseeing, taking it easy as you Americans say.' The man ordered two small glasses of Heineken and told the waitress to put them on his tab.

'What do you do in England, are you in business?' Lambert wondered if people could understand the norms of casual conversation anymore.

'I publish seed catalogues, actually,' Lambert said sarcastically, 'you know, flowers and vegetables.' The little bore thought for a moment and then said, 'You can't make much money out of that.'

Lambert was astounded. 'Why, have you published any seed catalogues recently?' Looking increasingly like Mr Magoo, he seemed impervious to Lambert's ridiculing remark.

'No, actually I make mouthwash; it's a booming market out here in Eastern Europe.' This was obviously his favourite subject and as he burbled on, his black suited and slightly paunchy companion joined them.

'This is Emile Shicklbaum, he's in banking and I'm Richard Hampton. I make toothpaste as well as mouthwash.' And then with a very serious face he announced, 'Emile, Michael here is in seed catalogues, and he publishes them in England.'

Despite its greasy appearance, his fish and chips were a

welcome sight when they finally turned up, and an ideal excuse to escape the somewhat unexpected corporate level of inane chitchat. He demolished the forlorn products of a burgeoning Bulgarian frozen food industry, together with two gooey packets of ketchup which arrived in a small basket. Ordering another pint of red beer, despite his promise to Arabella, it seemed that since he was now sitting in some occult world of Bulgarian Rotarians that the rules no longer applied. Leaving a few minutes later, both men waved at him and shouted, 'We'll see you tomorrow night!' And returning their wave Lambert thought to himself, 'Not if I can help it!'

When he got to his room, once more he picked up the dog-eared copy of the *Balkan Western News*, which had been found on *Fienna*, and looked through the pages. It was the spring 2000 edition and on the front cover there was a cartoon picture of someone called Penko Stanev who was a comedian. If only he could come across someone like him, through some chance meeting in the bar, instead of the suits and corporate bores.

What Lambert did not want, was to use an interpreter other than Gloria because he had heard that they were often more concerned about their own personal circumstances than fulfilling a true interpretation. Gloria had warned him that the only truth was her truth and that historically the Byzantines were in the habit of killing the messenger, if the news was bad.

The magazine interview was about the comedian's

career and his TV appearances mimicking the current Bulgarian President, who had a somewhat protruding jaw and a rather pronounced nose.

Apparently the prevailing comic vogue was political satire. It was now one year on from the election of King Gregory III as Prime Minister and Bulgarian politics had probably changed. But he wondered how close Side had really been to the politics of the day. The magazine announced that it was the sixtieth edition, so in any event by then Side had been publishing his monthly magazine for five years. He must have seen some considerable changes in that time, or perhaps none at all.

In his article called the 'Editor Rambles On,' he had not been particularly polite about the Bulgarian administration and neither was the article steeped in any optimism. It seemed as though the errant editor was prone to speak the truth when necessary. Other than that, the articles were mainly about people's lives, some political analysis and an interview with an EU ambassador about Bulgaria's prospects for entry into the EU and their imminent entry into NATO.

At the end there were the 'Funny Pages' with some cartoons and an American Financial expert whose answer to every question was '*a feasibility study,*' including questions about his wife. When in the sketch he is asked if he married her after a feasibility study, he replies, '*no, only after I had carried out some due diligence!*' So Side obviously had a sense of humour, but did his reading public? Judging by the man Richard Hampton, the answer was a definite no.

From the pages of the magazine it seemed that although much was about presenting the country in a pleasing light, presumably for visitors like himself, it also seemed to laugh at the expat community, certain politicians and many of the foreign business leaders.

Then there was a section concerning the training of paramedics in Bulgaria, which brought him back to Sergeant Park and his passing comments about the golden ten minutes on the M4 motorway.

In the magazine article it suggested that the leading cause of death of people between 1 and 44 years of age was trauma and that 20% of those could be saved though a quick response. 'Poor old Liam Side,' he thought, 'it was too late for him by the time the Reading paramedics had arrived.' But so far, Lambert could not see a sufficient motive for murder, only lingering congratulations for the editor's burgeoning satire.

Sleep being the best option, Lambert jumped into bed and turned on the TV. The BBC news was as usual about Israel and the Palestine problem, but also about some talks taking place in Macedonia. None of these countries seemed capable of maintaining peace, despite the efforts of George Robertson and Colin Powell, who had both begun new rounds of shuttle diplomacy. Although very little endured for long, fundamentalism seemed to be tearing the world apart, much of which was on the doorstep of Bulgaria. CNN told the same story, but then he discovered a local channel.

Although he couldn't understand a word, it was clear that despite an unhealthy air of optimism, Bulgaria was still falling to bits at the seams. There were reports of disgusting hospitals, children suffering from meningitis, usually followed by a meaningless formal press conference. In fact there were talking heads sprouting everywhere, which simply confirmed to Lambert, that Bulgaria was unquestionably a third-world country. Then his mobile rang.

'Mike, I am sorry to phone you so late, but I had to tell you about a conversation I have just had with a Vera Kolova. Apparently she and Side have been friends for many years. She speaks reasonable English and she said she could meet you tomorrow afternoon if you like. She'll pick you up from your hotel. I gave her your phone number and she'll phone you about four o'clock, if that's all right?'

Good for Gloria, but one thing was now becoming clear; Side may have been in this part of this world before, as well as after the changes and so he was an old hand and nobody's fool.

'*Gospodin Georgi Panov, Da! Da! Ot Ventzia, Da! Da! Namma problem.*' The yellow Daewoo taxi swiftly took off from the entrance of the Radisson Hotel. Although each moment seemed to be the cause for considerable angst from the bellicose driver, it was clear that he obviously believed that his was the only vehicle on the road and regarded any hindrance to his progress as a personal slight.

'*Pederast!*' he shouted at any given moment, turning to smile at his passenger. The insults to his automotive integrity were immense and only seemed to diminish, as they took to the Greek road leading to the outskirts of Sofia and the suburb of Ventzia. Turning left into a fair sized village, Lambert could actually see signs directing them to the house of Georgi Panov in English. It was positively surreal, rather like something out of a bad Hollywood film.

Ascending a steep hill, almost at once the taxi skidded to a halt on the gravel track and three dogs started to bark behind a wrought iron gate. '*Gospodin Panov tucka*,' the taxi driver said laughing and he waved his arm and made a '*Che Che Che*' noise as though he were sword fighting. Ten Leva later, Lambert was confronted by an enormous man.

At six foot two inches, Lambert was no midget but this man seemed to tower over him. Although approximately sixty, he seemed very powerful indeed. 'Welcome to Ventzia,' his enormous hand shook Lambert's in a torturous grip, but his smile was friendly revealing a perfect set of capped white teeth. 'It's nice to meet a relative of Liam. You must find it unusual here in my country, or have you been here before?'

The trip through the garden proved a little haphazard, as the three dogs jumped and barked. Then almost as quickly as they had appeared they disappeared with a wag of Panov's finger. 'As you English say, it is important to let them know who their master is!'

Sitting by the pool was an attractive younger woman. 'This is my girlfriend Zhivka. We have been together for eight years now,' he unexpectedly announced. Rising from her sun lounger she smiled, 'How do you do Mr Lambert, would you like something to drink?'

With the formalities over and a glass of Devin water in his hand, Lambert now had to break the very morbid ice and to confront the issue of Side's death. 'I'm afraid that what I am about to tell you will be somewhat of a shock, so you will have to forgive me.' The couple looked at each other with apprehension.

Lambert continued, 'I am sorry to have to tell you this, but Liam Side is dead. He was murdered in England. I must also inform you that I am not a relative, as my colleague told you on the phone, but the investigating Police officer on the case. I am sorry for the deception but it was unfortunately necessary.'

'Oh! I am so sorry. Oh! My God this is terrible news Mr Lambert. Don't worry, I understand, it's okay.' The expression of pain seemed completely genuine, his mouth turned down at the corners, making his large black moustache seem even larger as his grimace increased. Staring silently into the swimming pool, Zhivka sniffed and then got up and quietly walked into the house.

'How did it happen?' Lambert told him all he knew, and Panov repeated over and over, 'My God this is terrible news!' Finally he looked at Lambert, pursed his lips and shook his head.

'Poor man, he was so lonely too!'

'Listen Mr Panov, the reason I am here is because we know nothing about him, and—how can I say this delicately?—the British Embassy is unlikely to be able to help much, except with some basic background information. And your local police would also find it difficult to cooperate with me at this stage.'

The large man lifted both hands as if to say don't explain, 'My country is going through a great upheaval at the moment and there will have to be many changes almost everywhere, so I know what you say only too well.' After a while Panov started to speak.

'I knew him for many years, firstly in London which is where I actually met him. It was at a party at Stringfellows. Later we would meet and have the occasional meal together, generally in Fulham. There was a little Mexican restaurant in Greyhound Road I remember, you had to take your own wine there and they charged you for opening the bottle.' So Side had lived in London. 'Can you remember what he did for a living and did he seem to have much money?'

'He always had cash on him, and a lot of credit cards. He told me once that he was something in the property business, which is why he came to see my apartment and how I first met him. He wanted to buy it and renovate it. It was in the mid-80s and Earls Court was becoming fashionable. I think he called himself a *runner* for some big property company in the Channel Isles; it all seemed very vague to me at the time. You see I lived in London for a few years before coming back to help my country, just before the changes.'

Lambert tried to work out how there had been no records of Side, either from the Inland Revenue or the Ministry of Social Security; perhaps the Land Registry might have some information. 'Are you quite sure he was who he said he was?' Lambert asked.

'What do I know? He could have been an undercover policeman for all I knew. In this country half the population was in the Security Service or were informers, so why should your country be any different?' Lambert had the feeling that he was under suspicion too.

'Mr Panov, I'm just a humble detective from Thames Valley Serious Crime Squad and to be quite honest, I hate spooks because to me they all seem so pointless.'

'Not in my country Mr Lambert, because here in Bulgaria they continue to run practically everything! Every day another MP is revealed as an ex-member of the Darzhavna Sigurnost and sometimes I wonder what my file says?' Lambert recognized the conspiracy theory and it was abundantly clear that Panov had suspected Side at the very outset, but now things had greatly changed.

'When I first talked to him about Bulgaria he didn't even know where it was; I was astonished. Finally I got fed up and suggested that he came to see for himself. It was during Christmas 1985. I was living temporarily in an area called Mladost in one of those tower blocks close to the airport. Things were very different in those days.'

'How would you describe Side as a person? Was he posh or working class and could you distinguish his accent?' Panov laughed, it was as though he was being interrogated by a child.

'Look Mr Lambert, I have travelled all over the world

and have met people as far removed from one another as Henry Kissinger, Clinton, Saddam Hussein, Kohl, Margaret Thatcher and much of the British aristocracy, so I do understand your question. If the question is, "Was he Scottish, Welsh or Irish?", he didn't sound it and talked with a typically middle class English accent much as you do yourself. There are a lot of Scottish, Welsh and Irish families living in London who send their children to public schools, as well as a lot of, well, ex-IRA terrorists and nobodies. It's a big city; you should know that, and there are all sorts of people who are not what they say they are! Maybe that is what makes it so interesting.'

It was about midday and the sun was getting very hot, so they decided to move onto the balcony. 'How long have you been a detective Mike; by the way, may I call you Mike? Please call me George, everyone does.'

It was a good question and one which he hadn't really thought about much, nor had he added up the years. It was an honest question. 'Perhaps too long,' he smiled philosophically, 'about twelve years actually. Before that I was a uniformed copper in the Metropolitan Police and prior to that a professional soldier. So George, that's my life story so far!'

The big man laughed and then adjusted his large Balkan moustache, with the thumb and first finger of his right hand. 'He was a good man you know.' Panov opened a bottle of red Melnik wine and poured out two glasses. Standing on the balcony they clinked glasses and Panov tipped a little of his wine onto a nearby flower bed. 'This is our toast to the dead Mike; it is the only time we really cry.' The tears in his eyes seemed genuine, and then it was over.

Looking very seriously at Lambert the big man went on, 'Liam, with very little money did more to help our two cultures to understand each other than anyone. He was the first to publish anything in English and I believe he suffered for it. It was during the resurrection of the blue communists or the red democrats in 1995. They tried everything to stop him publishing or to frighten him, but it never worked. So they unsuccessfully tried to use him in any way possible and finally to set him up. Slander was and still is a criminal offence in Bulgaria, although you wouldn't know it by reading our national newspapers. He was the only person who wrote honestly about me and I suspect most of the others.'

The tall figure moved once more into the house, where miraculously some food had appeared from nowhere and onto the kitchen table. Zhivka had created a typical Bulgarian meal whilst they were talking. The table was covered with little dishes comprising various sorts of salad, a large plate of different types of ham and sausage, together with some good fresh bread.

Panov looked at Lambert and said, 'If you had known him you would have liked him. He hated all the phony receptions and having to meet these half-witted diplomats. In their turn they were only nice to him because he might publish a flattering article about them and he despised them for it; although there were also some notable exceptions. I go to these parties for my own reasons, but mainly to show everybody that I am still alive and well and still in the political game as they say. But he was right, when he called them pretentious fools.'

Lambert remembered reading various articles in the magazine about ambassadors and business people. Boring and conceited, their self-importance was out of all proportion to their actual status in such a small Balkan country. 'Why on earth did Side put up with it for so long George?'

'I think in the end it was his little daughter Patricia who kept him here. Without her he didn't have any real reason to remain here in Sofia, but by then he was too committed. Because of his daughter he had to put up with her Russian mother. It was the sting in the tail as you English would say!'

Panov shovelled a large forkful of potato salad into his mouth and munching with considerable concentration considered his next point. 'She is crazy. Russians! Hmm! They are all crazy!'

'Was the magazine his only source of income? There couldn't have been too many magazine sales surely? It's not a big City and there are not that many foreigners living here in Sofia after all.' If the people Liam Side had to put up with were anything like the two silly Americans he'd met in the pub the night before or all those pretentious embassy types, he must have been extremely dedicated to his calling.

'No he did other things, mainly with property and if I remember correctly, he worked a bit for a telephone company finding sites for their transmitting stations.

Sometimes he put on parties for visiting bankers and friends from London,' he laughed, 'but he actually gave the magazine away for nothing Mike. That's what surprised us Bulgarians because we hate giving things away! He told me once that he relied entirely on the advertisers to pay his bills!'

So he had friends from London who came to Sofia. Lambert wondered who they might have been. Panov shook his head once more, throwing a piece of sausage to one of the dogs to catch. 'But, they didn't do much except buy some bank debt and a few Brady bonds. They just used to talk big and argue with the so-called local financial consultants and the usual hangers-on from the national bank. I never took them too seriously. They were in and out—how you say—like a fiddler's elbow? They didn't invest real money, not for my people anyway.'

'Why did you come back to Bulgaria George?' They were sitting once more on the balcony, nursing their small sour black espresso coffees and munching fresh green figs. The pink insides had a soapy taste and the skins were wet from the garden tap.

'I was a professional sportsman. I was a world professional épée champion. I lived in Hollywood for a while and then in London. Perhaps it was time for me to come home and help my country.' He noisily sipped his little strong coffee and then gazed into the past. 'And it has been twenty very hard years for me too. First I was fighting the red democrats, then the blue communists and now we have a King in charge! How strangely the world turns!' Then with a whimsical smile,

'But we must be positive; Liam was. He never gave up despite all the tricks and games everyone played and he never complained. He was a tough little bastard and I'm very sorry he's gone, I truly am.'

The trip back to the hotel was uneventful, and the only shock was the charge at the end of the journey. The gypsy driver wanted thirty dollars, so Lambert gave him ten Leva and told him to fuck off. Suddenly he too was becoming a little prejudiced, if not over aggressive and it was a shock to him, because it had been such an easy transition.

It was very hot and he was a little edgy. It was just after two in the afternoon so Lambert went to his room and lay on the bed. Cooling down in the delicious air conditioning he ran over his conversation with Panov.

What was a man like Panov doing in a country so lacking in the basic comforts of life? It certainly wasn't designed for the self-indulgent, or was it? If he had lived in Hollywood and London in the past, as a sophisticated man, where did he find the level of culture or kindred spirits he would have known before? Bulgaria was obviously a very tough society and given to very little compromise.

Perhaps in his own country Panov could pretend to be all the things he had never really been in his past. With assumed—or quasi—celebrity, maybe he could now present himself in any way he pleased. The devastation of this hopeless little Balkan country may have become a convenient refuge for him, but was this also true of Liam Side?

Judging by Lambert's conversations so far, there seemed very little real communication between people. Didn't people laugh at the funny side of life? It seemed that conversation simply amounted to the dramatic pronouncement of an individual's continued existence and a condemnation of their painfully tiny world.

Lambert was beginning to miss the banter of the English streets and the warmth of people who were comfortable with their life. Bulgaria seemed a place of theatre, but not a place of comedy. Was it only about deception, or was there something else? Perhaps they were outcasts from an over-caring Europe, or was Bulgaria some faux pas of history and a place where people casually assumed different characters whenever it was convenient?

Vera Kolova phoned exactly on time at four o'clock that afternoon, just as Lambert climbed out of the shower. 'I'm with a friend of me at the moment and we go shopping, so I will come to your hotel at five o'clock. I park outside in my blue BMW, and then we can go for a coffee and cakes and talk somewhere.'

Lambert hated tears but he knew that was exactly what would happen. Maybe the truth was that he was getting close to tears himself. But he had only heard a part of Liam Side's story. The thought of a character like Side being an idealist and—according to Panov— an uncompromising democrat, seemed just a little far-fetched to the Reading policeman.

But a year is a long time if you are very ill and he

might have deteriorated fast. He could also have been a different man, but that remained to be seen. The dead-man on the boat alive would have been in no condition to be some popular legend, an angel of enlightenment or a supporter of naff diplomacy. If he was dying of cancer, he must have known he was unwell. So, where did he get all his energy from for such hard work? Then there was the possibility of some ongoing love affair. How Side stayed so active would remain quite a mystery to the English detective for some time to come.

Lambert was dreading Vera Kolova's arrival at five o'clock, but when she finally appeared he was definitely not prepared for it. Sitting and smiling in an immaculate and fairly new 7 Series BMW, Vera Kolova was blonde, beautiful and apparently very happy.

Lambert knew that her state of mind wouldn't last for long, nor could he imagine the final outcome of their encounter. Climbing into the car Lambert quietly introduced himself to her and then at great speed, she made for the motorway. 'It is such a nice afternoon I thought we could go to this little bar and restaurant I know, just under the mountain, where they make wonderful snacks and deserts. It is an old Party restaurant.'

Running past the City on the ring road the car was comfortable and cool. As they drove, they listened to a tape of an Orthodox choir singing. It sounded similar to a Gregorian chant. Although he was a jazzman, he still remembered the choir music during his boarding school days away from home, his visits to St John's College in Cambridge, and an outing with his school house to the Ardingly College music festival.

The smell of her perfume invaded the gloom of his thoughts. Used to the grim reality of police work, he knew how to control his feelings, which were becoming raw and over exposed in the strangeness of this Balkan setting. The BMW drove over the pitted roads and up into the mountain. Vera Kolova swerved to miss the old Ladas and Moscovitch motorcars which zigzagged their way down the mountain road missing them by inches. They seemed to be more intent on evading the holes in the road than the oncoming traffic.

The conversation was about life in England, the Bulgarian economy and of course the new Government. 'Do you hear about us in London, and the new Prime Minister? Do you think that things will change? It's been a circus over here for so long.' She swerved down a dirt track and came to a halt next to an old Chavda bus which had a flat tyre. There seemed to be no other vehicles in sight. Lambert got out of the car into the cool air of the mountain and looked at the panoramic view of the City which was now spread out beneath him.

Through the haze it was ugly and uninteresting. Sitting deep on a plain all he could see were the tops of concrete apartment blocks. As if dropped from the sky like some gigantic decaying monument to socialism, it sat silently festering between two very beautiful mountain ranges. Having finished making a cell phone call, Vera Kolova switched off her mobile and made for the entrance of the restaurant. 'It used to be so good here in the old days, and the view is so beautiful!' Lambert could only wonder at her concept of beauty and the myopia which produced such an illusion.

'I haven't been here since mother of me died three month ago, they were very kind to us and the food is very good.' Lambert dreaded the next part of the conversation. She seemed so successful and so self-confident, but he knew from experience that the tears would start to roll as her world became smaller and more painful. They walked through the empty building, past old tables and chairs, the table slips with holes, the stage set for some evening entertainment; perhaps a wedding.

Arriving in the sunny garden at the rear, the plastic tables and chairs looked brighter and the checked table cloths no longer bore the signs of neglect. '*Doberden Gosposhitsa Kolova*,' the waiter made grand gestures despite the simplicity of his open-air café, '*az ima malka masa tuka*.' He waved to a corner table in the shade of a Weeping Willow tree and then disappeared from sight.

Lambert asked, 'How well do you know Liam, Ms Kolova?' and she smiled, the red lipstick slightly smearing her white teeth. She had tried to make herself attractive for the occasion and it seemed unkind to simply announce Side's death. 'Not that well recently I'm afraid, that is why I am here, to try and get to know more about him.'

She looked at Lambert with half closed eyes and lit a cigarette as though she was studying him. Throwing the match onto the ground she suddenly asked, 'You are a policeman?' Her rhetorical question didn't really shock him and he just smiled weakly and nodded. 'We've found a man who fits his description on a river boat in England, whom we believe has been murdered. I'm sorry, but it might be him.'

'How you know it's Liam?' Her eyes didn't change, they just narrowed even more as she blew the smoke from her flat Maurati Turkish cigarette to one side.

Lambert made a stab at mending the moment. 'In answer to your first question, yes, I am a British police detective from Reading which is where the man was found. I am sorry if I have misled you in any way Ms Kolova, but I have to be very discreet with this inquiry for all sorts of diplomatic reasons which I am sure you will understand.' Her face became so forlorn that Lambert put his hand on her arm which she quickly pulled away.

'In answer to your second question, we are not 100% sure it is him. Since I have been here, I am becoming less convinced because his circumstances do not seem to fit the facts.' He lit a Victory cigarette and put the pack on the table together with his Zippo lighter.

'I see you like our Bulgarian cigarettes then.' Lambert put his right hand over his eyes, and opening the first and second fingers, he looked at her with his left eye. Lambert said, 'This is becoming very difficult for me. Why don't we have a drink, Ms Kolova?'

The whisky helped, as did the bottle of Merlot that followed. The ashtray was replaced by a huge plate of chips with white cheese sprinkled over the top, and Lambert asked, 'When did you last see Liam?'

She looked quietly at him as if remembering some distant moment they might have had together. 'About a year ago. I thought he was free again and we could get back together. I've always loved him from the moment we first met in the eighties. I always believed that we would finally be together one day.' She wept like a little girl for a minute, her beautiful face looking at Lambert as if he could share her grief.

'He was so clever and so lonely. He told me once that all I had was my money and he didn't want that. He said he had his own money and wanted something more than that.' Her round Slavic face didn't really need any makeup and Lambert found it increasingly easier to understand her attraction to a man like Side.

'He lived with different women, but they didn't treat him correctly. He was a fool with women, because he was so lonely. I was lonely too but still he was the only one.'

Lambert remarked that it seemed that many of the foreigners shared the same fate as Side and how the bars of Sofia were lined with English speaking girls and women, who waited their chance with a new face in town. Vera Kolev looked downcast. 'These girls don't want to work, and won't work. They want to go to restaurants, and you know…!'

Her voice trailed off and she looked despondently at her glass of deep red wine. 'I could have given him everything he ever wanted, but perhaps I was too old for him. Silly old fool!' Her face brightened and she once again tipped a little of her wine into a concrete flower tub full of green rather foul smelling plants.

'To Liam, if what you say is true and he is really dead.' Her eyes were full of tears, as she dabbed her eyes with a paper napkin from the rack on the little table and noisily blew her nose. 'You see Mr Lambert, I loved him.'

On the way back to his hotel Vera Kolova was very quiet. 'He left some folders at me house when I saw him last time and he also gave me some of those magazines to read. The file was full of letters and some emails, but I didn't read them; they were about his friends and family. I only fast looked at the magazines, because my English is no good and anyway what can you tell me about Bulgaria that I don't already know?'

Later she said, 'You free tomorrow?' Her invitation seemed to be the antidote to a thoroughly dead Sunday. Missing an oncoming vehicle by a few inches she glanced at him and smiled, 'Sofia is a big mess with all the roads and pavements being mended. It's a circus here, you will see!' Driving past the new apartment blocks and the surrounding areas of semi-derelict land, they drove into the city down past an enormous radio tower and then into the main shopping area.

The shops were full of Western looking clothes, and at eight o'clock at night were still open for business. The bored looking shop assistants sat outside their shops on plastic stools, smoking and drinking espresso coffee from small plastic cups. Nearly empty, the old yellow trams trundled along their rickety rails, advertising airlines, chocolate bars and mobile telephones.

'You like jazz, I find a radio programme.' Suddenly

thc car was full of the sounds of the Dave Pike trio playing Besme Mucho. Bill Evans was on piano, Dave Pike on vibraphone and Herbie Lewis on double bass; it was a favourite track for Lambert.

'We have many bands like this in Bulgaria. You go to Jazz clubs with those girls?' This revelation was not in Peter Carney's book, but it sounded promising. But Lambert came out with the most over-used excuse known to any man: 'I am a married man Vera, but if the music is good maybe I can go somewhere tonight if there is time.' She laughed, 'You not know these girls and you are handsome man!'

The Radisson Hotel seemed very quiet, although there were people lounging around outside Flanagan's sitting beneath the umbrellas. They were mainly trippers, who like him were wearing leisure clothes. As he made for the lift to his room, through the glass door to the bar he could just distinguish a few of the refugees from the previous night. 'Same conversation, but this time in trainers,' Lambert laughed to himself, preferring the comfort of his cool room away from the pseudo-corporate conversations of the previous evening. He immediately phoned home when he returned to his room.

'Kate, it's Daddy, is mummy there?' In the background he could hear Samanda galloping around on the parquet floor in the living room, and then the sound of muffled voices.

'Daddy, she is saying awful things about you, I can't tell you what they are over the phone and she won't come and talk to you.' The gossiping neighbours had now invented a new seminal reason for his presence in Bulgaria. It was sure to be because of that bloody fool Prothero and his hairdresser wife Fiona.

'Darling, tell everyone that I am all right and not to worry. I am getting lots of information about my case and I will be back in a few days.' She told him that she loved him, that he wasn't to worry and that things would be better when he came back. Lambert believed that the jury might still be out on that account. Arabella was a bloody self-righteous hypocritical spoilt bitch.

According to the young receptionist in the Radisson the big jazz venue which was called *Swinging Hall*, didn't get going until about midnight, but she told him about a hole in the ground called *La Strada* which was only a street away. That evening, after a short stroll through the badly lit cobbled street, he found the dark entrance to the club. Down some rather broken steps it was situated underneath a theatre of the same name. The theatre itself was obviously closed and the photos in the glass cabinet outside looked a bit old and sun-bleached.

Inside the walls of the jazz club were painted black throughout and it had a slightly tatty quality which Lambert could easily associate with most of the English jazz clubs of the sixties. Around the room there were black and white photographs of all the great historical figures of jazz, which loomed over the cheap and battered tin tables and chairs. Dizzy Gillespie, Satchmo, Miles Davis and Charlie Parker youthfully smiled down on a chattering crowd of mainly students and younger people. There were no suits in the large open planned club which seemed exclusively for the locals. In a murky corner there was a bar selling mainly cheap Bulgarian beer and the stage was littered with a comprehensive display of rather dated electronics.

An old Fender Rhodes stage piano stood next to a battered upright Russian piano, with a chair on which someone had placed a pile of music. It was just the right height for the man who sat practicing his arpeggios up and down the worn piano keys. Opposite the stage, a sound engineer sat in a large booth shouting instructions to the musicians who were setting up their instruments.

Four large speakers loomed over the stage, and two battered playbacks stood pointing inwards towards the musicians. Fighting with an input plug a young man was trying to control the volume of an old Hammond organ, which he then swung into position adjacent to the smiling pianist.

The electric bass player was struggling with his fretless guitar. It was far too loud and the feedback made him wince. After the sound engineer had reduced the volume, he swung his long Rock 'n' Roll hair from side to side and talked to people in the audience who he obviously knew well. The drummer was absent and there was a Fender acoustic guitar with an electric bridge sitting on a high-backed chair at the rear of the stage. Lambert realised that musicians were the same the world over, and never seemed to want to begin to play.

Finally the pianist turned to the band and shouted

out *'Muchachos robota! Viva la Cuba!'* Slowly the drummer, who was thin and athletic, climbed onto the stage and sat on his revolving stool. Using one stick he started to play a Latino riff on the bell of his riveted symbol and then in staccato he played in double time on his high hat.

The base guitarist joined in with a sliding base chord and suddenly the whole band came to life. The acoustic guitarist appeared from nowhere, and the Hammond organ started to feed in blues chords taking the offbeat from the Cuban pianist. The trumpeter stood up from a table at the front of the stage, the tenor sax player lent against the bar and they started to blow hundreds of beautiful notes.

In this drab little Bulgarian club which smelt of piss and neglect, the beauty of their music transported Lambert into an entirely new world. Far away from the death of Liam Side, Lambert had once more successfully navigated his way back to a very special private place in his heart. It was where he could finally stand alone, silently in happiness and deep into the absorbing world of jazz. Tonight he would forget about Arabella.

After a few minutes a beautiful black girl got up onto the stage, smiled and with a deep husky voice, began to sing *Girl from Ipanema*. The Latino rhythms and the controlled vibrato of her voice blended perfectly with the band. In the background the sound of an old Moog softly created a harmony with her voice, the band playing their breaks and the jazz guitarist playing lush cords in the background. With smooth arpeggios and lilting harmony, it brought a new image to the emotionally failing eyesight of the middle-aged policeman who—for the moment at least—was far away from home.

London 1996. Antony Kwong is looking thoughtfully through the window of his fourth floor office at the passing traffic on the City Road. He knows that it is not the smartest address in London, but as a fringe banker he is not out to impress his customers. He personally controls a global trading and confirming house, which exists discreetly in the outer reaches of business finance and far away from public scrutiny. It deals exclusively with governments or very large international companies worldwide.

Antony is not his given name. When he was a schoolboy in Hong Kong his English master awarded each student an Anglicised name, because he could not actually pronounce or remember their Chinese forenames. One day, with twenty students in his class, he wrote twenty names on the blackboard starting with Antony and ending with Winston. Depending on who arrived in class early or who was late, determined the first letter of each name and Antony Kwong had come to school early that day.

The name Antony has remained with him from then onwards. He is not Hong Kong Chinese but from Taiwan, and as the son of a long dead officer in the Chaing Kia-shek Nationalist Army, he therefore comes from a wealthy Mandarin family. His only interest in life is money, which is interspersed—not untypically—with frequent visits from London's many call girls and regular visits to Gerrard Street in London's Soho district. It is here that he consumes plentiful amounts of his favourite food at his private table in the Fook Lam Sun restaurant.

Usually alone, Antony Kwong sits in silence while he ingests his morning meal of dim sum. When he returns in the evening, he blithely breathes in the familiar aroma of five spices and sucks in the delicious rice noodles which splash soup onto his face. Antony Kwong is round and fat and self-indulgent.

Although conciliatory and generous to his long neglected wife in Taipei, in her middle age she has learnt to appreciate the benefits of hard cash and rarely misses his presence. How he makes his money is another matter and remains to most, a subject clouded in mystery. In a war-torn world, it is not only iron ore and rice that fill the holds of his ships, but it is often far deadlier items which make his bank account swell. His guiding mantra is that with credit comes knowledge and with knowledge comes power.

Although he talks of friendship with the leaders of many countries, in truth they are often his victims too. That is why he has led a strangely inconspicuous life; by hiding in the forgiving shadows of London's multicultural society and—forever alone—it is where he imagines he is totally safe.

In his office there is a large number of fax machines, which due to his business paranoia are connected to most of his incoming telephones lines. He can read English far better than speaking it, or repeating it, which he often needs to do to be understood. Faxes are legal documents in business circles, but they are also evidence of his activities. Standing next to his bank of fax machines is a very powerful paper shredding machine and on the office shelves there are many unopened boxes of fax paper.

There are a number of singular reasons why he fosters ties with Peru, but in the end, it is mainly due to the personality of President Takahashi himself. Although he is of Japanese descent there are more similarities than differences between the two men. Peru possesses its own sizable Chinese population and has done so since the 1850s. So Takahashi is familiar with their culture and China has remained a substantial trading partner over the years.

Whilst Antony Kwong's late father studied at the Baoding Japanese Military College and was of Mandarin Chinese origin, Takahashi's father was a humble Japanese fisherman who found his way to Peru almost by chance. But despite the apparent lack of patriarchal synergy, there is one major similarity, which is their undisputed mutual desire for money and power.

Antony Kwong's influence does not stop there, because there is one other dynamic in his relationship with Peru. It is his burgeoning association with Vladamiro Ilich Rizotis Pinero, and it has made this unlikely trio very rich indeed. The son of a Peruvian communist of Greek origin, Pinero is now the de-facto

Minister of the Interior in Peru and a very powerful man indeed.

Graduating from the American Army School in Panama, Vladimiro Pinero in the past has worked for the CIA in Central America, but now, with a plethora of contradictions and contrasting venues at his disposal, it is he who gives Antony Kwong the unlikely commission to deliver 10,000 AK 47 rifles to the FARC rebels in nearby Colombia and the acquisition from Belorussia of a squadron of MiG 29s for the Peruvian Airforce.

What seems incongruous to Kwong is how this consignment of weapons seem to be at odds with two marked political extremes; the right wing Fascist government of Peru and the Communist insurgents of Colombia. Although it matters little to Antony Kwong who has what and for what purpose, he wonders why Vladimiro Pinero, as the Peruvian Minister of the Interior, is prepared to take such a political risk. There can only be one answer and that is greed. This is something Kwong totally understands and thoroughly condones.

To Antony Kwong greed has always been a given and dealing with corrupt governments is his speciality. Trans shipping items from one destination to another is also easy for someone who controls a vast shipping fleet, even if it means transferring a cargo at sea. The Pacific is a very large area of water and almost impossible to police. Even with sophisticated spy satellites, the Americans have discovered that they cannot be everywhere in the world at the same time.

Kwong is also a master of deception and is well aware

of how to organise the packing and labelling of illegal cargos. This alone has accounted for much of his success in the past, together with the tampering of ships' manifests as they go from port to port. Bribing customs officials with often huge amounts of money has helped Antony Kwong to develop a grateful and loyal following, because there are many ports and countries which do not object in practice to the trafficking of large consignments of weapons, drugs and occasionally, of very young women.

In many cases the trade in arms is specifically linked to the cocaine trade, because any self-respecting *liberation army* is required to strictly control their production areas and naturally that means guns. Antony Kwong is a facilitator for these trades and is one of an exclusive band who maintains a wicked hold on the world of addiction and death.

But he also needs Vladimiro Pinero to take care of his *End User Certificates* and to keep the United Nations and the WTO happy. This is just as true of Pinero who in turn needs Antony Kwong to fix and finance his deals. It is a very cosy relationship.

It was Sunday morning and Michael Lambert sat outside Flanagan's, with a pint of Guinness. It was more like black lager than stout and despite the froth, which looked reasonably authentic, there was little else to recommend it. In the distance he saw the bobbing head of Richard Hampton going through his routine having recently discovered a new victim, but Lambert averted his gaze in order to consider his present position more fully.

He had recently consumed a rather large so-called *Irish Breakfast*, and was unsure of the wisdom of having done so. The toothpick reminded him of the appalling quality of Bulgarian sausages, a piece of bone having demolished one of his older fillings. As he sipped his black lager he went through a long list of unknowns.

What was not totally clear to him was whether the murdered man was actually Liam Side at all. Considering Eddie Singh's remarks about the dead man's antecedence being of Spanish origin, it rather confounded the issue since there was no corroborating information anywhere to be found regarding the man Liam Side.

He had tried to track him through the UK Social Security and health system, the tax system, through the various armed service organisations, and extensively through police files. It was possible that the man was from the Republic of Ireland, but Eire now shared its information with the UK and had done so for some while. There was no information forthcoming concerning the victim's fingerprints and it took time for the police to track people down—with any certainty— through their DNA.

Somerset House had not revealed any name changes, nor was there any information forthcoming from the passport authorities. There were no UK passports issued in the name of Liam Side nor was there a driving licence. This only left the Bulgarian authorities and the

Americans as a source of information. There was also an outside chance that the Canadians and Aussies might have some knowledge of the victim's nationality. That was why Lambert had been interested in how he actually spoke, in order to narrow down the origin of the dead man.

There was an outside possibility that the US authorities might have some knowledge of Liam Side even if these activities were generally unknown to the British Government, and for once they might decide to help. The Yanks kept tabs on anyone that they came across, particularly any Irish and British citizens. The final possibility was that Liam Side was a spook, who was working under an assumed name at the Balkan Western News. Such an undercover activity might have accounted for angst amongst some, but was hardly a reason for murder.

Lambert paid his bill and went into the reception area looking for a newspaper. There was the usual *New York Herald Tribune*, but very little else, just *Newsweek* and *Geographica*. Apart from the ongoing saga of Kosovo which had virtually come to a halt by 1999, there was little of interest in the newspaper and so Lambert splashed out on a rather expensive copy of *Newsweek*. In it was a story about Peru and the flight of their enigmatic President Alberto Takahashi to Japan. It was a story involving the embezzlement of millions of dollars, and the flight of his right-hand man Vladamiro Pinero.

Having only read some of the article, Lambert took the lift, and returned once more to his hotel bedroom.

At one o'clock his mobile phone woke him from a doze. He had been relaxing in his room by an open window and looking out on the square.

It was Vera Kolova. She wondered if he would like her to collect him from the hotel that afternoon to take him to her house which was close to the Military Academy. She told him that she had a nice quiet shady garden where he could sit and read in peace, through the files that Liam Side had left her to look after.

CHAPTER FOUR

VERA KOLOVA sat behind the wheel of her BMW waiting for Lambert to leave the hotel. It was another hot day. As she dressed that morning, she thought about meeting the enigmatic English policeman with pleasure, although she was still unsure if he had told her everything he knew about Liam Side or his alleged murder on the Kennet and Avon Canal. Somehow there were details missing, especially when it came to the simple question of why he was there in the first place.

In the past Liam had rarely mentioned England to her and although it was clear that he went there from time to time, he was far more likely to have gone to Greece for a summer holiday than to take a trip on an English river boat. Then there were details about his identification. Although the photographs that the detective had shown her resembled Liam in essence, there was something strange about his appearance.

It was difficult to put her finger on the exact reason, because the Liam Side who she knew always wore jeans and a tee shirt. He had never owned a blazer as far as she could remember and if he needed to go somewhere formal, he would wear the same old-fashioned Irish thorn-proof suit with a red knitted tie. It was his only suit. If anything, Liam was famous for being a little bit scruffy, but the photograph on the narrow boat was of a prosperous well-dressed businessman. She had looked at the photographs very carefully. Dressed in smart clothes with an expensive haircut and a gold Rolex Oyster wristwatch, he could hardly have been more different from the man she had known. Liam always claimed that he only owned a cheap plastic Swatchwatch, which he had purchased at the Tzum department store in the city centre.

Mike Lambert had somehow endeared himself to Vera because he appeared to be a compassionate man. Believing Liam Side to be dead he still referred to him in kindly terms, not wishing to upset her with the gory details of his murder.

Perhaps he believed that one should show respect to people in death, as in life, and it did not cost him anything to refer to Liam Side in a dignified way. That is why she had telephoned a friend from the past. It was in order for Lambert to glean some accurate background information about Liam's activities in Bulgaria. She believed that the English policeman deserved to know at least some of the truth.

Until quite recently Lt. Col. Yuri Vassilev had been the deputy director of The Ministry of The Interior main passport office in Maria Louisa Boulevard in Sofia. A rancorous argument with his deeply prejudiced boss had recently convinced him to return to normal police duty. As the newly appointed Chief of Police in Pristina, he was now seconded to the KFOR administration. Pristina was a place where he had recently experienced a distinct feeling of freedom, despite the plight of the poor beleaguered Kosovans themselves.

Col. Stressov, his ex-bureau chief in Sofia, still clung onto the poisonous views of the old regime and heartily enjoyed intimidating and humiliating foreigners who needed to stay for any length of time in Bulgaria. Occasionally an individual would *see the light*, pay a sizable bribe to Col. Stressov and become an exception to the rule, when their application swiftly progressed to a satisfactory conclusion. To encourage similar payments, Stressov's reasons for not issuing an internal passport or for finding fault with a written application were legion, and in terms of his inventiveness, were on a par with the bureaucratic fantasies of Franz Kafka.

Although Yuri Vassilev had come from the same background as Stressov, he was not cast from the same mould and so the foreigner-hating antics of the police authorities were all anathema to him. The consequence was that European Union countries now made it difficult for the locals to travel, which was hardly surprising bearing in mind the difficulties experienced in trying to operate a normal business in Bulgaria. A 'tit for tat' restrictive programme was in full swing, although official accession into the EU was only a few years away from final approval.

Lambert finally emerged from the hotel. He was decked

out in a smart short-sleeved white shirt and grey trousers. Carrying a large box of chocolates, he was quite unlike the remnants of the lunchtime drinkers in Flanagan's, and looked clear eyed and attentive as he climbed into the passenger seat of the BMW. Vera Koleva seemed pleased to see him and told him about the friend they were about to meet at her home in Sofia.

When they finally arrived in Momchil Voivoda Street, Lambert was impressed with the simplicity of her house. Having expected something a little more ornate and brash, he was now better able to understand his attractive hostess. Sitting in the garden reading that morning's copy of *The Duma* was a tough looking man, with very distinctive and penetrating blue eyes.

'Mr Lambert, I would like you to meet my friend Lt. Col. Yuri Vassilev. He is a policeman like you and he is home on leave from Kosovo.'

The two policemen shook hands and Lambert sat down on a tin chair next to the policeman. Vassilev had been chain smoking so there were quite a number of dog ends in the ashtray, which stood next to a practically empty packet of Kent cigarettes and a Zippo lighter.

Lambert remembered from earlier days in England, how easy it was for professional policemen to relax in one another's company despite coming from different countries. Cheerfully asking, 'How long are you home for Colonel?', he was surprised at how well the Bulgarian policeman spoke English when he answered his question.

'Just a few days, Chief Inspector Lambert,' he said

with a wry smile, 'You see, I have been checking up on you already! How is the Thames Valley Division these days?'

Lambert felt a little exposed but, realising that the Bulgarian policeman only meant to be on good terms, he replied, 'You certainly keep your fingers on the pulse Colonel, which is more than I could do on a Sunday afternoon in Reading.'

A chilled bottle of Han Krum dry white wine, an assortment of nuts and nibbles and some black olives appeared from the house and Vera Koleva sat down between the two policemen. The clean ashtray she brought with her became full within minutes as all three smoked their particular brand of cigarettes. Lambert had many questions on his mind, but he thought that he would start at the beginning. 'Did you know Liam Side well, Colonel?'

The Bulgarian policeman seemed to think for a moment. 'Yes, we met on a number of occasions, Mr Lambert. The first time was when he was being messed about by my old boss and for no reason at all. Being one day late for an internal passport renewal application was not a proper reason for denying him a five-year pass. The majority of western businessmen easily had that after one year; if they worked for people like Price Waterhouse Coopers, or KPMG. It was obvious that Col. Stressov was playing silly games and trying to intimidate Mr Side.'

'Why do you think it happened? Didn't he consider him to be like all the rest of the foreigners?'

Vassilev stubbed out his umpteenth Kent cigarette and lit up a newer version. 'It was the magazine, Mr Lambert; you see, in our country we believe that any magazine or newspaper must have some powerful business or political party behind it. The authorities could not believe that a foreigner would come to Bulgaria and start a publication without some ulterior motive. It's the conspiracy theory in action, Mr Lambert, and from his file it was clear that he was suspected of being an agent of either the Americans or the British Government.'

Lambert was intrigued. 'Did you personally believe it, Colonel? Surely you would need some evidence at least in order to suspect someone?'

'I did at first, because just after the changes there were literally hundreds of small companies and NGOs appearing from all over Europe and the West. This was particularly true of the Americans who had a raft of phony so-called "Business Consultants" pretending to help Bulgarians to create investment plans and feasibility studies for the totally non-performing banks.'

He went on: 'Then there were some educational foundations and university representations arriving from the US mostly sponsored by USAid. You see, it was partly my job to investigate them, or more particularly the foreign staff who came with them. When I dug around in their past, I soon discovered that many of the American lecturers or managers had been in the US armed services, which obviously was where they had been recruited from in the first place.'

Lambert twisted his wine glass around for a moment. 'So what, you thought that Side was the same and that his news magazine was a cover for something else?' It seemed odd to Lambert that so much suspicion could be heaped onto one individual without a firm reason. 'And, when did you change your mind, Colonel, and when was your moment of doubt?'

'He came to see me and told me that he now had a little daughter. We already knew he was living at the time with a Russian woman in Vassil Levski Street. He admitted to me that he would have left Bulgaria like a shot, were it not for his daughter. But we also knew about the Russian woman for another reason. This was because she was in the country illegally. The Russians were our closest ally before the changes and we didn't want to upset them in any way, so it was agreed to leave Side alone for the time being and to issue him with another one-year pass.'

'Am I right in saying that Side was quite a rarity in Sofia and that his only perceived crime was that of being an idealist?' The ramifications of post-Cold War thinking were becoming horrifyingly evident to the provincial English policeman, as he tried to deal with his opposite number's analysis and his ex-Communist view. 'Can you remember when and where his UK passport was issued?'

'My dear Chief Inspector, Mr Side was not an Englishman; he was born and bred in Africa!'

The afternoon progressed and very soon the mosquitoes started to bite and they moved from the garden into the house. Looking around Lambert noticed how the furniture seemed to come from another time, probably gleaned from the Stalinist era; it spoke of family hand-me-downs and, interposed with eclectic pieces of bric-à-brac from around the world, the inevitable passage of time.

It also seemed that Vera Kolova had been to other places in the world apart from those within the communist bloc. There was a plastic gondola from Venice with an electric bulb and flex, a wooden elephant from the Punjab and some tribal masks from Africa.

He particularly noticed how few books there were in the sitting room, which simply confirmed that Vera Kolova was no intellect. Lambert asked his hostess, 'Where did all these things come from? Did people give them to you?' She looked round the room and then smiled at him.

'I was an air hostess when I was younger and I flew with the national carrier all round the world. I was ex-President Zhivkov's personal air hostess when he made his visits to other countries. We went to many places together in Europe and the Middle East. That is, everywhere except Great Britain. Georgi Markov saw to that. Comrade Zhivkov was never invited there—unlike the Romanian President Ceausescu—it was so unfair!'

At seven o'clock that evening, Yuri Vassilev made his apologies and left. But before he did he told Lambert that he would help him if he could, because he still had friends at Maria Louisa and access to police files.

But it was now time to look through Side's effects and at the files which he had stored before he disappeared off the radar. 'When did you last see Mr Side, and do you remember what month it was, Vera?'

'It was about a year ago, Michael, in July of last year. It was just as the elections started and took over the media. I remember him saying to me that all Bulgaria had to offer the world was gasbags, more gasbags and talking heads. He said that it was life imitating art and that he had watched quite enough Samuel Becket and Harold Pinter in the past. He told me once, that he might write a book about Bulgaria one day, if only he could think of anything to say. He was right of course; it is a circus here, that's all.'

It was a cardboard box with Kellogg's Cornflakes written on the side. The top was open, and a number of magazines had been shoved inside. They were copies of *The Balkan Western News* and very similar to the one they found on the narrow boat. There were about sixty different editions which must have covered the whole period of publication, recording five years of changing fortunes in South Eastern Europe.

Lambert put them to one side and then removed a box file. Underneath he saw there were also two buff files, which he placed on the table and began to inspect. Vera Kolova was in the kitchen. He could hear the sound of her coffee percolator bubbling and the rattling of cups and saucers.

The first buff file appeared to contain a stack of household utility bills which seemed to cover a considerable number of years, judging by the dates which were printed on them. But he was little interested in this file and quickly put it to one side. The second buff file was marked *Private and Personal*, and contained a number of what seemed to be contracts and legal documents; all of which were in Bulgarian.

He made this out from the many official stamps and signatures which had been applied, and it appeared that these documents might be for anything ranging from property leases and agreements to court documents. So he also put this file to one side and finally opened the big box file. This proved to be far more rewarding and in time would tell Lambert a quite different story about the *Kennet Narrow Boat Mystery*.

Nearly all the contents were in English and were a mixture of letters, fading faxes and photocopies. They had been kept in date order and bull-clipped into subject matters which he could see were partly about business, together with some private matters involving a London lawyer.

What took his particular attention was a folder containing a cash flow and feasibility study. It concerned a proposed development project involving the renting of apartments in Sofia, the refurbishment and the re-letting of these units to foreign companies. Tucked in the front cover were copies of letters sent by various banks and investors. On the back inside cover there were some names and telephone numbers. Lambert would research these at a later date.

The letters to the London lawyer were mainly about Side's daughter Patricia. In them he clearly wanted to find out what her status was concerning citizenship, by asking whether she was South African, Bulgarian or Russian. There was a copy of what he took to be a Bulgarian birth certificate, attached to one particular lawyer's letter, and a two-page photocopy of his internal Bulgarian passport on which particular things had been specifically recorded in Cyrillic script.

Finally at the bottom he found a box of floppy disks and an out-of-date South African passport which had been stamped *GEKANSELLEER/CANCELLED*. It had been stamped by the South African embassy in Sofia. This was the most interesting item in the whole box file and one which would lead him to seek out the South African embassy.

Vera agreed to let Mike take the box file and the file containing Bulgarian legal documents back to his hotel. She knew that he would look after the contents but, as he explained to her, he needed photocopies of all the relevant documents and there was a business bureau with a copying machine at his hotel.

In the morning he would spend time inspecting documents, and faxing them to Gloria Hislop in Reading. He remembered Gloria's words to him before he left, telling him to be sure that she was the one and only translator. Vera also agreed to let him take the floppy disks which he could read on his laptop when he returned to his room at the Radisson Hotel that evening.

The trip back to the square was uneventful and Lambert asked Vera what she did as a job. 'I have a hotel in Bruges,' she turned to him and smiled, 'It has fifty rooms and it keeps me busy most of the time. It is a commercial hotel for business people.'

'Where do you live when you are in Belgium?' Lambert was surprised at the unassuming nature of the woman, realising how modest and successful she must be in business.

'I have my room there at the hotel but this is my home because this is where my true friends are.'

When they arrived at the Radisson, it was getting on for ten o'clock at night and despite Lambert's offer of a drink in the bar, Vera Kolova chose to go home. Nodding her head she said by way of explanation, 'All the crazies drive around Sofia at night, so you have to be careful! But I will be here this week in Sofia and you have my phone number.' And so they left it at that and he told her that he would phone in the next two days to arrange the return of the files and the floppy disks.

His room was cool and he sat for a while watching the BBC news on the cable service. On it was a short item about the possible extradition of ex-President Takahashi to Peru from Japan, where he had been in hiding for some months. It told of delays and procrastination by the Japanese government and its reluctance to send him back to Peru, which was his naturalised home.

Lambert's mobile sprang to life and shocked him out of his thoughts. It had been a long day and there was much to consider. 'Hello Mike? It's Gloria speaking, I've got some weird news for you. There has been a break in at your house in Sonning. Has anyone phoned you about it yet? Your Mr Durant wants you to telephone him in the morning; apparently he could not get through to Bulgaria. He told me that nothing has been taken, so they must have been looking for something in particular. Either that or they wanted to upset your wife, Mike. She's hopping mad! Do you think it is anything to do with our murder mystery?'

Lambert was dumbfounded and didn't really know how to answer Gloria. 'Well, it could be, I suppose; whoever these people are they don't seem to be frightened of anyone, hence the break in on the narrow boat in the police boatyard. But to be safe, tomorrow I will arrange for a patrol car to keep an eye on you, Gloria.' They did seem to be very determined to find something. He added, 'And I suggest that you securely lock up all our information somewhere until I get back.'

'This apartment is a bit like *Fort Knox*, Mike. It would take a very determined thief to break in here, but I will take your advice and double check all the doors and windows before I go to bed.' Her voice sounded just a little fearful and he really did not want to frighten her in any way.

'Is there anything else for me Gloria, or can it all wait until tomorrow?' Mike Lambert did not want to speak too much on the phone in case someone was monitoring his call. A very un-British thought he knew, but since his conversation with Col. Vassilev he now realised that all things were possible in Bulgaria and that he would be very wise to keep his unofficial police presence a secret.

He had to keep reminding himself that he was not on his home turf and that he could quite easily become a victim himself unless he was very careful. She went on by saying, 'That's okay Mike, there is nothing new here, but I thought I would touch base with you since I hadn't heard from you for a bit. I just wanted to know that you were all right, that's all.'

Lambert seemed to be surrounded by caring women now he was far away from his permanently miffed wife Arabella. He knew that she would not be very happy if she believed that the Sonning break-in was something to do with his police work. In future he would refer to it as a botched burglary; of which there were many in the Reading area, but he strongly suspected that it was not.

'Gloria, I have got to go through some papers tonight and I thought I would fax some of the documents which are in Cyrillic to you tomorrow, so that you can give me some positive feedback.' Once more he asked her to be careful and to carefully lock up her apartment.

He switched off his mobile phone and decided to buy a public phone card from the hotel reception the following morning, which he would use for any future calls to Gloria. Considering the most recent events in Sonning he felt it wise to be as secretive as possible and a public telephone was the best solution and perfectly anonymous.

Lambert was tired so he took a shower and then lay on the bed mulling over the day's events. He was sure that both Vera Kolova and Yuri Vassilev were essentially telling him the truth and that the documents he had brought from her home were genuine and had not been doctored in any way.

The events in England were also quite clear to him including the murder. The facts surrounding the man's death could not be so easily explained, because so far there was no motive. It seemed to him that there might also be some doubt as to the identity of the murdered man, although on balance it still appeared to be Liam Side. But what if it wasn't?

There was an easy answer to that question. If it was not him, where was he? Putting aside the identity of the dead man on the boat for a moment, he believed it was time to start digging around a bit more into the background of Liam Side. The two obvious places to start a search were the British Embassy and the South African mission in Sofia. However it occurred to him that without an official mandate from Interpol or permission from the Bulgarian authorities, all his enquiries would have to be unquestionably on the old QT.

Lambert awoke at three in the morning only to find all the lights on and the TV blaring away. Getting up, he double locked the entrance door to the room, turned off the TV set, put on his tee shirt and shorts and climbed into bed. Everything else would now have to wait until the morning.

The clamour of the early morning traffic in the square somehow crept past the double glazing and the balcony shutters, rescuing him from a deep but troubled sleep. It was now seven o'clock in the morning and Lambert got out of bed with a sense of resolve. He had a lot to do in the few days left to him before his return to England. Realising that he was two hours ahead of the UK, he thought that he would put off any phone calls to Arabella until later on. He was anticipating the usual tirade that she administered on such occasions, together with the customary admonishments about his income status; but she could wait.

After an indifferent breakfast in the first floor restaurant, Lambert went in search of a City map. The receptionist was helpful and didn't seem to resent having to work for her salary. It was now eight o'clock but there was still no sign of movement in the business centre. Looking through the window he could see a number of computer screens which sat on various desks and a large plain paper copier. On the reception desk just inside the bureau there was a small Brother Fax machine, which doubled as a telephone and would hopefully solve some of his communication problems later on with Gloria Hislop.

The map he received from the receptionist was a glossy City-centre one, with all the major buildings well marked and easy to distinguish. He could see the British, French, German and US embassies, but there was no sign of the South African embassy. This time, the receptionist reached over the counter and handed Lambert a small glossy brochure advertising the various entertainments on offer in Sofia. She told him that the address and telephone of the South African embassy should be in it somewhere. Finally he bought a 50-Leva BTC local phone card.

Before doing anything else, he went back to his room

to look at the contents of the box file. Sitting in the window seat he first inspected the development project. The sight of all the different fringe bankers and financiers was an eye opener for Lambert, considering *the black marks* that Bulgaria had received in the British press as a destination for investment.

None of them were familiar names and the British high street banks were nowhere to be seen. There was a mixture of Hedge Fund operators and London property developers with a few private Investment banks that were connected to firms of Chartered Surveyors or Solicitors. But there was one unusual letter which was different from the rest.

It was from a company called Yellow Sea Industries and Shipping Incorporated. In it there was a firm offer for finance subject to an annual return of 30%. The offer was for ten tranches of 20,000 GBP, to be paid to Liam Side's company Balkan Side Ltd., over a period of two years.

The proposed investor operated from an office somewhere at the top end of The City Road in London, together with a head office in Lin Hong North Road in Taipei. What was odd was the remainder of the address, which said Taiwan (Formosa) in The Republic of China. How odd this Taiwanese address seemed to Lambert, when as other people would naturally believe, Taiwan was regarded as being quite independent from mainland China. When he returned to England he would find out a little bit more about their business dealings.

The rest of the letters were either straight refusals, or

offers in principal subject to a variety of conditions, not unlike those expected from a building society or a joint stock bank. They all wanted huge returns on their investment which made Lambert's eyes water a little, but were much the same as the proposed Taiwanese offer of finance. Their reasons seemed mainly connected to risk. Lambert put this file to one side so that he could photocopy the contents later. He then moved onto the London lawyer's correspondence which concerned Liam Side's daughter Patricia.

This was a protracted exchange of letters where it was clear that the London lawyer was trying to build up some fees. Each evasive reply to one of Side's letters came with another question for him. This continued on eight further occasions, until it was evident that Side was losing confidence in his chosen lawyer. From the various comments made, it was obvious that his lawyer was more at home with property matters than general practice issues. It left Lambert with the impression that they must have known one another in the past, perhaps when Side was property dealing in London. This was something else he would have to follow up later. Lambert put a number of the Bulgarian documents to one side from this section, all to be photocopied and then faxed for translation to Gloria later that day.

He then turned to a bunch of papers which seemed to be covered by a series of codes. He had no idea what they represented, but were certainly a mystery which had to be solved at some point. There were fourteen sections in all, with two sub-sections each. Within each sub-section there were a series of Cyrillic letters followed by some random numbers and finally a date. This much he could understand and the dates referred in the list ranged from late 1979 to early 1981. So, whatever these codes concerned they appeared to be over twenty years old.

Lambert put these aside to be copied and then went on to the cancelled passport. The date of issue was January 1990 and it was a standard ten-year South African passport. It was issued to Side by the Department of the Interior in Northern Cape Provence and in it was a slip confirming payment of 400 Rand. The identity photograph was obviously of a much younger man but not dissimilar to the photograph of the murder victim.

It meant that a new passport must have been issued in January 2000, which by Lambert's reckoning would probably have emanated from the consular section of the South African embassy in Sofia. But what was of major interest were the entrance and exit cross border stamps, which littered the pages of the old passport, because what was unusual was that most of them were for the Bulgarian Dragoman border crossing into Serbia. Covering a period of three years and starting from early in 1997 up to the day of the passport's cancellation, this had been the approximate time of the NATO bombardment of Serbia and the consequent invasion of Kosovo by IFOR.

Liam Side had been presented to Lambert by both Vera Kolova and Yuri Vassilev as a peaceful and almost academic man, but their description of him was beginning to be belied by the facts. Why would a man, beset with Side's accumulated problems, risk his life in a belligerent country which was at war with the West? There was either a lot that the two did not know, or they were keeping something back from him. Perhaps the answer would be found at either the British or the South African embassies.

Returning to the hotel reception and realising that he might have a language difficulty, Lambert asked the receptionist to get him a taxi to take him to the British Embassy. It was now close to eleven in the morning and he had to get a move on because he had a full day ahead of him. Arriving at the embassy in Moskovska Street he paid the driver ten Leva and walked up to the reception kiosk. Having stated his business, the electronic door opened which allowed him access to the reception area. After a few minutes he was met by an older man who explained to Lambert that he was the security officer. Edwin Page looked at the policeman's warrant card and asked him to accompany him to his office.

'I was a copper too before I took on this lot!' Edwin Page was a policeman from the old school. 'My wife Mable and I were getting fed up with Penge and thought we deserved a change and so here we are!'

He was a jolly man and it was a great boost to Lambert's feeling of isolation to meet both an Englishman and a fellow copper. 'What can I do you for Chief Inspector?'

'You may have read that a murder took place just

outside Reading on a narrow boat which was moored on the Kennet and Avon Canal. We are having difficulty in identifying the murder victim, but we believe it might be a man who lived here in Sofia. We think his name was Liam Side and that he was the owner of an English language news magazine called *The Balkan Western News*.'

The look on Page's face told a story all of its own. '*That* man! Well, I'm not surprised. He was a total pain in the bum as far as the embassy is concerned and there won't be many who will miss him here, believe me.'

The look of surprise on Lambert's face was a picture in itself, because he was expecting at least a few kind words of condolence from this humdrum embassy security man. 'I thought he was a pillar of the expat community Mr Page; now you surprise me. I have read some past copies of his magazine and they seemed very complimentary to most Embassies, even to the less important countries and their presence in Bulgaria.'

Giving Lambert a knowing look, Edwin Page was quite forward in his reply. 'You see, Mr Lambert, that was true of the British Embassy as well, until an English friend of Side got mugged one day and phoned the embassy for help. You see, he had lost all his documents as well as his money and you know what that can be like in a foreign country?'

He went on: 'When he phoned the Consular Section, one of our English ladies working here told this man to pull himself together and, amongst other things, advised him to sort it out himself. Not unnaturally he went to the newspapers and that is where Side got into the act. He wrote an article called "The Easter Bunny Loses his Money", and then all hell broke loose.' Edwin Page offered Lambert one of his Victory cigarettes, which he refused, and then kept shaking his head as the story unfolded.

'The ambassador got hauled over the coals by the Foreign Office and a copy of this magazine even appeared in front of a Parliamentary Committee at the House of Lords. That's why we didn't like him very much, Mr Lambert, and why he has remained persona-non-grata ever since. The ambassador even accused him once of being a traitor!'

Harking back to Chief Superintendent Burrows' remarks about diplomats being useless, and according to the story he had just heard, it occurred to Lambert that Burrows might well have been right. But at least the Embassy might be good for something, especially if they possessed a good secure and modern fax machine.

'I was informed by someone in authority that he was in fact a South African. Did you know that, Mr Page?' The embassy policeman looked very puzzled as he absorbed Lambert's last observation.

'But he was so English. I met him on a few occasions and he sounded—well, how can I put it—severely middle class, for want of a better expression.'

'The most important issue for me Mr Page is not where he came from, but why he was allegedly found dead on the Kennet and Avon canal. My main problem now is a simple matter of identification. The killers and their motive will have to wait.'

'Of course the embassy will be delighted to offer you any Consular Assistance that you may require, Mr Lambert; and I will check our records of course, but I am afraid that there is very little I can tell you about this man, other than what I just told you.'

It was however agreed that Mike Lambert could use the embassy's combined fax copier machine, and having given the security officer Gloria Hislop's fax number in Reading, the documents requiring translation were duly sent to her, together with a complete photocopy of Side's old South African passport and the various pages within. Whilst this was happening, Chief Inspector Lambert sat in *Little England*, and drank a mug of Tetley's tea.

Leaving the sleepy Sofia embassy that morning, with the documents and cancelled passport safely secreted in his pocket, Lambert was convinced that the embassy staff were living in some pre-World War Two time warp, underlining the Chief Superintendent's views on diplomacy in general.

Walking down Moskovska he chanced upon a public telephone which was jutting out into the street from an adjoining block next to the embassy. Taking out his pre-paid telephone card he tapped out Gloria Hislop's telephone number.

'Gloria, it's Mike here. Look, I have just faxed some documents to you care of the British embassy and I thought that I would briefly explain to you what I want you to do. First of all have you received them yet?'

'They came through about ten minutes ago, and as far as I can see they are perfectly readable. So, what's the story?'

'I have managed to get my hands on most of Side's documents, but it now seems that he was not exactly as we presupposed. For a start, he is not British but in fact a South African. Secondly, he was not only involved in publishing, but he had other business interests as well, which might not be quite as straightforward as we thought. He also had a family of sorts in Sofia, because he fathered a young daughter by some Russian woman here in the capital. So there are suddenly various personal aspects of his life that we need to clear up.'

Lambert had the ability to deal in minute details without losing sight of the big picture. Speculation was not one of his many attributes, which was something he happily left to the spooks, or for *so-called journalists* to provide for the yellow newspapers, especially when the facts were running out.

'If I can just run through what I have Mike, there is a lot of stuff from a South African passport; about twenty pages from what I can see, and there are two pages from what looks like of one of those internal passports that the victims of Communism had to carry around with them. And what else is there? Oh right! There is a Bulgarian birth certificate and a further one from *The Maichin Dom—or Mother's House*—at 2 Zdravka Street Sofia 1431. This last one confirms the names of the father and mother, the name of the daughter which is stated as Patricia Liamova Side, her weight at birth, his internal passport number, and it also confirms that there were no complications or problems at birth.'

'What about his internal passport, Gloria? Does that give any further information? I will run out of time if I'm not careful, because I am leaving on Friday first thing, and I don't want to waste my time unnecessarily.'

Gloria went on, 'That document also confirms the date and place of the birth and the child's name, confirming him to be the natural father. There is also a note of his present address which is somewhere in Vassil Levski Street, Sofia, but there are a few other things I need to check out from my Bulgarian dictionary, all of which I will need to study for an hour or so.'

Promising to telephone Gloria that evening Lambert rang off, and then contacting Reading Police Station, he asked for Sergeant Durant who immediately answered his phone. 'George, I hear that we have had a break-in at home?' Lambert went straight to the point.

'Yes Boss, it was the local plod who answered the call. Of course they wandered all over the house poking around and ruining the crime scene—no surprise there—so there was little or no evidence indicating who the culprits were. I heard the call on the radio and went along more or less out of interest. Then the fingerprint boys arrived and dusted all your lovely antique furniture with nice silver powder. Arabella shouted about and called us all a bunch of twerps, and then I went home.'

George Durant went on, 'from what I could see it was a jemmy job, Boss, and not a very sophisticated one either. None of your toffee-nosed neighbours apparently saw or heard anything. There were no tyre or foot marks that I could see near the property. The publican at the Bull said there was a car left in his car park—which was gone by morning—but he said that it was not so unusual with the drinkers around Sonning. So there is nothing much to report. Got to be the phone, hasn't it?'

'Did you say anything to Arabella George? Does she have any idea what it was all about?' Lambert wanted to keep her in the dark about his present investigation, but he also wanted to know what to say when he phoned her up.

'No, I just said it was a botched break-in and that if anything was missing, she was to tell the plod and they would keep a lookout for any stolen items. Meanwhile she was to check all the door locks and window catches and to inform her insurance company about any damage that might have occurred. Not much more to tell you really.'

'Okay, George. Well, briefly, I am getting on quite well with the case, but I want you to check out two items for me. One is a firm of Solicitors in Hammersmith, and the other is a Taiwanese shipping company in the fringe city in London, but I want you to check it out personally this time; keep it to yourself and maintain a very low profile.'

'What about the spooks Boss, I hear from the Super that they are getting interested in our murder; what shall I do if they start earwigging about? And why are they so interested in a stiff on a bloody narrow boat?'

'I gather that they think he is an IRA suspect, but you can tell the Super that I can prove that he is in fact a South African. That should put them off for a bit. Tomorrow, you can go and see Gloria Hislop and she will give you a copy of Side's old passport, which you can then give to our digestively challenged Superintendent. Oh, and by the way, while you are with him you can tell him that he was right about the British diplomats and I thoroughly agree with him that they are all permanently out to lunch!'

Finally it was time to telephone his wife, which he chose to do from his room through the Radisson Hotel switchboard. He needed to make it look as though he made all his calls via this route, in order to divert suspicion by any prying eyes. But this could happen after he had consumed at least one pint of the local bitter. Walking into the city centre down Moskovska Street, he finally arrived at Tsar Osvoboditel Boulevard. Walking through the communal gardens and onto the Parliament Square, he arrived once more at the Radisson.

In an odd sort of way Flannigan's bar seemed to be a comfortable refuge at midday, with only one odd couple occupying a table outside overlooking the square. They were engaged in a heated argument and angrily prodding a Sofia City map with their forefingers. The disagreement seemed mainly about which way up the map should be, but in the end, they just got up and left.

Lighting a Victory cigarette, Lambert blew the smoke up into the clear blue sky then took a first long draught of the consoling brown liquid before him. It seemed to hit the spot immediately. As he relaxed, almost at once his mind started to circle around the events so far. This reverie started with the murder case, which somehow evolved to thoughts of home and Arabella, which finally descended into the matter of him remaining in the UK at all. Acting as a gentle reminder, his trip to Sofia had somehow revealed to him that, despite the passing of the years, he still might possess the courage for one final transformation.

What the hell was he doing with his life? Even the inscrutable Colonel Yuri Vassilev had opted for a career change as a policeman and he was well into his fifties. Was he, Lambert, now destined to replace his dyspeptic Chief Superintendent, to continue putting up with his hellish domestic home life, and thereafter slowly drift into some premature dotage? No, that was never going to happen! But why were these thoughts occurring to him today? For that there was an easy answer. It was because at this very moment in time, he could simply please himself. Personal freedom was the one thing that he had never really been allowed.

The hustle and bustle of his life had all started from the time he left school. First came the army, to be closely followed by his commission and training at The Royal Military College. Then there had been a further four years at The Royal Military College of Science and finally the award of a BSc (Eng) degree. This was followed by marriage to Arabella, the birth of Jedd and Kate and then finally—on reaching retirement from the British Army—he was propelled into a career with a very demanding Police force. It was as though there had been no time to breathe.

Certainly there had been no time to dream, but right now Lambert knew he had to face a cross examination from Arabella and her usual tirade. As he made his way into the hotel reception area to collect his door key-card, the receptionist handed him a handwritten message. It was from someone called Thomas Biko. The message asked him to phone after three o'clock that afternoon, so that they could make an appointment to meet later in the day. It didn't mention what it was about.

Back in his room, Lambert looked out over the Narodnie Square from his sunny balcony. The traffic was jammed up, and the horns were working overtime in the humid early afternoon. He closed the aluminium doors to the balcony and turned on the air conditioning. Dialling his familiar home number, the receiver was picked up almost immediately and Arabella's strangely calm voice answered.

'It's Michael; I'm phoning from the hotel, can you hear me okay?' Suddenly her voice became harsh as she realized her husband was on the phone, together with the all too familiar sound of her peeved aggression that he had come to know so well.

'Well, how is the whore capital of Europe? Is it living up to your expectations, Michael? Just got out of bed have you in time for some brunch, or have you only just got back from some all-night assignation?'

The glaring hypocrisy of her accusations was quite baffling, but he went on regardless. 'I heard from

Durant that we have had a burglary; was there anything stolen? He didn't seem to think so.' Lambert believed he could bypass the invective for a while.

'They made a bit of a mess getting in through the French door from the garden, but I think Samanda put them off by barking. She was in her kitchen basket and the racket must have woken me up because I came down the stairs shouting and waving your old police truncheon. It must have frightened them to death, because they ran off like a shot and escaped through the front door.'

'Did you get a good look at them? Did you see their faces at all and could you identify them if need be?'

Arabella started to swear like a sailor. 'Fuck me Michael, don't you ever stop all your policeman crap! Why don't you ask me how I am, and if I was hurt? Why can't you behave like a normal husband and show some concern about my feelings for a change?'

'Did you give a description to the uniforms when they arrived and did the intruders say anything which you could hear?'

The phone was slammed down and then there was only the sound of buzzing. As far as Lambert was concerned, it was not only a typical end to one of their conversations, but today was an even greater reason to simply give up altogether!

CHAPTER FIVE

AT THREE O'CLOCK that afternoon, Lambert telephoned the man called Thomas Biko from a public phone in the square. He had no idea who this man might be, and how or why he had tracked him down to the Radisson Hotel. The surprise was that, when the call was finally answered at just after 3 p.m., a voice informed him that he was speaking to the South African Embassy in Sofia.

When he asked for a Mr Thomas Biko and announced who he was, the receptionist further surprised him by her response. 'Ah yes Mr Lambert, the Ambassador was expecting your call, I will put you through to him right away.'

After two minutes, a deep African voice asked, 'Is that you Mr Lambert? Thank you for returning my call so promptly. I understand that you are interested in a South African citizen called Liam Side. I believe we have a mutual friend in Colonel Vassilev, who you apparently met recently. It was he who informed me of your interest in this man. How can I help you?'

Lambert was astonished at how rapidly the diplomatic grapevine worked. It was pretty clear that

Vera's friend had been quite serious in his promise to help him solve the murder. To get an ambassador's attention so quickly was a very useful imperative for the Reading policeman, considering the little time he had left in Sofia.

'Yes Mr Ambassador, how kind of you to contact me. I met Vassilev only yesterday as a matter of fact, and we spent the afternoon discussing Mr Side. Although I am here unofficially, I think I should inform you that Thames Valley Police have a special interest in Mr Side and if it is possible, I would like to speak to you more fully about him in private? Perhaps I could meet you sometime today—if that's okay with you—just say when and where?'

'What about four o'clock today Mr Lambert? I have a meeting in a few minutes which should be finished by then.' And so it was agreed to meet at the South African Embassy.

Looking in his entertainment guide of Sofia, the Englishman quickly discovered the embassy address in Vassil Aprilov Street. It appeared to be situated just behind the Sofia University building in an area called Doctors Gardens. Looking at his city map, Lambert realised that he could easily walk there from his hotel and he got himself ready to go.

Climbing into his grey slacks, white shirt and blue blazer, he carefully tied his Cavalry and Guards Club tie, all of which was the nearest thing he had to formal attire. He hoped that the ambassador would understand his casual appearance. With Side's cancelled passport in his pocket, together with some of Collingwood's photos of the dead man, a notebook and his police warrant card, he made for the lift. When he reached the ground floor, he walked through the almost empty reception area and out once more into the summer square.

The heat was oppressive and he could easily appreciate why the neighbouring country of Greece took a siesta during the afternoon. Very little was moving and even the taxi drivers seemed more relaxed and less prone to lean on their car horns. The shopkeepers sat close to their air conditioning units and smoked their strong Balkan cigarettes. Taking little notice of the passers-by, they were glued to their TV sets, which were at most times a distinctive feature of their day. In their world, the customer always came last and to serve anybody in this oppressive heat was to offer someone a considerable favour.

Turning right, Lambert walked along a narrow road which took him past an ornate and historical looking building which seemed abandoned and was fast becoming derelict. Perhaps like other parts of the eastern bloc there was little value put on history which, considering their communist past, the Bulgarians had every right to ignore. Walking down into the underpass, Lambert realized that Sofia was hiding a secret subterranean world from him, because there were shops, restaurants and even a disreputable looking nightclub secreted beneath the main road.

Climbing the stairs at the far end of the underpass, Lambert emerged next to the University and walking behind the main building, he passed through a garden area with some old broken seats and a coffee stall. It was full of jolly students who seemed to be unaware of the doom and gloom that was repeated daily in the media, or the constant complaints by the bar staff of the Irish pub. They seemed only too pleased to grumble about their ill-chosen nationality. Lambert had heard somewhere that Bulgaria was considered to be the unhappiest country in Europe. This seemed as much to do with the mentality of the citizens of Sofia, as the politics of the day.

Turning right into the main street, Lambert walked past one bar or restaurant after another, which somehow belied the myth that Bulgaria was on its last legs. Finally he got to Vassil Aprilov Street and turning left, he discovered the South African Embassy lying back off the road. Occupying a beautiful house surrounded by a fine mature garden, he walked past the flowering cherry trees and entered through the front door of the building. He was greeted there by an extremely hefty young white man who, in a somewhat abrupt manner, asked him who he was and what he wanted.

'My name is Chief Inspector Lambert and I have come here at the invitation of Ambassador Biko. Perhaps you would kindly tell him that I have arrived.'

The young man flexed his shoulders as if he was going to a training session at a gym and left the room. On his return and in an equally brusque manner, he glared at him and then said, 'Come this way would you? Our Ambassador is expecting you.'

Lambert was unaccustomed to South Africans in general and put this young man's behaviour down to a cultural glitch; in any case there were plenty in the UK who showed little respect for any kind of authority, including senior British policemen.

As he entered the room, sitting before him was an elderly black man wearing an immaculate morning suit. Standing up from behind his desk, he held out his hand to the Chief Inspector. 'Welcome to the South African Embassy Mr Lambert. Now, how can I help you?'

As the story of the Kennet and Avon narrow boat murder unfolded, Ambassador Biko started to look very sad. 'You sound a little unsure about the actual identity of the murdered man, Chief Inspector. Is it possible that the person you discovered on the boat might be someone else?' Although Thomas Biko appeared to be well into his seventies, he seemed to have a sound grasp of the realities of the Reading murder enquiry.

He went on: 'You see, I come from a country where a man's identity is often in dispute. Until 1995 we all lived under a constant cloud of innuendo and denial, so many of my people were wrongly identified. If you have the dead man's fingerprints and the forensic analysis of his DNA, we might be able to help you with the identification directly from our embassy here in Sofia, Chief Inspector. Mr Coetzee, who is our first Secretary, can assist you if you can fax us this information.'

The ambassador smiled at the English Policeman. 'We can easily bypass Interpol—who seem to be quite useless anyway—and get the information you require directly with the help of our Department of the Interior in Pretoria. But I would ask that the information be faxed directly to us from the Reading police, Mr Lambert, and as soon as possible because our Mr Coetzee will be going on leave next week.'

Lambert looked around the room and immediately felt at home in the company of so much antique furniture. 'Did you know Liam Side well, Mr Ambassador? I can't imagine that there are many South Africans living in Bulgaria,' Lambert said removing the cancelled passport and the various photographs from inside his blazer pocket. 'Perhaps you would take a look at these photos for a moment. I also have his previous cancelled passport here, which he left behind with a lady friend. She has kindly let me borrow it for a day or two.'

Thomas Biko picked up the passport first and looked at it with concentrated interest. It was as though he was saying goodbye to an old friend. He leafed through its contents and then put it down once more on the desk. Picking up the photos of the dead man he then removed a magnifying glass from the top drawer of his desk and looked at the sitting figure in his smart cavalry twill trousers and striped shirt.

'I can tell you one thing, Chief Inspector, and that is this passport is quite authentic, there is no question about that. But, I am not so sure about the pictures of the murder victim. He does look quite similar I agree, because in answer to your question about how well I knew Liam Side, the answer is very well indeed.'

He handed back the cancelled passport and sat back

in his chair. 'You were right when you said that there must be only a few South Africans in Sofia, Chief Inspector, but take it from me, there was no one quite like Liam Side. He was a real gentleman and although he was not a supporter of the ANC, he was most certainly a truly modern South African!'

It was obvious to Lambert that the old man had been fond of Side. Through Thomas Biko's last remarks, the character of Side had suddenly been greatly rehabilitated in the policeman's mind and was no longer tainted by the witterings of the ex-London copper Edwin Page, which in his mind he now put to one side as being simple prejudice.

While Lambert was seated in the cool quiet atmosphere of the ambassador's office, the door suddenly opened and the muscular young man, who had greeted him so abruptly on arrival, entered the room carrying a large silver tray. On it was a blue Spode teapot, a bowl of sugar, together with two cups and saucers, a small milk jug and a tea strainer. Smiling at the ambassador in a way that Lambert could only describe as with considerable respect, the young man silently left the room, quietly closing the door behind him.

'I hope that you will join me in a cup of English tea Mr Lambert, it is four o'clock after all?' He smiled with humour and proceeded to remove a large red box of McVities biscuits from a nearby cupboard. 'I am sure that these biscuits will be familiar to you, although they are rather difficult to buy here in Sofia, but they are the only ones I really like.'

'Can you tell me a little more about Mr Side, Sir, and how he came to be in Sofia in the first place? Also, as you knew him so well, I would like to know a little bit about his past life if possible?'

Ambassador Biko poured out two very strong cups of tea and sat back once more in his wing backed office chair. On the wall behind him was a large smiling photograph of Nelson Mandela. The old man asked Lambert if he would like some milk in his tea and placed the bowl containing sugar lumps next to his cup. Evading the question of why Side came to Sofia, the ambassador carefully inspected the policeman sitting before him.

'He was a very good man, Mr Lambert, because when I first came to Sofia I knew precisely nothing and absolutely nobody and he tried very hard to help me. In the past I was a Senior Lecturer at the University of Fort Hare in South Africa, but more to the point I was in the Department of Political Science at the University. There were very few black specialists in Political Science during the time of our struggles and so when the changes occurred in 1995, and because of my close involvement with the ANC, I was offered the post of Ambassador to Bulgaria. You see, they honestly believed that I had rather more wisdom and ability than was strictly true.'

Sipping his strong red tea he went on, 'my country has had an Embassy in Sofia for many years; after all, where else was there for a pariah state such as South Africa to go? There was a full international embargo on our country's activities, which was exclusively due to our then government's misguided belief in apartheid. It seems odd to say this to you now, but not much has changed in the last few years, and South Africa still needs the continued help of certain ex-communist countries, because in many respects we are still operating at the same level.'

'In which way was Mr Side helping you, Ambassador? Can you be more specific?' For the life of him Lambert could not imagine how a little country like Bulgaria could contribute to the dormant economy of a huge country, so rich in natural resources, like South Africa. 'What sort of things did your country need and what was he able to do for you precisely?'

'He sometimes referred to himself as a *Procurement Agent*, when it came to business matters, because he knew so many people, and due to his contacts through his news magazine, he could easily track down the things that we needed. After all, he had met far more people here than any of the embassy staff, and he had also been in the country for far longer than any of us. You see, we had experienced such an enormous sea-change at home, and apart from one or two locally employed staff, everyone at the embassy was untried, untested and thoroughly inexperienced. So meeting Liam was a great boon for us all.'

'Can you give me an idea of what you were actually looking for with his assistance?' Even after three days in Sofia, for Lambert, it was easy to observe how rundown and basic the country was, so as the story unfolded he became even more perplexed.

'Well, there were the townships for a start. We needed

people to build cheap housing for our ordinary citizens. They had been living in slums for years under apartheid. The wealthy landowners and businessmen either didn't care or claimed they didn't even know about the plight of the blacks, and so it was a case of not only being out of sight, but out of mind, Mr Lambert. When the ANC came to power all this was due to change, but of course it didn't happen. The country was short of cash and so we needed to do things on the cheap and where better to start, than a country like Bulgaria?'

Discovering the three remaining ginger biscuits and putting them in his saucer, the ambassador carefully inspected his depleted stock of McVities biscuits and then pushed the tin box towards his guest. 'At the time few could perform even the most basic everyday tasks at home, because my country was excluded from any foreign training programs and university courses. With the emigration of our best minds to other countries, or the brain drain as it is colloquially referred to, our technical standards become severely depleted. Not only that, but we needed all sorts of plant and equipment; tractors, diggers, forklift trucks, busses—you name it— and that meant that we were restricted to mainly dealing at the time with the Soviets and the Comecon countries. They in turn needed us because of our natural resources. Now, after all the political claims and the resultant publicity, very little has really actually changed.'

Dipping his last ginger nut biscuit into his cup, Thomas Biko shook his head. 'That is the reason we needed all the help we could get. Not only had we lost our traditional western trading partners, but we had also lost the culture of dealing with them when we re-emerged from the international boycott and this included our banks.'

It was five thirty by the time their meeting drew to a close, but they agreed to meet the following day. The ambassador gave Lambert his business card and suggested that the following morning would be a good time to make contact, allowing him time to discuss matters with Mr Coetzee and after receiving the faxed fingerprints and DNA analysis from the Thames Valley Police. Firmly shaking him by the hand, the old man walked with Lambert to the door of his office and politely wished him good afternoon. He asked the policeman to give him a phone call in the late morning to arrange a meeting.

The walk back to the Radisson was calm, and apart from tripping over a number of potholes in the pavement, it was quite uneventful. By now it was five forty-five local time, which meant that the time in Reading was three forty-five and his office would be fully functioning. Stopping by a public phone, he inserted his pre-paid card and dialled a familiar number. George Durant sounded a little breathless, as though he had been running up the stairs. 'Afternoon Boss, what's happening in Eastern Europe this afternoon? How's the local totty?'

Lambert missed his friendly team in Reading. 'You

don't want to believe all you are told George, and anyway I have been too busy today to look around. Now listen, I have got some important things to tell you. Firstly, I have visited the British Embassy, who tell me that Liam Side was persona non grata, but also that they were totally unaware he was even a South African. So, you can tell the Super that I have drawn a blank there— which won't surprise him one little bit—but I have now got the full cooperation of the South African Ambassador, a Mr Thomas Biko, who said quite the opposite. According to him Side was a star and helped them considerably with their problems in Bulgaria. Apparently our man was a little bit more than just a journalist, but just how much more, we will find out in due course.'

George Durant had also been busy. 'Well, I have got some news as well, Boss. When I checked Side out with the Passport Office in Petty France, they said that they had never heard of him, as you already know yourself. But what I forgot to tell you was that I also checked with the Immigration Authorities and it appears that a Liam Side entered the country this July in a private aircraft which landed at Blackbushe Airport near Camberley. The records show that he had come from the Municipal Airport in Grimbergen near Brussels. That is why it has taken so long to track him down. They also confirmed that he had arrived on a South African passport, so it is beginning to tally up. However, the immigration official at Blackbush mentioned that he was apparently unwell and had to be collected by wheelchair from the plane and assisted through customs. There is no specific information about his two companions.'

Lambert was not so confident. 'It might be a little more complicated than we originally believed, George, and we now need to be even more certain of the victim's identity. But if you do what I ask straightaway George, we might get the result we are looking for by tomorrow. According to Mr Biko the South African Ambassador, the first secretary at their Embassy in Sofia—a certain Mr Coetzee—can apparently bypass Interpol for us and go directly to the South African Department of the Interior in Pretoria. I guess he is the embassy spook; we all have one!'

Sergeant Durant scribbled down the embassy fax number, and the coordinates of Mr Coetzee. 'If you fax the dead man's fingerprints straight away George, together with Eddie Singh's DNA analysis, Coetzee can then send all this information on to his pals in Pretoria. This way we can confirm the victim's identity directly from their computer files which I am led to believe are very reliable. Then we will know for sure, if Mr Side is the man we have got in the freezer.'

George Durant said that he would send this information at once, but was slow to put down the phone. 'Haven't you forgotten to ask me something, Boss, something rather more important than our ever present murder?'

Surprised by the question, Lambert thought for a moment and looking up to the heavens for some celestial inspiration, it suddenly dawned on him what his sergeant was referring to. 'Of course, the cricket match, how did we do yesterday at the Jacks Booth?'

'They hammered us, Boss. I was out for three, but I have to tell you, Adams was brilliant. He was up to seventy-two before one of those two Jamaican lads knocked out his off stump. We were all out for 187, and they romped home with five wickets to spare. The only way we can beat that Reading Second Team in the future Boss, is if we arrest those two lads beforehand; I'm telling you, they are both magic.'

Back once more at the hotel, Lambert thought that from now on, he would give Arabella a miss. Any conversation with her at present was futile and now with the comforting benefit of distance, it was becoming clear to him that it was time to throw in the towel and for them to split up. Both Kate and Jedd were practically off their hands and if not entirely out of their hair, recently they had been showing encouraging signs of independence.

Lambert suspected all along that his wife was having an affair, not least because of her accusations and the jealousy which often disguised undisclosed betrayal. This at least he had discovered during the course of his career as a police detective. The main reason for domestic violence by either of the alleged injured parties in a marriage could be explained easily by reason of jealousy or guilt. It was usually a case of the pot calling the kettle black, although his circumstances were different because unlike his wife, he had absolutely nothing to hide.

It was cool and relaxing to be back in his hotel room, and due to a phenomenal surplice of hot water, soap, shampoo and Turkey towelling bathrobes, he decided on a luxurious soak in the spacious Jacuzzi. It was time to have a think.

Rolling down the window blind and turning up the air conditioning, the sound of hot water pouring amongst the bubbles reminded him of things past, and happier times when there had been family harmony. He remembered the sound of children running around the house, and his wife shouting up the stairs telling everyone that tea was ready. It was at a time when there seemed to be more reason to life, and a growing sense of fulfilment. It was all so long ago.

An hour later and securely wrapped in his bathrobe, Lambert laid in silence on the king sized bed and inspected the ceiling. The question was what to do on a Monday night in Sofia. Sitting by the window, Lambert opened the blind revealing the crowded square below and putting on his shorts and a tee shirt, he made for the Irish Pub.

The bar was full of suits and briefcases. Mainly comprising American businessmen, the accent of choice was a kind of mid-Atlantic drawl, even by the locals. Probably attached in some way to the many burgeoning NGOs, imported East Coast American Universities, finance corporations, human and civil rights organisations and charities, they seemed to be entirely preoccupied in repeating the clichés so often heard on CNN and the Discovery Channels.

Doing the right thing in Bulgaria, Bulgaria going forward, and finally being proactive, seemed to encompass that day's business speak, the standard word of exclamation being *awesome*. The eager-eyed locals were also busy pretending to admire their grey haired mentors, who willingly bathed in their unending flattery, their omnipotence, manifesting itself for the first and probably the very last time in their boring and predictable lives.

Lambert decided to stick to fish and chips. It had not been bad the first time round, so at least he was able to hold out some hope for a similar result. Consuming a pint of red beer in just a few minutes, he sat at the bar next to other refugees from distant lands. What did he do? *They were in telephones.* Where did he live? *They came from Tel Aviv.* Was he married? *They were married and had two kids and a wallet full of photographs.* But the final question seemed to be the most important one of all; it was *what car do you drive?* They all talked like provincial travelling salesman, which in fact was what most of them probably were. But no one had ever heard of an Alvis TF 21!

With the reassuring arrival of his deep fried fish, it was Lambert's excuse to find a spare table somewhere at the back of the bar in order to eat in peace, but also to retreat from the inane conversation he was reluctantly overhearing. It was not as though he was above indulging in idle banter; which he did all the time at work in Reading, but he had more serious things to consider.

Having consumed this most recent delivery of processed food, he paid the bill and decided to raid the mini-bar in his room, in order to escape from the sea of suits and their adoring minions. It was also to evade the approaching figure of the American mouthwash mogul. Giving him a polite wave, Lambert made for the lift.

The floppy disks were much the same as the papers in the various files; indeed, they also contained many copies of documents he had already inspected. So it occurred to him to copy the discs onto the hard drive of his laptop and to print them up on his return to England. But before that, he would need to inspect each document and to read where possible the information contained in the discs. If he was going to be on top form the following day with Ambassador Biko, he needed to do his homework.

Clearly an intelligent African, the ageing diplomat would not tell him everything he needed to know, because most of the joint affairs between the South Africans and Side would quite rightly have been considered as private—if not secret. But what was more important to him, were the assurances from the man Coetzee concerning the matter of identity. If the dead man's identity could not be confirmed, the case would have to remain open, and he might be forced to talk to the spooks in London.

Many of the discs were copies of trading accounts, and for VAT returns. Once more in Cyrillic they were easily distinguishable as financial records for the news magazine. With an approximate turnover of ten thousand Leva a month, by the time he had paid off the overheads and the staff, what remained was a modest salary even by Bulgarian standards. One could only assume that he somehow managed to get by and that rents in Sofia were cheap. But, he could also see from these accounts that the day-to-day requirements of his immediate dependants were fully taken care of, although there were obviously few luxuries to be otherwise had.

That evening the Chief Inspector faxed a number of documents to Gloria from the folder which contained the Bulgarian contracts and legal documents. What was important to know more about, was Liam Side's private life in the Bulgarian capital.

The business bureau was open in the hotel reception area and there were a few suits staring at computer screens, some playing solitaire. The girl behind the bureau reception desk was smoking a slim dark cigarette and drinking espresso coffee out of a little plastic cup. How these people slept at night was a mystery to Lambert, who observed the 'no coffee after 2 p.m.' rule. Conveniently the more important papers slipped easily out of their plastic sleeves, ready to be sent by the Brother Fax machine on her desk.

It took a few attempts to get all of the documents off; involving a number of redials and discussions about whether the documents had been received or not. Dependant on the somewhat unreliable confirmation system and a substandard telephone line, the confusion about the cost became quite heated at one point, but after an hour of discussion he left the little office with a thick pile of photocopies, a receipt and a horrible headache. Returning to his room he was glad to raid the bar and to consume both of the two miniature Grouse whiskies in quick succession. He sat on the balcony and lit up a Victory cigarette.

Back in the room, he made a quick call to Gloria Hislop. It was now seven o'clock in England and although the evening had just begun, she would still be at her desk or watching TV. This time he dialled her number on his handy and got through to her immediately. The reception was good via the local GSM provider which was partly owned by the Austrians. 'Gloria, it's Mike, can you hear me all right?'

She seemed very pleased to listen to his voice. 'I wondered if you would phone me this evening Mike. I have got rather a lot of your faxes through from the Radisson business centre, and I am just going through them now. They seem to be mostly concerning rental agreements but there are one or two other documents concerning his daughter Patricia. I need to read these very carefully. So I will study them tonight and report back tomorrow if that's okay with you Mike? By the way, there is not much to report about this morning's faxes sent from the British Embassy, but I will go into that in a minute. But first your Sergeant Durant came round this afternoon and collected a copy of the passport details and the letter from that lawyer in Hammersmith. I also gave him the coordinates of that Chinese bloke in London.'

Lambert was impressed by the way she worked and was pleased to feel her on his side. She then continued on a more serious note. 'Mike, about the internal passport which you sent this morning from the British Embassy. Our man seems to have had a dickens of a problem with the authorities in Bulgaria and he had been within a hair's breadth of being chucked out of the country on a number of occasions. It is obvious that he had a hard time there, especially when it came to registering his daughter as a Bulgarian citizen, which she obviously is. After all, she was born there and by international convention she is by rights a citizen in her country of birth.'

Mike Lambert thought for a moment. 'But we don't know anything about the Russian woman either, other than the documents from the Mother and Child maternity hospital. Can you dig around and see if there are any details anywhere relating to the mother? At least if I had her full name and her national or internal passport number, it might help to track her down, even if she is an illegal which I am told she might well be. I don't even know if she is still in the country Gloria, but I can find out more tomorrow from a Colonel Vassilev, if he is still in Sofia.'

The rest could wait, and Gloria Hislop promised to go through all the faxed documents by the following morning and to make some sense of them. The local time was now ten o'clock at night, and the choices were an early night with the cable TV or a further visit to the nearby jazz club at La Strada. The Chief Inspector went back to his laptop.

It was clear from one of the floppy disks that Balkan Side Ltd, which was Side's main business vehicle, had been involved with the Africans for some time. Although he claimed to be no businessman, Michael Lambert could follow the money as well as most police detectives. According to the accounts, various payments had been made to Side, to cover his expenses for trips made on behalf of customers to different parts of the Eastern Bloc, in order to tie down the purchase of mainly new plant and equipment. This ranged from tractors and diggers from Minsk to mining equipment from Moscow and St Petersburg. Much of the second-hand or used equipment he supplied came from Bulgaria itself, Romania and Serbia.

He had also bought some specialist equipment from the UK; including platform trucks, gantry cranes, and Coles heavy-lift mobile cranes. There had been quite a comprehensive number of vehicles of one sort or another destined for Durban. This would account in part for some of the entry stamps in Side's old national passport because it would have been completely necessary to visit these countries at some point.

Very often it was '*the singer and not the song,*' that mattered when doing business in ex-communist countries, and where *the messenger* was sometimes more important than the actual buyers or sellers. It might also have been that the messenger could be shot. Side was the messenger, and consequently it was he who would experience most of the dangers. Surely there must have been some sort of reward for his efforts, although his accounts stated otherwise. Maybe he was paid in cash by the seller?

The morning came too soon; sunlight crept through his shutters and brought the world alive once more. It had been two o'clock before Lambert finally switched the light out and gone to sleep. What concerned him this morning—prior to consuming an alleged Irish Breakfast—was if Durant had carried out yesterday's orders to send the prints and DNA of the dead man to Coetzee at the South African Embassy. It was seven o'clock in Sofia and just a little early to wake up his assistant in Reading. Lambert would take his time and phone Durant at 10 a.m. Sofia time.

It would be another scorching day, but at eight o'clock the air was still fresh despite the car fumes generated by the traffic in the square. Lambert took his first coffee of the day, ordered the proscribed Fenian fry-up and considered his progress on the case. Although Durant had cleverly tracked down the UK entry point of Liam Side to Blackbushe Airport, the make or break reality continued to depend on the South African computer in Pretoria. What if it said that Side was not the murdered man?

Then who was the victim and why was Side involved—as he clearly was—by reason of the wheelchair-bound man's arrival in England. The fact of his presence in the UK would never constitute a coincidence in Lambert's mind. After the heart-stopping Irish Breakfast, the policeman paid his restaurant bill and wandered into the square.

Turning left, he crossed the square and on reaching the main road, he crossed over and walked past the side of the Sobranie Parliament building towards the cathedral. He had about an hour to kill, and since it was nine o'clock he decided to go into the Nevski Museum to look at the collection of Icons, but to no avail. Once more the museum was closed.

Instead he went to the St Sofia church which was to the left of the cathedral. Originally built in the 6th Century it was a contemporary of the famous Hagia Sophia in modern-day Istanbul. The capital of Bulgaria was named after this church, which went through various transformations over time, including use as a Mosque during the Ottoman period. In a city blighted by ugly crumbling buildings it was good to know that at least one original building remained.

In the street next to the cathedral, the antique and bric-à-brac market was beginning to come alive and Lambert walked through the market looking at items on sale. Mostly reproduction mementoes from Russia, there were the usual choices of Russian dolls, military caps, Astrakhan hats with a red star attached, and a plethora of used militaria including daggers, night vision devices, old cameras and assorted railway timepieces.

Emerging at the far end of the market, Lambert found a public telephone and inserted his pre-paid card. 'George, is that you?' He could hear the sound of traffic over the receiver. 'Did you manage to send off those prints and the DNA analysis to that man Coetzee?' A few expletives and criticism of other road users' driving skills, and it was obvious that George Durant was still on his way to work.

'I sent it all off by fax Boss, just as you said and received a complementary receipt back. So don't worry, they have definitely got it all.' The cursing continued and so Lambert cut the call short, telling his sergeant that he would phone later on. Turning left into the main road and crossing it, he turned left once again and returned to the hotel.

Outside a clap of thunder announced a summer storm and the sky opened up and the rain began to pour down. He would give it another hour before he phoned Ambassador Biko to confirm that morning's appointment and so he returned to his room. He finally made his phone call to Ambassador Biko who agreed to see Lambert at twelve thirty in his office, but little else was said.

CHAPTER SIX

SOFIA 1998. The wind rushes through the apartment from one open balcony door to the next. The sky grows dark, and in the distance he can hear a distant rumble as it travels around the mountain. It is then that the lightning begins to flash over the city, and the thunderclaps boom; first next to the Vitosha mountain, and then overhead. There is a scream; it comes from the sitting room and Liam Side runs there to discover his daughter curled up on the sofa. She is hugging a threadbare toy dog.

Patricia is frightened; she jumps into his arms and cries. Being three years old has its compensations when life is fun, but fear makes her doubt the reality of the cotton-wool world with which he has so deliberately tried to surround her, one that—he knows only too well—doesn't really exist. In the end he turns on the television set and she sits with her head on his lap watching the cartoon channel. The catastrophe is now over. As they watch the TV program, he weeps silently. He realises that the only thing left for him in the Balkans is his innocent little daughter.

It might have been described by some as a moment

of indiscreet passion, to be closely followed by the reality of—the official Eastern European means of birth control—an abortion. But no, whatever he feels about the outcome—the shouting, the abuse, the violence, the hate and the accusations—the one redeeming feature emanating from the unwholesome relationship with the Russian woman is the love he shares with his little daughter. It is she who has made it all seem worthwhile.

Five years in Sofia has been turbulent and troublesome. Dealing with the culture—as it is generally known by nearly all the bewildered foreigners—is more than just an academic subject. He has lived with and amongst Bulgarians, and with great difficulty he has tried to relate to them. At a time when he should have been in England, back home in South Africa or at least in some more civilised surroundings, he has chosen to remain in a place of intrigue, corruption and divisiveness. Love in the Balkans is the tool of the weak against the strong. Because in the end, it is passion that counts, and then of course there is money.

By the time communism had turned the fabric of the Bulgarian Orthodox Church into the mediocre servant of socialism, sex had come to be regarded as a recreational activity and love spurned by most Balkan women, in favour of power and wealth.

The world which Liam Side presently inhabits with its shallow social paradoxes is often hard to bear. To say that he has been bored would be totally untrue, but to say that he has been happy is also a painful exaggeration. In the end he has left Natalia the Russian woman to live with a Bulgarian woman, and now his list of regrets is beginning to mount, in direct proportion to his peccadilloes.

The news magazine has been his salvation, and it has occupied his thoughts and much of his time. In a country where *knowing people* is a mainstream preoccupation, it is also a highly regarded and essential route to self-improvement. Those he knows—the high and the very often self-proclaimed mighty—are many and various. But save for his most intimate staff and a few western drinking companions, he has few if any friends and often experiences a deep feeling of isolation within the world he occupies.

Simultaneously, the outside world has—little by little—become less interested in any of the Balkan players and become immune to the empty political statements which their leaders make. As a journalist he is often hard put to write about the slow movement of the political paradigm, or even to represent it as real. But the truth is that nothing has really changed in fifty years. What has made the world take notice of this small backward Balkan country is its next door neighbour Serbia. Now the NATO troops come to Sofia for R & R, they drink the bars dry and fraternise with the local bar girls. They in turn relieve them of their money by telling the soldiers tales and by making many unreal and cynical promises.

In the end Serbia has proved that polite political demands by the West have to be reinforced by *baseball-bat inducements*, and it is fast becoming obvious that the

Balkans is a place where the truth can be casually replaced by a lie. For the sake of expediency, both have the same significance, especially if you get what you want. What really fascinates all the players is the brinkmanship involved, which usually takes the West to the edge. This makes the Balkan people laugh.

The bombing has now stopped in Serbia and so has the endless analysis. Gone are the censored accounts of yesterday's NATO activities, the Serbian denials of genocide and the Western apologies for their so-called collateral damage. The tanks have rolled into Kosovo and CNN now shows smiling and waving people in Pristina, happily inviting the soldiers of Europe and America onto their devastated soil. Past the gutted villages, the fallow farms, the thin and sorry people, and the ominous burial grounds of the innocent, the tanks rumble on towards a forlorn hope of just peace.

Milosevic has proved that evil exists in the Balkans and that each Western move has to be tested, as has every strength and weakness. In his apparently defunct *socialist paradise*, it is the endgame that matters and not the outcome. What is winning and losing, as long as your opponent doesn't win? The strange perversion of such thoughts often pervades the soul of Liam Side, a man who none would say is an easy touch, more so that he is a hard-nosed bastard.

The sky begins to clear and the child now sleeps curled up with Rush her favourite fluffy toy; its dog's ears cover her nose, and its paw is touching her mouth. The birds begin to sing and the sound of an airliner taking off from the city airport breaks the silence of his vigil.

His dream of kindness and compassion is a forlorn hope that needs to be left in the past. Time is running out for him and he knows it. Is this the failure of an uncompromising challenge or the beginning of another? The answer rather depends on the next few days and the response to his most recent email. But, how had it all started?

London 1993. It is winter and the cold wind blows down the river Thames over a dark and inhospitable London. It chills the black leafless trees, and chases away the clouds which deaden the moon's bright light, making the Thames' waters seem even deeper, darker and just a little depressing. It seems hard to imagine that in 1989 the events in Eastern Europe would have changed the World so dramatically.

A man who has known great fear and exhilaration in his time, Liam Side stands in the saloon bar of the Bull at Barnes Bridge drinking a pint of Fullers beer. He is listening to the sound of jazz which creeps past the padded doors that lead into the jazz club next door.

Through these doors he can hear the rising notes of *A Night in Tunisia*, as the band plays their final spot for the night. He orders a last beer from Jim the landlord and gets ready to go back to Grove Road and to his girlfriend Pansy. Pansy is a travel agent, and has been his companion since his arrival from South Africa in 1980. She comes from Cape Town.

These days the couple rarely speak to each other,

except about money and possessions, which all seems so banal. Love has been replaced by a kind of politeness, and passion by occasional warmth. The never-ending parties given by local couples in Barnes— George and Fiona, Jack and Margo and all the mutually galvanised names that litter their social diary—simply provoke an indisputable reason to leave the party on the dot of midnight.

London in the eighties was different. Money seemed to come from nowhere and life had become an enormous pile of easily affordable luxuries. There was always another businessman who wanted to discuss a particular deal. 'A nice little part possession property in Balham, Liam, I reckon you could double your money in two months.' And he often did. 'If you give me a couple of grand on the contract, you can have it tomorrow!' That is how it was done then.

It wasn't so difficult and the property market in London was still workable. So the wheels kept on turning and the money came rolling in. There was never a doubt in anybody's mind that things would remain the same forever, but then the property slump arrived and the start of a long and painful decline began.

Suddenly, the banks became aggressive and a sea-change occurred. The old bank managers, many of whom were friends, began to disappear. The new breed of bank manager didn't seem to care about your past, or for your future much, it was only here and now that mattered.

'Mr Side, I realise that your company has banked

with us for some years, and I know all about your unblemished track record, but the whole philosophy within the banking system has changed quite dramatically and we need our money on time, whoever you are.' The writing was on the wall.

With all his highly geared investments which were held in a Jersey-based Property Company, Liam Side, as many others also experienced, had no choice but to divest himself of everything he owned and as quickly as possible. Involving the sale of some fifty tenanted houses, apartments, shops and upperparts, it seems that his favourite question is *Can you exchange contracts next Friday?* Very often the actual agreed price seemed rather unimportant.

He could see that most of his contempories were having a hard time too, but what was the reason behind it all? Inevitably it was about politics, the mismanagement of a sophisticated economy, the arrogance of Margaret Thatcher and her virtual dictatorship. It was also about a bank rate of 20%. Thatcher's house of cards was beginning to collapse around her and—as in the imagination of Alice in Wonderland—the self-important Queen of Hearts was no longer able to strut around her blighted garden.

Nightly on TV, all there was to be seen was the greyness of John Major—quoting one cliché after another in his rather puny voice—telling the country that *there is no gain without pain!*

Liam Side was well aware of where the pain was, and perfectly aware of the painful remedy. In a way he was glad that things were about to change and that his life would never be the same again. And what about Pansy? Would she weather the storm with him, or grab what she could and run? She ran.

Sofia 1998. It is five years on, and looking out of the balcony window Liam Side can smell the scent of the old Linden tree that eclipses the upper part of the house where he now lives in Borova Gora. He tidies up the leaves which have been strewn over the parquet floor by the wind, sweeps them into a plastic dustpan and then tips them over the side of the balcony. He watches them float away, losing themselves amongst the other leaves on the glistening wet road below.

The phone rings. 'Ah, Mr Biko, I wondered if you would call. I can see you tomorrow if that's okay. What time would suit you?'—It is now seven o'clock in the evening and he is due to return Patricia to her mother by eight o'clock sharp—'Okay, that's fine Mr Ambassador, I will be in your office at midday tomorrow; we can go through it all then.'

Liam Side goes on: 'That's right Sir, and I am due to be in Minsk the following day. We can arrange the Letters of Credit from there. Our buyers are still using the Standard Chartered Bank I presume? Yes, it is very easy doing business with the Belarusians because their enterprises still have the old banking procedures, unlike the Bulgarians. That ended with the changes.'

Sofia 2001. By the time he had dressed, Lambert was

ready for his walk to the South African Embassy. The rain had stopped and the sun was once again in the sky. The atmosphere was fresh now the streets had been drenched by the sudden squall. Walking past the derelict old building on his right-hand side, he retraced his steps from the previous day and descended into the underpass.

He was a little early when he arrived at Vassil Aprilov Street, and the tough looking young man asked him to wait. This time he was more polite and asked Lambert if he would like some tea or coffee. Lambert settled for a mug of Nescafe. Within ten minutes or so, he was invited to join Ambassador Biko and the mysterious Mr Coetzee.

When he entered the office, he could see that both men had been deep in conversation and were looking a little concerned. 'Good day Chief Inspector,' the Ambassador waved him towards a vacant chair before his desk, 'please sit down, we have a lot to discuss.'

The Ambassador introduced him to Coetzee, and immediately the English policeman was impressed by the man he saw before him. Lambert half rose from his chair for a moment and shook hands with the tough looking white man.

Coetzee was wearing a lightweight Safari suit with short sleeves. He had closely cropped grey hair and penetrating brown eyes and was most certainly unlike the normal run of the mill diplomat that one might expect and appeared more like a seasoned soldier. In his fifties, his leathery brown face told of many days in the sun—and not the superficial suntan one might associate with a week on a beach in Lanzaroti—but somewhere cruel like the desert.

The ambassador had a sheaf of papers before him and Lambert could easily see that it was an official looking fax. Mr Coetzee was first to break the ice. 'Chief Inspector, you may not know this, but in order to get a driving licence in South Africa, not only do you have to take a comprehensive driving test as in most countries, but to finally receive the licence itself, first you have to be fingerprinted. In our country we find that this is the quickest way to identify an individual.'

Ambassador Biko then interrupted his colleague. 'According to our records at the DLTC in Pretoria, the fingerprints which were provided by Thames Valley Police of Liam Side don't match up, and unless something remarkable transpires as a result of the DNA analysis that you also provided, I am afraid that I must inform you that the dead man you discovered on the riverboat in Reading, is not Liam Side but someone else, Mr Lambert.'

To say that Michael Lambert looked disappointed would be an exaggeration, although the truth was that he was looking for an easy solution to at least a part of the case. He asked if he could receive a Photostat copy of their report, and both men agreed. This meant that he now had the authentic fingerprints of Liam Side.

Ambassador Biko then said, 'I am sorry to say that I am rather pleased with this result, Chief Inspector, although you must be a little disappointed as the investigating officer. You see, we all like and trust Liam

Side at this embassy and this time yesterday, we both believed that we had lost a very good friend.' Biko shook his head and gazed at the report. 'In fact, it was very hard for me, under the circumstances, to contain myself when we spoke about him. I am sure you will understand, Mr Lambert.'

Mr Coetzee gazed at the English policeman as if to determine his strength of purpose. 'You have come as a bit of a shock to us, Mr Lambert, and you will have to forgive me if I treat you with some hesitation. You see, we have had very little to do with the Brits for many years, due to the embargo we experienced in South Africa, and this meeting today represents quite a novelty for me at least! I also have no idea about the protocols involved, but I would ask of you one thing, that you keep us informed about your investigation, if or when you are able to track down Mr Side. You see, he is not only a good friend of ours as you now know, but we also have some important outstanding business with him that needs to be cleared up, or we will all be in very big trouble.'

Coetzee looked curiously at Lambert. 'As I have already said to you, I don't know the official protocols involved, but if you don't mind putting up with my ignorance in this matter and we can bypass the usual time wasters, it is possible that we might even be able to help you to get to the bottom of your case more quickly. What do you say, Chief Inspector, is that a deal?'

Lambert rarely did anything by the book and eager to remain on good terms, he agreed wholeheartedly. 'I agree to share my information with you, Mr Coetzee, but it is with the proviso that you fill me in with as much background information on Liam Side as you can muster.' Lambert went on, 'Because I have every reason to believe that he is connected in some way or other to this murder.'

Lambert went on to describe the alleged arrival of Liam Side by small private plane into Blackbushe Airport near Camberley in Surrey. He explained that his assistant George Durant—who was always thorough in his investigation—had enjoyed a good chat with the local immigration official.

At the time this officer had expressed surprise at the dishevelled condition of the man in the wheelchair, but had finally let him into the country because the Belgian pilot of the Piper Cherokee had told him that the ailing man—who he referred to as Liam Side—had been taken ill with food poisoning whilst on a trip to Brussels. They said that he'd hired the four-seater PA 28 in Grimbergen, especially for the trip to the UK.

Lambert went on: 'Their story was that they were apparently on their way to the Cromwell Private Hospital in London. They also explained that the ill man also suffered from Type 1 diabetes and that he needed urgent treatment due to the likelihood of him going into a coma due to his low glucose levels. That was all Durant knew when I last spoke to him.'

Looking at his watch, Lambert suggested that they went out for a good lunch, to one of the many restaurants in Doctors Gardens and on the dot of two o'clock, the three men left the old embassy building in

Vassil Aprilov Street and found their way to a discreet little restaurant nearby, called The 33 Chairs.

Situated in Professor Assen Zlatarov Street, it seemed that Lambert could finally get away from his most recent diet of fried food. The English speaking waiter suggested that they might like to try the house speciality—a whole stewed rabbit each! This turned out to be a good choice for the three men, who all claimed not to have eaten rabbit for many years.

Of course, in the end the conversation turned to Liam Side. They all agreed that he was probably still alive; possibly somewhere in the Balkans and that it was unlikely that it was him who had been wheeled through the provincial UK airport at Blackbush.

How and why this had all played out became clearer when Ambassador Biko began to describe the life of his fellow countryman. As they sat sipping their red Melnik wine, the conversation turned into a fascinating journey, which took the English policeman on a trip through Central Europe into the heart of Africa.

'You see, Mr Lambert,' the elderly black man continued, 'Africa is a very big country, but in the same way that some Americans in the past believed their newly found country to be a good place to reinvent themselves, this was also true of South Africa in the early years. We have always been a refuge from religious intolerance, as well as presenting an opportunity for many disenfranchised Europeans to improve their lives.'

It appeared that Side emanated from old South African stock and his great grandfather Karel Szeidovitz had immigrated to Bloemfontein in the 1870s. Szeidovitz came from what was then called the Pale of Settlement in Poland. In those days pioneers travelled to Africa from many parts of the world, to what was soon to become The Orange Free State. It was a magnet for many who needed to escape from the anti-Semitism of the time and the first Jewish settlers arrived in the Bloemfontein area as early as 1813.

It was nearing the end of the lunch, and all three men were sipping strong espresso coffee together with a glass of Rakia. Ambassador Biko went on, 'this was the time when Karel Szeidovitz chose to anglicise his family name to Side—which many did in those days—in order to sit more comfortably next to their English, German or Dutch colonial neighbours. Perhaps he hoped to hide his origins by integrating anonymously with the many new pioneers who were by then beginning to populate the town. It was 1870 after all, Mr Lambert, and prejudice was not unknown.'

He continued: 'Many of the Jewish settlers had been farmers; in and around the Shtetls of central Europe, but the great majority were traders. In Africa they found both a new home and new hope, and also a place to start a new life for themselves amongst the many other pioneers, who had arrived from a severely divided Europe.'

It was an interesting history lesson in itself, and Lambert could easily understand why Ambassador Biko had been appointed to a university post in Political Science.

And so the story continued: 'Moving further north, in the 1880s Cecil Rhodes arrived in what was then called Matabeleland, and on behalf of the British South Africa Company, he took control of the area. By 1890 he was sending Pioneer Columns of well-armed Europeans into the territory, and by 1895 the area had been renamed Rhodesia after Cecil Rhodes himself and the area south of the Zambezi was to be known thereafter as Southern Rhodesia.'

Coetzee then took over the story. 'By 1923 it became a self-governing British colony, and it was in the autumn of 1925 that Liam Side's grandfather Ebenezer bought the family farm in the Karoi district, just 200 km northwest of Salisbury, which is now called Harare.

'Situated in the land of the Shona people close to the provincial town of Tengwe, it occupied 1,200 acres of arable land and was destined to be entirely devoted to producing tobacco leaf, in order to satisfy the growing demands of the London tobacco auction markets and the hungry tobacco processing factories in Northern Ireland and Liverpool. Nestling in a shady wooded copse and surrounded by enveloping Gum trees, this was where Ebenezer Side built a traditional African farmhouse with tobacco drying sheds, a warehouse and servants' quarters.

'It had a thatched roof made of bulrushes, hardwood shutters, raised and rendered Dutch gables. It would be the family home for three generations and a place of wealth, happiness and harmony. They called it Valley End Plantation. This was where Liam Karel Side and his brother Johan were born, but it was also where their mother and father were murdered by the ZANU militants. When the Bush War started in 1966, his parents had been two of the first white casualties and the first of many murders which were to follow.

'Side was due to return home to Valley End Plantation from Bloemfontein when he had completed his studies. Firstly as a boarder at Grey College, an early South African public school, followed by three years at The University of Orange Free State where he studied Natural and Agricultural Sciences. Liam Side was getting ready for the life of a Rhodesian farmer. Afterwards he stayed awhile with one of his second cousins in Bloemfontein, finally returning to Tengwe on receiving news of his parents' tragic double murder. When he finally arrived home, his brother Johan was armed to the teeth and the family farmhouse had been turned into a fortress.

'The walls surrounding the compound were now tipped with broken glass, and the fences strewn with razor wire. Each window was caged with wrought iron bars, and inside each room there was a fully loaded rifle or pistol ready for use. Side's brother Johan had a Walther PK strapped to his belt, with a separate ammunition pouch and a machete in a leather sheath. When they were finally on their own, both men sat and wept. After the funeral, they had stood silently by their parents' grave and planned their revenge, and Liam Side swore that he would never weep again.

'Seven years later, when the Bush War began to

escalate, Liam left his brother Johan to run the tobacco plantation on his own and joined the Selous Scout Regiment to become a regular Bush soldier. A specialist regiment famous for its brave acts—according to the Rhodesian white minority at least—it was also accused of genocide by the black leaders, who finally took power in 1979.'

Coetzee lit up his Briar pipe, and blew a cloud of aromatic Dutch tobacco into the air. 'You see Mr Lambert, young Major Side, as he was by then, had already become hardened to war and was sick of it. Side knew that his future in Rhodesia was looking bleak so in 1973 he decided to move to South Africa, something which he could do quite easily because of his grandfather's original citizenship.'

Ambassador Biko picked up the story as Coetzee puffed away at his pipe. 'Afterwards all that remained politically was for ZANU and ZAPU to fight it out with each other, which they did until Nkomo and Mugabe finally made their peace. What happened to Liam's brother Johan is unclear because Zimbabwe is now a wreck and with all the sanctions imposed on the Mugabe regime by the west, I can't imagine what might have become of the family farm. So, you can understand Chief Inspector, that Liam Side has had a very tough life indeed.'

While he was at it the Reading policeman decided to ask one final question. 'But, what happened to Side when he moved to South Africa?' He was searching for the whole story. 'Did he go into business?'

Lambert called the waiter over and asked for the bill, telling his guests that lunch was on him and that Thames Valley Police would pay. As they left the restaurant, Coetzee replied to the seemingly almost forgotten question. 'More or less what he does now Mr Lambert, as you might have already gathered, because since that time he has worked one way or another, for the South African Government.'

The two diplomats politely shook the policeman's hand, thanked him for lunch and promised to stay in touch. He confirmed that he would contact them as soon as he had anything positive to tell them, which understandably might take some while. Leaving them that day it occurred to Lambert that many essential years had been lost to the civilised world through the hegemony of politics and the ravages of racism. How long would the killing go on for? For that reason alone Lambert was warming to his new quarry and his apparent rejection of war.

Lambert believed that it was high time for him to take a break from his enquiries, and in order to consider the many changes which had occurred in his original understanding of the *Kennet Narrow Boat Mystery*, he made once more for the Radisson Hotel, a warm bath and an air-conditioned room. That evening he telephoned Colonel Vassilev and agreed to meet him for a drink. They met in the bar in Flanagan's where they ordered two pints of Guinness.

The bald-headed American was nearby with a roly-poly and rather rumpled man. As soon as he saw Lambert and Vassilev together, he made his way towards them and introduced his companion. 'This is John Ernst,' he announced, 'and he is an accountant at Price Fotheringay the well-known financial advisors. John, this is Michael Lambert, and he is an established English publisher of seed catalogues, and I don't know your colleague's name?'

Colonel Vassilev rose to his feet and cordially shook hands with the two men, and then formally announced, 'My name is Yuri Vassilev.' He spoke in a serious manner. 'And I too am a printer of seed catalogues, but only in the Bulgarian and Turkish language.'

CHAPTER SEVEN

MICHAEL LAMBERT and Colonel Vassilev got a little tired of toothpaste and mouthwash after a while, because there is only so much one can say about it. But at the same time, it was interesting to see how determined the American was to discuss his job function and that of Lambert and his entirely fictional publishing of seed catalogues. Maybe he thought that he had missed something rather important from their ongoing dialogue, and that somewhere within the hidden depths of seed catalogue publication, there might be a new business waiting for him sometime in the future.

Wishing the American bore and his scruffy companion a very good evening, the two policemen decided to leave Flanagan's for the more relaxing surroundings of a traditional Bulgarian restaurant. This was to be found at the Nicky Hotel, where Vassilev assured Lambert that by Bulgarian standards, it was the best food in town.

It was only a short walk from the Radisson and so they leisurely strolled down Sixth of September Street, crossed over Vitosha Boulevard, finally arriving at the

Nicky hotel in Neofit Rilski Street. It seemed strange to Lambert that a small three-star hotel could spawn such a popular restaurant, when there were so many others thereabouts to choose from. Walking through the hotel reception area, they finally came upon quite a large half-covered area at the rear, which had at one time probably been the hotel garden. The two men found themselves a discreet table to one side, where they sat and inspected the hugely extensive menu. Ordering two large Kamenitza beers, they smoked in silence for a while, before once more broaching the subject of Liam Side and his disappearance.

'The thing is Yuri, at some point, I will have to inform my masters about the findings from the fingerprint report that the South African authorities have provided. But, I also need to keep this under my hat meanwhile, until I have established the true identity of the murder victim.'

Vassilev had a knowing look on his face. It seemed he had already anticipated Lambert's last remark and the suggestion he would make in return. Stubbing out his Kent cigarette he leaned forward and said in a somewhat surreptitious way, 'I think I might be able to help you there, Michael. As you may know KFOR is a NATO-run programme, and as Police Chief in Pristina, I have access to much of the American information system, because they are my de-facto bosses. If you give me a clear copy of the victim's fingerprints, I can run them through their computer to see what it brings up when I return to Kosovo next week. I can't promise anything, but it will be much faster than our friends at

Interpol; that's for sure. But meanwhile Michael, now you have Liam Side's official fingerprints from Pretoria, you can run those through your British Police computers, when you finally return to the UK, and see if you come up with anything new.'

Lambert was well aware of Interpol's shortcomings and like most European policemen he felt that the recently established EU equivalent had been a long time in coming. At the very least, it would be easier for Europol to monitor Police activities and would discount any fears of corruption, which had dogged the reputation of international police organisations for years. 'What is the best way for you to stay in touch Yuri? I mean, right now I would like to keep things as quiet as possible, at least for a few more days.'

'What about good old SMS? We have got a good temporary GSM service in Pristina; it was installed by the Brits about a year ago, and it suits my purpose entirely. It can be monitored I know, but it's very unlikely and it is much more reliable than emails. They have to go through the American server in Kosovo and we are obviously carefully tracked by them.' Colonel Vassilev had kept in touch with current technology, and seemed to be as aware as Lambert, that their communications could be followed by their respective masters. 'That would be quite okay for short messages, Michael,' Vassilev smiled, 'and if you need to contact me at length, there is always a web based service like Yahoo or Hotmail. Why not get yourself a private email address, with one of those gobbledygook prefixes? That usually puts the Yanks off the scent if they get too interested.' Vassilev gave Lambert his email address on Yahoo and they turned the conversation round once more back onto police work.

'How long do you intend to continue in the police force, Yuri? I know that I am getting close to making an important decision. They have offered me my boss's job when he retires next year, but my instincts tell me that it is time to leave the force for good.' Lambert had never discussed this matter before with anyone.

'What will you do, Michael, I mean, for a job if you leave?' It was as if the Bulgarian policeman was emotionally locked into a world from which he could never escape. 'I can't imagine what I would do without this new job of mine in Kosovo. I am paid a western salary by KFOR, which is unknown for a policeman in Bulgaria of any rank! I can easily afford to keep my family fed, my children educated and my mistress happy too.' He smiled at Lambert, assuming that he too would share in the implied conspiracy, by offering the English policeman a sideways glance into his private life.

'It's not like that in England, Yuri.' The Chief Inspector seemed resigned to a fate of virtual celibacy. 'I'm afraid that I am presently severely married, but to be honest, I don't know for how much longer. Maybe I am due for a change of partners soon, who knows?'

Two great cast iron plates of sizzling meat and vegetables arrived at the table, together with a large mixed salad, some toast and two further large glass mugs of Kamenitza beer. Lambert had never seen so much food on one dish before. 'We are sometimes like the Greeks on these occasions Michael, because we Bulgarians like a full table when we eat out.' The Colonel stabbed a piece of chicken breast with his fork, and began to slice it up on his plate. 'For us Bulgarians, quantity is far more important than quality!'

Walking back through the city later that evening, it seemed that the two policemen had become firm friends. It transpired too that the Colonel was an avid reader of Western literature and had consumed many of the same books which the English policeman had enjoyed during his solitary holidays in France, away from the distractions of his family life.

'I have always been a writer of sorts Yuri,' Lambert remarked as they arrived back at the Radisson Hotel, 'and I always thought that there was a story in me somewhere, and right now, that is precisely what I would like to be doing with my time, I mean, when this case is over—perhaps next year.'

They stopped outside the Radisson for one last smoke, agreeing to meet up the evening before the Englishman's return to Reading, and once more confirmed that he would bring a clear photocopy of the Kennet and Avon murder victim's fingerprints with him for Yuri Vassilev to process. That night Lambert was in bed by eleven o'clock and fast asleep at exactly five minutes past.

The following morning, after a rather boring hotel breakfast, he realised that it was time for him to become better organised and to start piecing the puzzle together, because there were only a very few days left in Sofia for him to accomplish any kind of investigation.

It was now Wednesday, and due to his protracted absences and the somewhat unusual secrecy policy he had chosen to adopt, he had become a little out of touch with the day-to-day management of the case. So his first job that morning was to get up-to-date with Gloria Hislop. By now it was eight o'clock in the morning in Reading, and he knew that she would be at her desk. Lambert began to write some questions out for her in his police notebook.

Had she managed to get in touch with anyone else in Bulgaria?

Were there any results from her phone calls to South America?

Did she have any news concerning the Russian woman, and had she discovered either of her National or Internal Passport numbers?

What were the Cyrillic documents in the buff file about, the ones he had copied and faxed to her the day before?

Had there been any strangers watching her apartment, or unfamiliar vehicles parked outside? Were all her security cameras working okay?

As for Detective Sergeant George Durant, he was mainly interested in hearing how he had got on in London, because both the Hammersmith lawyer and the Chinese banker seemed somehow to fit into the equation somewhere. His questions for him were more general.

Had he tracked down Antony Kwong, and had he discovered any hidden truths about this enigmatic financier?

Was Footman the Hammersmith solicitor in the frame, or was he just something from Liam Side's past?

Had there been any further information forthcoming from Eddie Singh?

Did Superintendent Burrows now realise that Side was a naturalised South African?

Was there any further information from the immigration authorities, concerning Liam Side's entering and leaving the country?

Would he arrange for a squad car to keep an eye on Gloria Hislop?

Lambert put his police notepad into the top pocket of his polo shirt and his wallet, British passport and handy into the Samsonite pouch attached to his belt. After donning his trainers and Kate's Gucci sunglasses, once again he walked out into a humid Sofia summer's day in search of a BTC public phone. As before, he sauntered through the outdoor antique market by the Nevski Cathedral, but this time he was in search of some presents to take home with him to England. He remembered that people liked to collect pens for example, of which there were many on sale, but what fascinated him mostly were the Russian Railway timepieces.

Carefully winding up a watch to see if it ticked, Lambert spent 30 Leva on a somewhat distressed chrome watch for his assistant Sergeant Durant and a further twenty Leva for a Russian doll. He would present this doll to Gloria Hislop on his return to Reading. The doll he chose had Gorbachev's face on the outside, and inside were a series of dolls depicting the five previous communist leaders of the Soviet Union. He also noticed that there were quite a lot of stamps for sale in the market, which interested him enormously, but it would take an hour or so to inspect and evaluate them properly, which was something he decided to put off until the following day.

Returning once more to the same BTC public telephone as before, he punched in a familiar Reading number. 'Gloria, is that you?' Her cheery good morning made him feel thoroughly reassured. 'Is everything all right?' he asked.

She sounded very positive. 'I am fine, Mike, and I have got quite a lot to tell you this morning, because I have been rather busy whilst you have been carrying out your investigations in Sofia, and some of what I have to tell you is very important. But first let me go through the Bulgarian phone numbers. What surprised me was how many of them were out of date, and that most of those which did work, were for English or American people living in Sofia.'

Gloria went on: 'More or less they all said the same thing. Most said that they hadn't seen Liam Side for only a day or two. Apparently a lot of the expats go to the same pub. It's called J. J. Murphy's, and it's in a street called Karnigradska. I was told that it's just off Vitosha Boulevard which is, as you know, the main street in Sofia. When I asked them how well they knew our man, they all claimed that they were bosom buddies! My opinion is that they are just a bunch of hopeless drunks. I hear that booze is quite cheap in that part of the world.'

'Surely you can't apply that conclusion to everyone that you spoke to Gloria? I find it hard to believe that Sofia is populated exclusively by such people.' Having uttered this last statement, on reflection, Detective C.I. Lambert realised that there might be an element of truth in what she had just said, especially with his own recent experiences at Flanagan's, 'Gloria, there must surely be a few exceptions?'

'Well, most of them have no idea what Side did for a living for a start. Some even thought he was still publishing the *Balkan Western News* magazine. When I asked them if they had read a copy recently, most of them said that they found it too boring and that it didn't contain enough articles about football. When I told them it had not been published for nearly two years, they simply went silent. But I did have some luck with the Russian woman, Mike. I have tracked down her National Passport number; it was hidden away in all that stuff concerning the birth of their daughter Patricia.'

The Reading policeman wrote down the Russian passport number and decided to give it to Yuri Vassilev when they next met. He of all people should be able to get the information needed quite quickly through one of his old colleagues at the Marie Louisa passport office. Was she in the country, or had she taken their daughter abroad as suspected; that was the question? If Lambert could track down their daughter Patricia, he would probably find Liam Side at some point. 'What about the telephone numbers in South America, Gloria? Did you have any luck there when you phoned around?'

'I was gobsmacked when I discovered who I was phoning, Mike. The first call I made turned out to be to the Peruvian President's office, and the second one I tried turned out to be the home of a certain Mr Vladimiro Pinero. When I asked to speak to someone regarding a Mr Liam Side, I was politely asked if I ever read the newspapers! Well, I know those twerps in Sofia don't, but I do, Mike, and I couldn't believe my ears. It turns out that Pinero used to be the Minister of the Interior in Peru and has been on the run for some months now. Also, the President—who is apparently of Japanese descent—is lying doggo in Japan, and refuses to go home to face the music! I read recently in *The Times* I think it was, that the new government in Peru claims these two Herberts have stolen millions from the national budget and shed-loads from their local banks as well. These two gentlemen are not nice people, Mike!' Gloria Hislop smiled to herself because she could actually hear the Reading detective whistling to himself over the phone.

'Blimey; that bad, is it? It's getting to be a bit like Topsy's house Gloria! This case is getting bigger and bigger by the moment!'

Perhaps it was time to speak to the spooks, but something inside Lambert made him exercise his usual caution; after all, what Gloria had just confirmed to him was at best circumstantial and fell far short of lining up the Kennet and Avon murder with some sort of international intrigue. 'I will be back in Reading on Friday Gloria, and we can talk about that then—but before I go—did you have any luck with those official looking Bulgarian documents I sent to you?'

'Yes and no Mike, I mean, they were all more or less as you imagined—leases, agreements and day-to-day contracts—the only interesting one being a court document, in which Side gets joint custody of his daughter Patricia, together with a declaration from the Bulgarian court that she is a Bulgarian citizen. If as you suggest, the Russian woman may have left the country, it might well have been because she thought that Side could now exercise some control over their daughter, implying that he might have some continued control over the Russian woman as well!'

'Good point Gloria; I can see now why you have all those university degrees!' Of course she was right, but he still didn't have the Russian woman's exact address in Sofia and short of knocking on hundreds of doors in Vassil Levski Street, he would have to wait for Yuri Vassilev to do some digging around. Promising to catch up with Gloria first thing on Friday afternoon, Lambert now turned his attention to Sergeant George Durant.

He caught George Durant parking his car outside Thames Valley Police Headquarters. When he answered his cell phone, he seemed to be very busy remonstrating with the driver of a badly parked van. 'Sorry Boss, I will be with you in a moment after this twit has moved his sodding heap!' Seconds later the Sergeant was free of angst and back on duty. 'Morning Boss, and how can I help you this morning?'

'I really phoned George, to ask you how you got on yesterday. Did you find anything out about our Chinese friend? And about that lawyer in Hammersmith—what was his name? Ah yes, Mr Footman—what happened there?"

'I will start with the firm of Footman & Co., if you don't mind, Boss? From what I could glean by speaking to a nearby fellow lawyer—a Mr Lionel Krueger—Clive Footman is the main Conveyancing solicitor in this firm and rarely gets involved with any general practice issues at all, well, not if he can help it. Krueger told me that in the past he had faced him in court—over certain matrimonial matters—and that he was a total plonker. So, if our man was relying on him for any serious help, I would personally feel rather sorry for him. Krueger puts him down as a typical London legal hack and told me that the property boys probably use him because he does what he is told. Lionel Krueger is in general practice and only a small amount of his work is in property purchase and sales. He told me he doesn't have much to do with Footman & Co., on a local level at least, and so I think it better to forget him altogether Boss.'

Going on, Durant now changed gear: 'However, this Chinese character is altogether a very different kettle of fish, and I spent the greater part of yesterday chasing him up. Firstly, I went to his office address in the City Road, just off Old Street to have a look round and discovered that he only occupies a very small part of a much larger block, with a small suite of offices on the fourth floor. Built, I would reckon, about 1965; it is a very unimposing and quite featureless building. All there is to indicate the Chainman's presence in the building, is a small sign with his company name on it, which is attached to the wall just inside the entrance. Not much to report there, Boss, but I had quite a stroke of luck with the head porter—a certain Mr Ron Trimble—because he turned out to be an ex-copper from Notting Hill and he remembered you from the good old days.'

'Ron Trimble, yes I remember him, he got bashed up during the Notting Hill riots in the sixties, and then became the desk Sergeant—nice bloke—but surely, he must be getting on a bit now?' What a small world it really was. 'And did he have anything to say that might be of interest to us, George?'

'Well, he knew Kwong's home address in the Barbican for a start, because Kwong is in the habit of receiving private visitors at his apartment occasionally, and with that and certain important courier deliveries, he trusts Trimble to redirect people or parcels to his home at weekends and after hours. Trimble told me that the property owner he works for keeps the building open 24/7, which is why it is popular with foreigners like Kwong, who have to deal with different time zones through their international business activities.

'But before I left, he told me that the office buildings security is extremely tight. He told me that this is mainly because a lot of posh people turn up to see Kwong in their big limos—heads of state, ambassadors, military attachés, wealthy Arabs and so on—which Trimble has to deal with personally. You see, on arrival they have to sign a special book which Mr Kwong insists on keeping at the main desk. That's about it, Boss, except for Mr Trimble that is—who asked me to wish you all the very best—and after that I went off to the Barbican.'

'You did well George, and Trimble is obviously a good future contact for us too if we need him. Pity I wasn't there though, I would have liked to have spoken with him once again.' Lambert could always trust his roly-poly assistant George to do a thorough job. 'And what happened at the Barbican?'

'That is another story Boss, because for the first time in my life I managed to get myself nicked!' They both started to laugh as the story unfolded. 'You see, I was snooping around the block that Kwong lives in looking for the door to his maisonette, when a next door neighbour came out of her apartment. I asked if she had seen Mr Kwong, because I had a message for him. She said that she hadn't seen him recently, because he was often away on business, and that he came and went at odd hours. I then asked if she could give me a description of him—you know, short fat with *slanty eyes*—when she suddenly slipped back into her flat and slammed the door in my face. Next minute there are two heavies coming at me from both sides, one grabbing my arms, and the other cuffing me.'

The Detective Sergeant went on: 'I told them that I was a copper, and they told me that they would see about that when they got me to their Security Office. When we did eventually get there and they took off the cuffs, I showed them my Warrant Card—which I usually forget, lucky me—and they apologised. Apparently the security at the Barbican is also quite tight and this woman had phoned them to say that she thought I was either a burglar or a mugger, and definitely up to no good. To all accounts this is not the first time she has done this but they have to react anyway, even though they all think she is a bit barmy!'

What happened next proved to be a gift from the Gods. 'After they apologised to me for the umpteenth time, we all sat down and had a cuppa together. Quite frankly Boss, by then I was feeling totally knackered anyway—what with all the travelling, the traffic an' all— and so we finally got onto the subject of the Chinaman. It turns out that although he lives there on his own, he has frequent visits from some very high class *Ladies of the Night*. These security guys have recently had to accompany these girls to his door—because of certain scandals caused by the neighbours—and also to keep the girls' own minders away. Apparently when he first lived there he was not terribly discreet about his choice of *takeaways* and the other tenants started to complain about the many and varied visits. So the security company, by accompanying them to and from his door, manages to stop a lot of fuss from ensuing and everyone's happy.'

'He sounds like a real scumbag!' Lambert could never get his head round the idea of hookers. 'And he must be earning a bomb to pay for their professional services.' The picture in the Policeman's mind's eye was of a dissipated and emotionless man, who had no real connection with normal humanity and cared for little else, apart from money. 'What other gems of information did our security experts come up with then?'

'Rather like Trimble, it was also a story of occasional visits from *foreign big shots*—who apparently arrive at the Barbican accompanied by similar examples of the aforementioned girls—and they party until the early hours of the morning. These security guys think that this is more or less how he does his business; I think the present day expression is having a *Bunga Bunga* Party.'

'You have been busy George, pity about the handcuffs!' Lambert had rarely had to restrain anybody in the past. That was usually done by the uniforms because he typically came along with the questions later on. 'By the way, did you give Burrows my message about Liam Side being a South African? We don't want any nonsense from MI5 at the moment, especially since I am planning on having a word with Kwong sometime next week. The thing is George, despite the fact that he sounds like a walking cesspit, Kwong might have some useful information about our man and it's important for me to know if he actually went ahead with that offer of finance to Balkan Side Ltd., and if the deal finally went through?' Lambert knew he had to follow the money.

'I showed Burrows the photocopy of the passport Boss, and that seemed to do the trick, although I think he is more concerned about a certain Councillor Strang at the moment. She seems to be his local nemesis! Oh, and by the way Boss—I will know from Immigration for sure on Friday—but it seems that Liam Side might have entered the UK on four other separate occasions during the month of June, the last time just three days before he entered the country through Blackbush and before the murder on that narrow boat. The trouble is that it takes a lot of time to track these events down, because his arrivals and departures were unusually from four different airports.'

This told C. I. Lambert that anything further the pathologist Eddie Singh had to say, could in any case wait until Friday afternoon. All that remained for him to arrange was for George to organise a passing squad-car to keep an eye on Gloria's home in Southcote.

As far as Lambert was concerned, the future of his enquiry now rested entirely on the findings of his friend Yuri Vassilev, the fingerprint analysis, and the present whereabouts of the Russian woman and her daughter Patricia. Whatever the motive for murder might be, it would purely rely on the identity of the murder victim. Without this information, Thames Valley Police would simply be chasing shadows.

Lambert returned to the hotel, and phoned Vera

Kolova in order to make an appointment to return the documents he had on loan from her. The Chief Inspector had photocopies of all the necessary documents he needed and had downloaded the floppy disks onto his laptop. As far as he was concerned his investigation in Sofia was at an end. That is why his conscience allowed him to drop everything and to have a good time. When he finally touched base with Vera, it was agreed that she would come to the Radisson around eight that evening, and she happily accepted his invitation to go somewhere afterwards for dinner. With the rest of the day at his disposal, Lambert opened up Peter Carney's excellent guidebook on Bulgaria in order to choose where to go for the day. Thursday would be his last day for business, and together with a long search for any unusual and inexpensive postage stamps in the antique market to add to his already burgeoning collection, there was not much time left before his return to London.

When he got back to his hotel bedroom he found that it was being cleaned by the hotel staff, and excusing himself, he removed his laptop and other papers from the wardrobe together with the box of documents which Vera had entrusted to him. When he got to the ground floor, he put it all into one of the hotel's special security lockers next to the reception area, and placed the key in his Samsonite pouch; this information was far too valuable to risk, after so much trouble had been taken by him over the proceeding days.

Sitting on the bus taking both him and other eager

tourists to the Rila Monastery, the Englishman marvelled at the ease by which he was able to buy an all-inclusive ticket for the excursion. Unlike other things he had experienced in Sofia—especially the absurd antics at the business centre—the receptionist had simply taken his money and told him to wait twenty minutes for the bus to arrive at the hotel entrance. Up until then, he imagined that getting anything done in Bulgaria must be rather like swimming in treacle.

The tourist bus bullied its way through the Sofia City traffic and turning right at the Tzum department store, it found its way along Marie Louisa Boulevard and on to the Greek road leading to Sandanski. Passing by Pernik, Bobov Dol and Dupnitza, after about an hour it abruptly turned left off the main road and sped along a small winding local road, on up into the Rila Mountains and their ultimate destination.

Lambert wandered around the galleries looking into the little rooms that had at one time housed the many priests who would have once lived at the Monastery during the 19th Century. It was summer now, but Lambert could imagine how—on cold winter nights in the Rila Mountains and without proper heating—the Monks must have been very tough to withstand the biting winds and the icy conditions which would have unquestionably tried their faith and resolution as well. The Reading policeman also noticed how few priests were to be seen that day—no more than five—and that this beautiful building was no more than an historical decoration from the past. Communism must have put paid to the vitality of the Bulgarian Orthodox Church, existing only as a form of Christian insurance in a sea of discontent and doubt.

What also occurred to the Reading policeman—on a beautiful and relaxing sunny day in the distant and mysterious Rila Mountains of Bulgaria—was how far away he was from his treacherous carping wife and the milieu of their life together. He knew that it was time to make the final decision—not just concerning his relationship with Arabella or their two children—but about how he wished to spend the rest of his life. It was time to think about himself for a change.

Later that afternoon, after some indifferent grilled Kabapche and Kyufte—all wrapped up in a soggy bread roll with wilting lettuce and squashy tomato slices—it was time to return to Sofia and an evening with the charming Vera Koleva. Sitting on the bus nursing a bottle of Devin water and a mild case of indigestion, Lambert watched the passing scenery with interest.

As far as the eye could see, nothing seemed to have been properly finished and very few houses had been rendered or painted. The gardens were unkempt with shabby outbuildings and old Lada, Trabant and Moscovitch motorcars were parked on pavements. Goats seemed to wander as they pleased, despite the cajoling and the rage of their aged herders.

As the bus passed by Pernik and on into the suburbs of Sofia, although there were people milling around the shops and offices along their route, the backdrop to their lives seemed rather desolate to the English policeman, their faces withdrawn and their body language lacking any form of animation. Back into the City the tourist bus returned once more to the Radisson Hotel, to a degree of modernity and some personal comfort. Lambert was pleased to get out.

He was tired after his Rila trip and it was time to wash away the sweat and the dust of the journey. Returning to his room, he was surprised at the state it was in. He knew that the cleaners had been in that morning, because he had spoken to them, but on his return he found all the drawers and cupboard doors open, with his possessions spread all over the floor. The balcony window was ajar and the table tipped on its side, but he knew from experience that it was a very old trick. Whoever had rifled his room had come through the entrance door, and that could only mean one thing. Someone had given the intruders a duplicate key-card; it was as simple as that.

Returning downstairs to the hotel reception area, he reported the break-in to the manager. It was the same man he had spoken to on arrival, and although he was apologetic, he seemed to spend the next hour making excuses and attempting to absolve himself of every iota of responsibility. This was a side to the Bulgarian character which Lambert had not experienced before, and it was clear by his attitude that the good opinion of the Hotel owner towards him was far more important to this hotel manager, than a disgruntled hotel guest's complaints.

Before he returned to his room with the obsequious manager, Lambert quickly inspected his security locker and noted that the contents were intact. When they arrived at his room the manager asked if there was anything missing, and searching through the room Lambert confirmed that everything seemed to be there, any personal cash and documents having been secreted in the little wall safe. He dialled up his birth-date on the keyboard and the door sprang open, revealing the cash and private documents he had left there on his arrival. Lambert said, 'There seems to be nothing missing,' and the manager lifted up his arms, grimaced in a resigned and knowing Balkan way, and nodded his head.

'That is how we are in this country,' was his only comment, and as he turned to go he said, 'I will ask the staff if they saw anything unusual Sir, but it was probably the gypsies—it always is!' Ten minutes later the room was shipshape and the Englishman took to his Jacuzzi bubble bath for a long hard think. It had been a long day.

He had obviously been rumbled by his unknown adversaries. If it was the two Bulgarians who broke into the narrow boat in Reading—or those who had burgled his home in Sonning—they were obviously very determined to find out what he knew. If they were not the same two men—and he could discount the Gypsies, because they would have most certainly have taken something even as a memento—then perhaps he was dealing with a well-organised group of people. Who they could be made his mind boggle; then again, maybe it was not a question of who they were, but of who they might have been in the past. It was conceivable that he was dealing with the remnants of Bulgaria's Communist regime, refugees from which had become a kind of shadow security service.

'*Old habits die hard.*' Lambert was clear on that point, especially if there was money involved and particularly if there was nothing to lose. But, it demonstrated one simple thing to the Detective Chief Inspector; that he was getting closer to the truth about the Kennet and Avon Canal murder, although he didn't even know how, or why!

At eight o'clock Vera Kolova parked her BMW outside the hotel and was waiting in the reception area when Mike Lambert came out from the lift. They both looked pleased once more to see one another, and this time he gave her an affectionate kiss on the cheek. For an Englishman, this signalled an unconscious sign of a burgeoning European identity.

Carefully removing the box from the security locker, and relocking the door, he carried the files to her car and placed them in the trunk, whilst making sure that the car was securely locked and that the vehicle alarm was properly activated. Whoever it was that had earlier entered his hotel bedroom, would not chance being caught by the policemen who were on duty outside the Sobranie Parliament building opposite, so it was quite safe. Lambert said nothing of his break-in to Vera.

'Where we go tonight, Michael? You have found somewhere nice we can eat?' The truth was that he believed he had hit the jackpot, because they were both on their way to the Opera Club. Highly recommended by the hotel manager, after he had made the last of his many puny and repetitive apologies, it also had a good write up in the *Sofia Independent* newspaper.

'We go to the opera for a concert?' Perhaps Vera hated opera, but once more Lambert said nothing as they crossed the square, and entered the gardens next to St Sofia church and the outdoor antique market. The antique dealers were wrapping up their wares and putting them into their cars ready for the following day. Most of the stalls were now empty and the detritus of the day was being swept up by the street cleaners. Turning right into Rakovski Boulevard, they walked towards the National Opera house, but instead of entering the main building, they went down some side steps and entered a plush busy restaurant. Vera gasped in astonishment: 'Are we really in Sofia Michael? It's incredible!'

It was like walking into an Art Nouveau time capsule in Old Vienna and a world that had been long forgotten by anyone in Sofia. The *Maitre D'* turned out to be an Englishman who later told Lambert that he was originally from Essex but was married to a Bulgarian girl from Sofia. He showed the couple to a table by the small stage at the rear of the restaurant and told them to ask for *Richard* if they needed anything. He also told them he was the manager of the restaurant, which had been open for only a year and that most of his customers were wealthy businessmen or foreign tourists.

The menu was not enormous, unlike the Nicky Hotel restaurant which seemed to go on forever, and with the usual choice of grilled meat or fish, it came with a choice of interesting sauces, salads and side dishes. They could see the American influence, one which the restaurant was obviously geared for. There were a lot of suits there, but unlike the thirsty habitués of Flanagan's these customers were obviously quite different and were from Brussels, London or Washington. It seemed to Lambert that they were all taking themselves very seriously and not simply out for a good time like Vera and himself. That is, until the waiters began to sing!

He'd noticed when he sat down that the waiters had a microphone set attached to their collar, but what he did not know was that all these microphones were connected to the intricate sound system in the club restaurant. Before they could order their meal, the band struck up, the music began and they were all suddenly transformed into the audience of the Andrew Lloyd Webber musical *Jesus Christ Superstar*. First they sang the theme song from the show, and this was followed by a girl singing *I don't know how to love him* from the stage. What was amazing was how this did not stop the waiters from waiting, or the customers asking for the usual things one asks for in restaurants. The whole event just seemed to fit together, and transformed the whole eating experience into an almost surreal occasion.

The food was great, although the service was understandably slow, the event suddenly interrupted by what appeared to be a drunk carrying a stepladder, who seemed determined to change a light bulb over the stage.

He could hardly climb the stepladder he was so drunk, and it rocked from side to side, looking as though he would crash to the ground at any moment. After changing the bulb, he finally slid down the ladder, fell over, got up, bowed and then carried the ladder out of the restaurant. 'Who is that man, Richard?' Lambert asked.

The restaurant manager laughed at the innocent question. 'That's the boss Sir, he used to be a Circus Clown many years ago, and he is always doing stuff like that for fun. You wouldn't know it, but he hardly ever drinks!'

The food arrived, and with a bottle of Melnik red wine to accompany the meal, he and Vera sank into an easy and intimate conversation about their lives so far and what they would like to do in the future. They talked about past relationships, the political changes in Eastern Europe and how she had escaped from Bulgaria in the mid-80s, more or less at the time when she had come across Liam Side.

They had met on a flight to Sofia which had been diverted due to bad weather in the capital, to the little town of Burgas on the Black Sea. After that, they had seen each other a few times and then lost touch when she met her husband, married and moved to Belgium.

'What happened to your husband Vera?' It seemed to Lambert from her remarks that she lived on her own in any case. 'Oh, he comes around from time to time; of course we are still friends, but these days it is just business.' But, it was here that Vera's story of the missing Belgian husband ended. After a final French digestive brandy, followed by some chocolate gateaux and a cup of espresso coffee, they slowly strolled back to the Hotel.

'I really enjoyed it tonight Vera, perhaps we could meet up again one of these days—maybe in Belgium if you are around—and I would very much like to keep in touch.' It was obvious to Vera Kolova that Lambert was no ladies' man and, still very unsure of his future, didn't really know what to say.

'Yes, I would like that very much Michael. I give you a card from my hotel in Bruges; you can always phone me there, or if I not there, I will be here in Sofia. Thank you for a wonderful evening, it has meant a lot to me.' She kissed him gently on the cheek, and the Reading policeman suddenly felt a terrible twinge of guilt. It was nothing to do with his attraction to Vera, but the fact that he had not told her the whole truth about Liam Side, or that he was probably still alive.

'I am due for some leave soon Vera. I was going as usual this summer to my little house in Normandy, but Bruges is not so far for me to drive from there. I could travel to Belgium in the morning and then you could perhaps show me around Bruges in the afternoon. I don't know Belgium very well at all.'

And so it was left, and as he watched her drive away in her BMW he mentally kicked himself. '*Why didn't I say more to her?*' Lambert knew that he would regret not doing so, even before the car had disappeared from view and he had once more returned to his hotel room.

The next morning was his last before his final return home to England and, taking his time, he emerged from his room at ten o'clock and rather later than usual. By then the hotel breakfast room was closed and so once more he found himself coerced into a heart-stopping Irish breakfast in Flanagan's. Despite the fumes, he sat outside under an umbrella, drinking the eponymous Irish tea which he somehow extracted from the pretentious café menu. It was another hot day, but with a slight breeze blowing across the square, it took the edge off the humidity which usually accompanied the heat in Sofia.

Paying his bill at the bar, he crossed the square once more and made for the outdoor antique market which by then was in full swing. It was obvious that not all dealers were specialists and that meant the quality and prices were very unpredictable and subject to the dealers' whims. What the Reading policeman tried to do was to isolate one good dealer who understood the international stamp trade, who had studied the realised auction prices, but that was rather a tall order.

Milan Boev was one such dealer, who sought out Lambert when it was clear to him that he knew what he was doing. 'Are you an American?' He looked quizzically at the Englishman, squinting through his John Lennon glasses. 'No, I come from London,' was Lambert's generic response. Nobody had ever heard of Reading in Bulgaria, and they were usually confused when he spelled it out for them. 'Are you interested in unusual postage stamps, I mean expensive ones? If you come with me I will show you some important Bulgarian stamps you may like to buy. These are not for everyone.' They walked to a stall which was full of Russian military hats and paraphernalia, with the usual watches and pens. 'I have them here in this packet; there are two you might like.'

They were in fairly good condition for their age, the first being a WW1 green 18 Leva stamp of a monoplane flying over the Rila Monastery, and the second was an 1879 10 Stotinka green Lion stamp. Both had been properly franked by the post office, with traces of the original adhesive on the back. To Lambert they looked quite perfect, but that depended on the price. 'How much do you want for the pair?' The dealer looked into the heavens for some inspiration. He knew that foreigners paid a lot of money for stamps which were right. 'I want 200 Leva, Englishman,' was his reply. The pungent smell of garlic filled the air as Lambert looked into the dealer's piggy eyes. 'I will give you fifty Leva for the two and that is all I am prepared to pay.' The squint had now given way to a laughing face. 'Do you think that we Bulgarians are fools?'

Lambert shrugged and moved away to a stall further up towards the Nevski Cathedral, and pretended to look at some pens. He smiled at the old lady whose stall it was, and carefully inspected a battered Parker pen which was worth precisely nothing to anyone. Someone was tugging his sleeve, and it was the myopic street trader. Standing stoically with a look of resignation on his face, 'The best I can do is 100 Leva Mister, I can't do less than that.'

Lambert counted out 100 Leva and held them in his left hand. Boev shrugged, handed over the stamps which Lambert then carefully inspected once more to check if they were the same ones. With a nod he finally let the man take the cash from his hand. Shrugging his shoulders, the trader smiled at the Englishman, and then disappeared once more into the crowd. But Lambert was a very happy man and, placing his two philatelic treasures into his wallet, for the third time in three days he headed for the nearby public telephone.

It was agreed that the two policemen would meet for a drink at seven that evening, in the hotel cocktail bar, where they were unlikely to meet anyone they knew. The Chief Inspector would then hand over a copy of the murder victim's fingerprints to Yuri Vassilev, and the passport number of the Russian woman. Lambert was due to leave the hotel very early the next morning and didn't want a late night. The Bulgarian policeman said he quite understood, and explained that he needed to spend some time with his family before returning to Pristina. With that evening's meeting arranged, Michael Lambert made for the National Art Gallery.

The flight home was uneventful. Despite the early hour, British Airways had a full complement of English newspapers on board for the passengers to read, together with a full English breakfast. With plenty of good filter coffee, the journey was relaxed, and it gave Lambert time to catch up with the news.

The *Independent* reported the continued refusal of the Japanese Government to return the ex-Peruvian President back to his country of origin, due to an ongoing legal dispute concerning his ethnic origins and his dual nationality. It seemed that constitutionally, Japan did not recognise any extradition proceedings against its citizens and was therefore not obliged to return him to face the wrath of the Peruvian judicial system. Attached to this article was a footnote concerning the whereabouts of his Peruvian henchman Vladimiro Pinero. He was presently alleged to be in hiding with the FARC gorillas in Colombia, where it was stated the Americans were hot on his trail. It was also reported that no recovery had been made of the missing millions, reputed to have been as much as 200 Million USD.

Going through immigration and then through customs was very easy for Lambert and before he knew it, he was back in the long-term car park looking at a rather grimy Alvis 21. The cost of its removal from the airport compound was also a bit of a surprise, but soon he was pleased to be back on English roads, after his week's stay in Sofia. The British habit of give and take once more governed people's driving habits and with the continued respect for classic cars shown by other road users, he was on his way back to Reading in no time at all. Parking his car in the Thames Valley Police car park he could not help but wonder how long these familiar surroundings would dominate his working day. The CD player was playing Art Tatum's *Begin the Beguine,* which brought the Reading policeman back to reality with a painful bump!

CHAPTER EIGHT

LAMBERT had little more to do other than report his activities to Superintendent Burrows. 'Did you enjoy your *jolly* Lambert? I heard from Durant that the Brits were good for some photocopies and few faxes! What did I tell you?' The older man sniggered to himself. 'There was a time when these embassies were run by proper English toffs and old soldiers a bit like yourself Lambert, not these numpty also-rans!'

Burrows was sitting in front of a great pile of correspondence which he was gamely attempting to read, but something very negative inside him was inhibiting the process. Opening his top drawer, he removed the bottle of pink unction and swallowed a tablespoonful. 'I can't take much more of this bullshit; I used to be a good copper once, Lambert; now all I am is a bloody clerk'.

'Why don't you delegate all this stuff to one of your more mature desk sergeants Sir, one of those nearing retirement for example? Then you can pick and choose what you want to deal with.' Lambert had seldom been so outspoken to Burrows, who had always maintained an aura of authority.

The Superintendent shook his head and with a weak smile, picked up the pile of correspondence before him and chucked it unceremoniously into his wastepaper bin. 'Is that how you would define delegation, Chief Inspector? If it is, then all my problems are now completely solved!' With a look of huge satisfaction on his face, he lent back in his creaking office chair, 'Well then, what happened in Sofia?'

'I am a lot further forward with the case than last week Sir, and we now more or less know the life story of our alleged murder victim. It was when I discovered that he was not a Brit—or a Paddy for that matter—that things started to gel and a clearer picture began to emerge. It seems that our Mr Side might well have been an agent for the South African Intelligence Service before he left Pretoria in 1980, which was when he moved to London. It also seems that he came to London with his then girlfriend—a Pansy something or other; we don't presently know her surname—who might well still be working here in the UK. Apparently she was a travel agent in South Africa, which at the time was one of the few legitimate ways of taking large amounts of money out of the country.'

Lambert sat down and with a wry smile went on, 'For all we know, he could well have remained a spook, but that was far from all he did. According to a local Bulgarian politician of his acquaintance—a certain Mr George Panov—Liam Side was very busy property dealing in London in the eighties, operating anonymously through a company registered in the

Channel Isles. He told me that they used to meet occasionally, when this Panov man lived in Earls Court, which would explain why there is no information concerning Side's tax or social security status, because—as a foreigner—he was operating offshore and outside the UK system.'

Referring to his notes, Lambert went on, 'It also seems that during that time he did most of his property transactions through a Hammersmith solicitor called Clive Footman who was also advising him on matters relating to his daughter Patricia who was born in Sofia, because Liam Side left the UK in 1993—after the London property market crashed around his ears—and then moved to Bulgaria. According to the present South African Ambassador in Sofia, a Mr Thomas Biko— appointed to his post by President Nelson Mandela in 1995 I believe—Liam Side helped his country a lot with their procurement needs from Eastern Europe. According to Biko, when the trade embargo was dropped after the abolition of apartheid in South Africa, they needed a lot of things quickly and Side assisted them in his role as some kind of Procurement Agent. Don't ask me how this all fitted in with his *news magazine*, but it seems that Liam Side had a lot of Eastern European contacts who could help with these purchases. This ranged from tractors and diggers made in Belorussia, mining equipment from Moscow and St Petersburg and a lot of second-hand plant and equipment from Serbia, Romania and Bulgaria. There were also deals made with certain Bulgarian contractors, to build some new townships in South Africa.'

Burrows gazed at Lambert and shook his head. 'My word, Lambert, you have been busy. Sergeant Durant tried to keep me informed of your activities as best he could, although it now seems that there have been some important results concerning this investigation closer to home. Am I right in saying there were four or more trips made between June and July to and from the UK by this man Side, the last one as a basket case through Blackbushe? Sounds to me like a deal gone wrong, Lambert. This is all about money, isn't it—it has to be?'

Lambert did not disagree with Burrows, although it was becoming clear that in the end the main evidence was likely to be provided through the good offices of Colonel Vassilev in Pristina; if and when he came up trumps with the dead man's fingerprints. Meanwhile he also had Side's fingerprints from Pretoria to run through the computer and a mysterious list of codes to decipher, on which account he decided to keep his Superintendent partially in the dark for the time being, or at least until he had made a real breakthrough with the case. There were also the two accomplices to deal with at some point, or were they quite simply assassins?

It was now time to go home, to face the music and to find out what surprises Arabella might have in store for him. But first he kept his promise and drove to Southcote to see Gloria Hislop. Ringing the front doorbell, a metallic voice said, 'There you are Mike, on time as usual I see, do come in,' and then the door opener buzzed.

'What was it like there?' Greeting him at the door of her apartment in her wheelchair, Gloria Hislop's gleaming face was a welcome sight.

'It was quite unlike anything I have experienced before Gloria, although rather too Machiavellian for my tastes, so I am very glad to be home.' Lambert looked quite different to her. Sitting in her apartment in his casual clothes, he appeared far more vulnerable than she remembered him.

'Did you find out what you needed Mike? I mean, seven days in a foreign country is not a long time really if you don't know the ropes.' She imagined his language problems and how he must have struggled to get around Sofia.

'It was surprisingly easy actually, Gloria, because many people speak English there, and once I had met Panov and Vera Kolova, things started to unravel quite quickly; especially when it became clear that Liam Side was in fact a South African.' Lambert smiled tiredly. 'How about you, did you see anyone suspiciously eyeballing you from the road?'

'There were a couple of men parked outside one day looking at a map, but I guess they must have just been lost. The uniforms came round quite regularly and knocked on the door to see if I was okay, but to tell you the truth Mike, I feel much safer now you are back in Reading.'

Home once more in Sonning, things were not quite so relaxed. The house felt empty and there was no sign of Samanda. He went into the living room and saw where the glass had been replaced, probably by Mr Paddick the local builder. The house had been cleaned and the kitchen was neat and tidy. Lambert got to work on his Braun filter coffee machine, and soon the room was full of the aroma of Arabica coffee, the bubble and hiss the sound of good things to come. On the hall table there was an envelope with his name on it. In it was a note from Arabella.

Dear Mike,

I hope you enjoyed your stay in Sofia, and that you haven't strained yourself in any way. Too much exertion for a man of your age is quite dangerous.

I have gone away for a few days to Brighton with a friend from the Maidenhead Guild of Artists—you have never met them, they live in Cookham—and I expect to be back by next weekend. I have left Samanda with Fiona Prothero with what little dog food we still have, so you will have to get some more delivered from the local kennels.

Kate has gone back to Wandsworth and I haven't heard from Jebb recently, I expect he is busy in the City.

There is plenty of stuff in the freezer.

Arabella.

Mike Lambert contemplated phoning his absent wife on her mobile, but then thought better of it. Knocking on his neighbour's front door, he could hear the clatter of Samanda's paws in the passageway. Fiona Prothero came to the door with Samanda who was wagging her tale and snuffling. 'Thank you for looking after her.' The Chief Inspector was pleased to see his white Labrador. 'I hope she wasn't too much trouble for you, Fiona?'

Fiona Prothero said nothing at all, stared at him for a moment and then slammed the door in his face. *'I see the gossips have been busy again!'* Lambert thought to himself, *'Arabella must have been trying very hard to build up a strong case for herself.'* As if by magic, it seemed that he had now become the guilty party.

He returned to the house and let Samanda into the garden where she galloped around, sniffing all her familiar places to reassure herself that she was once more back on familiar territory.

He was very tired from the journey and sitting in the kitchen sipping his strong black coffee, he imagined how nice it would have been to be made welcome once more in his own home. Taking his coffee with him he thoughtfully climbed the stairs. Entering the main bedroom—which they had once so contentedly shared—he went into the en suite bathroom, looked around for any signs of his wife's continued existence, turned on the bath taps and got ready for a long hot soak.

As he wallowed in the soft soapy water, Lambert realized that a long weekend on his own would probably be *just what the doctor ordered.* It was the perfect opportunity to check out the value of the two postage stamps he had purchased from the Sofia dealer, and a marvellous opportunity to get back in trim after his recent orgy of fried food. The sun was shining and a Saturday afternoon in the nets at Luton Park School would soon shed a few of his unwanted pounds and get him back into shape. It would also give him an opportunity to devote some time to his beloved Alvis 21, and to make her sparkle once more after his recent travels.

By Sunday Mike Lambert had come to realise that he might enjoy his own company a great deal more than he thought. He was able to tidy the garden and mow the lawn at his leisure, and now that the hosepipe ban was lifted, he was once again able to water with the garden hose and to get the sprinkler system working. By Sunday late afternoon he had cleaned the swimming pool, replaced the contents and replenished the chloride in the filtering system. The prize for his hard work was a long lingering swim in the cool welcoming water and an hour or so sunbathing in the remaining sunrays of a long summer's day.

Monday, however, was like any other working day when he returned to the usual routine of his office in Reading. He texted Colonel Vassilev from his GSM, to confirm that he was back at his police work and received an SMS saying *good luck*! Eddie Singh wanted to know what to do with the body of the murder victim, and Lambert advised him to wait a few more days before handing it over to the Coroner's Office. Sergeant Durant was pleased to see his Boss back at work, but for no other reason than to discuss the local cricket scores.

'We missed your strong steady hand at the crease Boss! I didn't mind standing in as Captain while you

were away, but we especially missed your batting skills.'
The tubby Sergeant had not attended net practice, two
days before, because he was on duty. 'Not much
happened at the nick this weekend Boss, one GBH, a
couple of sundry punch-ups, two or three domestics
and the usual drunks, but I left that up to the uniforms
to handle and concentrated on my report to Burrows.'

C. I. Lambert was not surprised. 'I want to see that
Chinese banker tomorrow if at all possible, George; I
know that he has got something hidden up his sleeve.
We can go together if you like—we'll take the Alvis. That
way, it will give you a break from driving and I haven't
had a spin *up the smoke* for ages.' After a week's absence
from Reading he knew he would have to spend all day
writing out his report and accounting for his expenses.
It was a normal Monday and a complete washout.

'What was the totty like in Bulgaria Boss? Did you
get what you were looking for?' Durant's cheerful
countenance saved him from a stern rebuke from
Lambert, who now realised that it was a well-known
destination for sex tourism.

'Don't you start,' he gave his Sergeant a withering
look, 'I've been getting black looks all day, and even my
next door neighbour refused to speak to me when I
collected the dog. Why can't anyone realise that I was
there on police business?'

'I'm only joking Boss!' George Durant had recently
read an article in the *News of the World* called 'Bonking
in Bulgaria,' which had involved a visiting British
Cabinet Minister. The arrogant twit had strongly denied

it of course. 'I don't suppose you read the gutter press much, do you, Boss?' But Lambert said nothing.

Later that day the Chief Inspector phoned Antony Kwong's London office in order to make an appointment to interview him. All his advertised phone lines seemed to be attached to various fax machines and so no one answered. Lambert was therefore forced to fax a letter to the Chinese banker, who oddly enough replied to him almost immediately.

In his fax Kwong agreed to meet the Reading Policeman at 2 o'clock the following afternoon in central London, at the Institute of Directors in Pall Mall. In his reply he confirmed that it was to discuss matters relating to a Mr Liam Side. Very formal and businesslike, at least the official police investigation could now proceed on the home front as well as abroad.

At midday the shining Alvis 21 glided almost silently from the Thames Valley Police headquarters with Michael Lambert at the wheel. His assistant Durant sat in the passenger seat wondering what had become of head banging Rock 'n' Roll, because although his boss's choice of music was not exactly an obstacle to their professional relationship, he conceded that it didn't help. 'Haven't you got something a bit jollier we can listen to Boss; something with some sort of tune in it?'

Lambert leaned over and switched his CD player off altogether. 'How's that Sergeant Durant, is that better for you?' The silence was deafening as they drove swiftly down the M4 motorway, up and over the Chiswick flyover.

With the hood down, any music would have been completely drowned by the sound of the teaming London-bound traffic. Lambert drove onwards to Hammersmith, turned off the flyover—hooked off down Hammersmith Road—and then, when he got to the Shepherds Bush roundabout, made his way along the Bayswater Road on up to Cumberland Gate and the top end of Hyde Park. Driving down Park Lane the Reading Policeman then turned right and drove into the Hyde Park underground car park.

After closing the hood and carefully locking the doors, the two men walked up to Regent Street and hailed a black cab. Arriving at the Institute of Directors a little early, they asked for Antony Kwong and were shown into a members lounge to await his arrival. On the dot of 2 p.m. the well rounded and enigmatic figure of Antony Kwong entered the room, accompanied by a thin reedy man in a scruffy suit.

The thin man was first to speak. 'Are you Chief Inspector Lambert, Sir? This is Mr Kwong, and I am his solicitor Hugh McNeil.' No offer of a handshake was made and turning to Sergeant Durant the thin man asked politely, 'And who may you be Sir, we were only expecting one visitor today.'

Lambert took the initiative and introduced his Sergeant to the two men and decided at once to get down to business. 'Look, it's kind of you to speak to me at such short notice Mr Kwong, but you may be able to help Thames Valley Police with our enquiries.' How banal his jargon sounded in the plush surroundings of the Institute of Directors, 'You see, it is about the recent murder of a certain Mr Liam Side, which took place approximately ten days ago on the Kennet and Avon Canal.'

The Chinese man seemed very stiff and formal and simply stared at the Chief Inspector and then back again at his lawyer as the dialog progressed, and there were no noticeable signs of comprehension displayed in his face that either of the two policemen could perceive.

'And how, pray, do you think my client Mr Kwong can help you, Sir? As you might have gathered, Mr Kwong does not speak English very well, and so he has asked me to attend this meeting—I speak a little Mandarin—so as to better understand your questions.' The slight Scottish burr indicated that Kwong's lawyer was perhaps from Edinburgh. McNeil turned once more and spoke inaudibly to his client before returning his attention to Lambert. 'Perhaps you would be good enough to enlighten us a little, Chief Inspector?'

'As no doubt your client will remember, Mr Liam Side came to see him two years ago, in order to arrange a loan for a building project he had in Sofia, the capital of Bulgaria. In his letter of offer to Side, Mr Kwong agreed to lend his company Balkan Side Ltd., an amount of 200,000 US Dollars; subject to various conditions, to pay for unspecified building work. I have a copy of this document here confirming that it would be paid out in 20,000 US Dollar tranches over a period of some two years, at an interest rate of 30%. What can Mr Kwong tell me about this project, and did Mr Side go ahead with the deal?'

Hugh McNeil spoke to his client in a very hushed voice, to which the Chinese man replied in Mandarin in a loud and somewhat dismissive way, as though he was laying down the law to his solicitor. Turning once more to the two policemen the lawyer announced, 'He remembers Mr Side but said that Mr Side did not agree with his conditions of offer, informing Mr Kwong that the interest rate was too high.'

'Mr McNeil, according to our investigation, Mr Kwong's offer to Side was almost identical to other offers he received, yet Side didn't consider any of the others and appears to have settled exclusively on Mr Kwong. Can he tell us why, and if there was any other business conducted between the two parties which might have influenced his decision?'

While Mr McNeil mumbled into the Chinese banker's ear, it was clear that Kwong was getting annoyed and was in danger of *losing face* since he was no longer in total control of the conversation. Whilst the Scottish lawyer remained calm his client was now becoming more agitated. Lambert removed the list of twenty-eight coded numbers from his briefcase and spread them out on the coffee table before him.

As he did so, the look on Antony Kwong's face changed completely and his arrogance seemed to shrink as his eyes absorbed the contents of the papers before him. 'Where you get that?' he demanded. 'This is Government business, you have no right to question me about this, this is secret business. I will speak to MI5; you not very important policemen, they will make big trouble for you!'

Lambert was nonplussed and not really surprised by the outburst. Was it that easy to knock this arrogant Chinese businessman off his high horse? Lambert continued to address the lawyer: 'Perhaps Mr Kwong— who seems to speak a great deal more English than he has led us to believe—might like to confirm to me what these numbers are for, Mr McNeil?'

The look on Antony Kwong's face resembled fear more than annoyance, so while the Chinese banker was being counselled by his scrawny solicitor, Lambert nonchalantly removed his notebook and placed his warrant card on the table before him, while he awaited his reply.

Looking as though an arrest was imminent was an old trick that the Reading policeman had used time and again to gently intimidate self-important people. They always believed that they would shortly be carted off in handcuffs, something which neither of the policemen ever carried around with them.

'My client informs me that they are probably jet engine numbers, Mr Lambert. He says that he has seen similar numbers in the past in the manifest of a ship travelling from Murmansk to Angola. Mr Kwong does not know any more than that. He says that they could be for any type of airplane because he is not an expert, Chief Inspector.' Having said that the two men got up to go, but the Reading policeman was not finished yet.

'Was Mr Kwong involved in Liam Side's business with these jet engines?' and turning his attention directly to Antony Kwong, 'because, Mr Kwong, I am inclined to think you know far more than you are letting on and—unless I am personally satisfied with your answers—I will get a warrant to search your offices whoever you think you know, be it someone from MI5 or the bloody Prime Minister himself! So please sit down until I have finished this interview, after which, I will tell you when you can go!'

If looks could kill, and by the way that Antony Kwong was glaring at Lambert, he should have been in his death throws and writhing in agony on the floor. Both he and McNeil sat down rather condescendingly while the Reading Policeman looked at his notebook. 'Twenty-eight engines sounds to me like a squadron of 14 fighter planes, Mr Kwong, and judging by the Cyrillic prefixes on each subdivision, I can only assume that they were of Russian or Ukraine manufacture. Would I be right in assuming that, Mr Kwong?'

Kwong was not a man to be easily intimidated, but he also knew that a search of his premises would reveal many other things which he would rather were kept secret. Finally Kwong quite clearly replied in English: 'Mr Side asked me to check out the authenticity of these engine passport numbers at the Russian Aircraft Corporation factory in Russia. I sell a lot of things to Russia and they are good trading partners with Taipei, but I refused to help him. That is why I withdrew my offer of finance to him, Mr Lambert, which is why you are here.'

Rising from his seat, Lambert announced that the interview was now at an end. Solicitor McNeil gave

Lambert his business card and confirmed his client's willingness to continue their discussion should it be necessary. The Chinaman glared once more at the two detectives and left the room shouting incomprehensively at McNeil, who trotted along behind him, more like an insignificant coolie than a London Solicitor. Lambert smiled at George Durant, put his effects back into his briefcase and invited his bemused assistant for a short walk to the Cavalry and Guards Club in Piccadilly, followed by a pint of beer.

They walked up to the end of Pall Mall, crossed the Piccadilly thoroughfare and then turned left towards the club. It was then that Lambert started to laugh out loud. George Durant hadn't really understood the reason behind his chief's line of questioning. 'What was all that about Boss, what the hell happened in there?' Sergeant Durant was way out of his league and utterly confused.

'Well George, I had no idea what those codes were when we went into that meeting this afternoon, and it would have taken some time for me to find out by going through the usual channels. That would probably have involved talking to the spooks at some stage, which I did not want if at all possible. What Kwong managed to do—by telling me what these numbers were for—was say that he was somehow personally involved in this case. You see, in Britain to act as an arms dealer without a licence, is a criminal offence. By his claiming that Side had *asked him* to check out these engine numbers at the MiG factory in Russia, I immediately realised that what he said was not precisely true and that he was lying, and it was Kwong who asked Side to check out the engine numbers, not the other way round. I suspect that Side got these numbers from the sellers, and then sent them to Kwong. That is why he knew what they were, because he himself had gone directly to the Russians to authenticate the engine numbers to see if the information was correct.'

Arriving in the reception area of the Cavalry and Guards club, Sergeant Noakes was pleased to see the Chief Inspector: 'Ah, Major Lambert, we haven't had the pleasure of your company at the club for some time. You are always most welcome here Sir.'

'Afternoon Sergeant Noakes, hope you don't mind but I have brought a colleague with me as a guest. We were on our way back to the sticks when we suddenly developed this dreadful thirst!'

'Well, you have come to the right place and if you don't mind signing in Major, I will arrange for two pints of our finest Young's best bitter to appear on the bar for you. Oh, by the way Sir, ten days ago—if you remember—you asked me if I had come across a member or guest called Mr Liam Side, and you spoke to me about him wearing one of our club ties and you showed me his photograph. Well since then, I have looked through our guest book and now I remember who he might be. It seems that in the past we have had the occasional visit from a man who answers to your description; he is one of our foreign reciprocal members. I remember him because he is—by our club standards—a rather scruffy individual who usually wears a rather tatty Irish tweed suit.' The three men walked into the bar, and the Chief Inspector and his assistant collected their two pint glasses and sat at an empty table.

The Club Sergeant went on: 'As you know from your own experience Sir, we have got some reasonably priced rooms at the club for visitors and so affiliated members from abroad very often come to stay for a day or two, instead of paying for an expensive local hotel. But this gentleman's name is not Liam Side, as you mentioned at the time, but is in fact a Major Leon Szeidovitz, who is a visiting member from the Harare Club in Zimbabwe. I am afraid that is all I can tell you Major.' Lambert was astounded by this information, and thanked Sergeant Noakes for his help.

As the two policemen sipped their Young's best bitter, Lambert told Durant about some of his more recent investigations in Sofia. He explained that although he had been successful at collecting information, until then the some parts of the puzzle he had unearthed in Sofia had not exactly fitted together. The reaction of the Chinese banker to his questions had been a massive bonus, and Noakes' most recent information about Leon Szeidovitz had now made the picture even clearer.

'You see George, if Liam Side was busy in Eastern Europe buying up plant and equipment for the South Africans, Kwong might have easily come to the conclusion that he could also help him out with his—what shall we call it—more unorthodox business interests? There is not such a big difference between a large excavator and a fighter jet. They are both made out of metal and are both covered in registration numbers.' The question remaining was where could he have possibly been? Lambert did not know any arms dealers as such and knowledge of the murky world of weapon sales was hardly the remit of a provincial policeman and so the next step would be hard for him to accomplish on his own.

Having wished the Club Sergeant goodbye, the two men strolled down Park Lane, back once more to the underground car park. 'Isn't there some sort of arms control institute in Stockholm, Boss?' George Durant often came up with little gems like that. 'I think it is called SIPRI or something like that? I was recently reading about it in the paper; something to do with increased Russian arms sales to Iraq and Syria. I believe they call themselves some sort of think tank.'

They left the hood up on the gleaming Alvis on their return journey to Reading, but only in comparative silence, because of a local Berkshire pop music channel. It was Lambert's way of rewarding Durant for coming up with a good idea and his Sergeant now sat happy and relaxed, listening to his favourite songs from the sixties. By now it was six o'clock and the afternoon was practically over.

He dropped Durant off at the office and then made for the Reading Reference Library. Parking the Alvis in the Forbury Gardens, he knew that the library was due to close at seven o'clock that evening and if he was to track down the information he needed, he would have to get a move on. The receptionist had a grey and slightly depressed face and sat under a notice saying *Silence*. Lambert looked around the old galleried library and immediately sought help from her. She looked up at him with her moist brown eyes and glared at him rather unenthusiastically through her rimless spectacles.

'My name is Detective Chief Inspector Lambert and I need your help.' Brightening up at once, she responded with a perfectly manicured grin and fluttered her watery eyes. 'Oh yes Chief Inspector, of course, what do you need to know?'

Things had moved on since he had been a student and there were now computer screens dotted around the room, as well as the ageing microfiche machines which contained past copies of the *Evening Post* and the *Reading Mercury*. 'I need to know the coordinates of an organisation which I believe is called SIPRI. I think it is an anagram for the *Stockholm International Peace Research Institute*, and I wonder if you can possibly help me to track them down?'

Looking at her computer screen, it only took a few moments. 'Here we are Chief Inspector, it's not apparently in Stockholm itself but in a place called Signalistgatan, which is in Solna.' Leaving her desk she crossed the room and returned with a paper-backed catalogue. 'It says here that if you require any information you will need to speak to the Communications Director, and so you will need their phone number in Sweden, Chief Inspector. They are one hour ahead of us in England and I think it would be better to phone them in the morning, if you don't mind my suggestion.' She walked over to a photocopying machine and came back with a sheet of A4 with all the required details, and drew a ring around the relevant section. Lambert thanked her for her help. 'That's all right Chief Inspector, that's what we are here for, anytime.'

Lambert drove over Reading Bridge, turned right along Gosbrook Road and then into Briant's Avenue. Finally, he turned right at the Travellers' Rest, onto the Henley Road and home to Sonning Village. Parking the Alvis in the driveway, he let himself into the house and made for the kitchen. Samanda was in the garden and so he opened the door and let her in. He gave her the rest of the food which was left over from the day before and made a note to phone the kennels for a new consignment of dog food the next day. Samanda must have been quite hungry, because she bolted her food down as quickly as she could.

What had pleased Lambert the most was his purchase of the two Bulgarian postage stamps. Having spent about 40 Pounds on them, when he telephoned his friend Garrick at his shop in Church Street Kensington, he was given some very good news. 'They are worth about three hundred apiece Mike, perhaps a little bit more if they are perfect and properly franked, so you did well there. And I don't suppose you noticed, but they are also very light to carry around and there are no demands for receipts or letters of authentication at airports. Lucky old you!'

That night he slept like a top, and waking the following morning at seven, he made for the swimming pool and swam a few lengths before breakfast. Opening the fridge door he realised that apart from dog food, he would need to stock up for himself, so after a strong mug of coffee, Lambert made for the police canteen and some proper rations.

He was in his office by nine that morning, which meant that it was ten a.m. in Sweden. Dialling the number for the Communications Director at SIPRI, he was surprised when the telephone was answered by an Englishwoman. Lambert explained what the problem was and how the British police were in need of their assistance.

'We can track down a lot of information from engine numbers and chassis numbers, just like you do with ordinary everyday vehicles.' Laura Haughton was not in the least bit reticent. 'What I can do for you Chief Inspector is to have a word with one of our experts here, and put you directly in touch. We have all sorts of computerised information which we get quite straightforwardly from most of the arms manufacturers who willingly cooperate with us here in Solna. They in turn like to be sure they know where their stuff is going to—as well as us—so we check all *End User Certificates* and make sure these goods arrive where they should!'

Lambert calculated that he had over 400 GBP left over from his trip to Sofia and a money clip full of Bulgarian Leva. This amounted to about 30 GBP which he decided to keep for his own use, should he return to Sofia at any time in the near future. All his receipts were in order, except for taxi fares and one or two cheap restaurants. O'Brian, the Reading Administration Officer, chuckled when Lambert handed back the cash. 'It's really cheap there isn't it, Sir!' He counted the cash and then put it away in a drawer. 'But then again, the locals have to get by on about three hundred Leva a month so it's not cheap for them.' He put Lambert's expenses form together with the receipts into his in-tray.

Handing back the Travel Guide written by Peter Carney, the Chief Inspector thanked O'Brian for the loan of the book and told him how he had been to the Rila Monastery one afternoon. 'Bloody brilliant there, isn't it Guv? There are lots of interesting things to see in Bulgaria if you want, although most blokes go there on the piss or for the totty, don't they?'

When he returned to his office George Durant was sitting there reading the *Sun*. 'There's a bloke called Lindquist just called you, Boss, it's about them engine numbers. He said he could help you if you fax them to him. Look, he left his number—where is it, ah yes that's right—he said he was phoning from somewhere called Solna.'

Lambert removed the photocopies of the engine numbers from his briefcase and sat at his desk. If what Kwong had said about these numbers was correct, it certainly didn't account for the date at the end of each Passport number. He wondered what the date actually represented. Was it when the engines were manufactured, commissioned or installed? From his personal knowledge of light tanks, a military vehicle normally had to be re-commissioned every seven years or even totally replaced. It rather depended on how many hours a vehicle had been in service and the life expectancy after refurbishment or even sometimes a total rebuild. Lambert made the call to Solna.

It turned out that Henry Lindquist was a retired university professor. He openly explained to Lambert that most of the consultants at SIPRI were seconded from either NGOs, government departments, industry, were ex-military personnel or came from a variety of universities worldwide. It sounded very ad hoc, but it was obviously not. Lindquist made it clear from the start that SIPRI's objective was to generate publicity about the international trafficking of arms, whether legitimate or not, and for open public discussion.

Although Lambert supposed that his engine numbers were only a minute part of the equation, Lindquist disagreed. 'Mr Lambert, a squadron of well-armed modern jet fighters can decide the whole fate of a country, or even a continent for that matter. They are able to affect the balance of power and send any hope of peace, for some countries at least, back decades. American or European fighter planes may be the best in the world, Chief Inspector, but that rather depends where you happen to be in the world!'

Lindquist told the Reading policeman that he was coming to London shortly to attend a seminar at the LSE on arms proliferation, and invited Lambert to come along out of interest, as an observer. Meanwhile he gave the Chief Inspector a secure fax number and suggested that he send his Russian engine numbers straightaway.

Lambert was self-effacing and even modest about his part of the ongoing enquiries. 'I know it might seem a little beyond my remit as a provincial police officer, Mr Lindquist, but a murder has taken place and I need to know why it has occurred.'

During the afternoon, Lindquist was able to confirm by phone, that the engine numbers related to an infamous squadron of MiG 29s which had been sold by the Byelorussians to the Peruvian Government in 1996. This had come about as a result of their war with Ecuador and their total lack of any suitable fighter planes able to intercede in cross-border skirmishes. To all accounts, at the time the 14 planes were no longer airworthy, had not been flown for some while and were in need of a complete refurbishment and modernisation. He said that this would account for the dates attached to the engines indicating that they were quite old and therefore quite useless. Lindquist seemed to be a mine of information.

'The amount paid for them at the time was estimated to be 350 Million USD including procurement commissions, Mr Lambert, although the true value according to the Russian manufacturer was no more than 100 Million USD. Practically dysfunctional and in no state to fly, the 14 fighters planes were then transported by merchant ship to Peru from the

Ukrainian port of Odessa, offloaded at Port El Callao which is west of Lima, and transported onwards by train.' The university lecturer continued.

'We believe that the Peruvians must have cannibalised some parts from the different aircraft and got a few aircraft flying somehow, but when two of them crashed—one earlier this year in front of an official Peruvian anti-corruption panel which was checking the airworthiness of the fighters—the squadron was finally fully grounded. To all accounts, Chief Inspector, when the Russians discovered this deal had occurred behind their back—and that the Peruvians had not purchased similar fighter planes directly from them—they refused to carry out any work on the aircraft, claiming that their service contract was with the Belarusians and not with Peru. Later the Russians recanted and completed their renovation and upgrades required for the remaining aircraft, which involved some 110 Million USD. Since this summer things have remained stable, but of course there has been a change of Government in Peru, and the ex-President Takahashi and his accomplice Vladimiro Pinero, have both gone on the run.'

Lambert thanked Henry Lindquist for his information, and said that he greatly looked forward to meeting him and receiving his invitation to the forthcoming seminar in London. Sitting quietly behind his desk he looked at George, his assistant. He was occupied by the previous day's cricket scores in the *Sun* newspaper. Oblivious to Lambert's world of international bribery and corruption, it seemed unkind for his Boss to interrupt his concentration, although Detective Chief

Inspector Lambert was pleasantly preoccupied with his day's fruitful results.

Finally he had discovered the long awaited motive for the Kennet and Avon Canal murder. Superintendent Burrows had been absolutely right, and the murder was unquestionably all about money. It was the amount of money which was the problem. Dwarfing the proceeds of some piffling bank heist—which might amount to a hundred or so thousand pounds—if Lambert was right, the profits from this lucrative international scam could amount to as much as 200 Million USD. If the difference between a purchase price of 350 Million USD and the value of 100 Million USD mooted by the Russians was realistic, then allowing for commissions and any necessary *back handers*—agent's fees, transport costs and CIF costs to El Callao—this estimated profit must have gone into some very sizable pockets.

Even split ten or more ways it would have been quite enough reason to kill any man, including a man like Liam Side. It was therefore time to discover if the Hammersmith solicitor Mr Clive Footman had anything to do with any crimes of murder or fraud. Lambert interrupted George Durant's cricket reveries, and told him to go and get his police wheels because, once more, they were off to London. Durant made an appointment to meet the Hammersmith solicitor at five o'clock that afternoon.

Retracing their steps from the previous day, they were in King Street Hammersmith by four thirty and having parked in a convenient side street off the Goldhawk Road, they slowly walked to the premises of

Footman & Co. Stopping by the entrance to the office they saw that it was a small shop and upper-part. The front window of the shop was made of opaque glass with the words *solicitors' office* heavily engraved into it. There was a polished brass plate in the doorway with the firm's name and telephone number and a glass door had been inserted into the doorframe, making the office look bright and welcoming. Entering the office, they were greeted by a friendly girl who informed them that Mr Footman would shortly be available, and would they like some tea of coffee? Both men opted for a strong cup of instant coffee.

It was hard to see such a traditional firm of lawyers being implicated in a major international fraud, and Footman's secretary Tracy disarmingly dispelled any notion of double dealing. 'Oh, they are both very nice men,' she announced when asked how many solicitors worked there, 'there's Mr Footman on the first floor, and Mr Ashby is in the back office. He's our Assistant Solicitor, and then of course there is old Mr Abercrombie. He was Mr Footman's original partner—he is now retired—who helps out occasionally, and that is about all. Except me, of course, and I do everything else,' she said with a smile whilst carrying two rattling cups and saucers. When asked how long she had been there, it seemed that she had worked there since she had left school.

Mr Footman appeared to be quite different from the way Krueger had described him to Sergeant Durant. Poking his head around the door, he smiled and simply said, 'This way chaps, if you don't mind the rickety stairs.'

Once they were sitting in his office it was clear that he was just a friendly everyday solicitor. In his shirtsleeves and wearing some rather colourful braces, Lambert could not help but notice his tie. 'Royal Scots cavalry isn't it, Mr Footman?'

'Well done, Chief Inspector, finally someone has recognized my tie! The old *Bird Catchers*; you are quite right—*Second to None* as they say—but alas no more since 1971. I was long gone by then though, only National Service I'm afraid, all mainly spent with our German friends.' He seemed amiable enough, hardly vying for a place in some rogues gallery. 'I know you have come a long way to see me, so tell me, how can I help you two blokes this afternoon?'

When Lambert had trotted out the usual preamble to the alleged murder of Liam Side, and that they had come to see him in order to discover more about Side's London activities, Footman suddenly looked rather shocked. 'Oh dear, I am so sorry to hear this, he was such a nice man. Oh dear, I am sorry.' The two policemen looked rather embarrassed by the solicitor's emotional response. 'I'm afraid you didn't tell me over the phone that he was dead, Mr Lambert, how terribly sad,' he said staring into the distance and wrinkling his brow.

'I'm awfully sorry Sir, but we thought you already knew about it. We came here to try to get some background information from you since it seems you were his London lawyer.

'Yes well, the word *were* does seem to be the right one, doesn't it? We did all his Conveyancing here; you probably know he was fairly active in the world of property at one time. In fact he actually found me this office a few years ago. Although, he worked offshore most of the time—a South African you know—he did his darnedest to make it work here in the UK. Very lonely fellow it seemed to me. Never met his live-in girlfriend—Pansy, was it? Had rather a disrupted life—what with the murder of his parents, and with all that stuff in South Africa, he couldn't wait to get out—and now this! Poor sod.'

'I was in Sofia recently, and amongst his belongings I found some letters addressed to him from your firm, it was about his daughter Patricia. Can you tell me more about this, Mr Footman?' Clive Footman sat forward in his chair and looked despairingly from right to left, and then leaned back into his chair and for a moment he simply stared at the Reading Policeman without speaking.

'Well, the poor man was being buggered around in Bulgaria—sounds par for the course doesn't it—and simply couldn't get a straight answer from anyone. Didn't know what to do, and asked me if I could help. Don't do that stuff really—mainly Conveyancing here you see—and I said I would ask around. Even asked that sneering little reptile Krueger, but he was no help at all. Didn't charge Liam a bean—he was sort of a friend really—then he suddenly went quiet. So, I quite wrongly thought he had done a runner—back to South Africa perhaps—but it appears now that I was very wrong, wasn't I, Mr Lambert?'

'Do you have any idea why he originally went to Bulgaria, Mr Footman? There has never been any satisfactory explanation so far why he went there in the first place.'

'It was that man Panov if I remember. I met him

once—big tall chap with a deep voice and a large black moustache. Told me he was standing for office in Bulgaria or some nonsense. I wouldn't vote for him—bit of clown really—waved his arms about a lot and talked about Hollywood. You met him, Chief Inspector? He seemed to have some sort of hold over Liam Side—don't know why. When all hell let loose in the property market, Liam simply pushed off to Sofia. Keeping his head down perhaps I thought, but who knows? He might have owed some money or it might have been that bloody Russian woman—we'll never know now—sorry I can't be more help to you.'

George Durant drove the police Ford Escort 2000 back to Reading in no time at all. He was a very accomplished driver and drove aggressively touching all the margins and all the limits. By the time they got back it was well past seven and the police canteen was beckoning to Lambert. It was time for an unhealthy and stodgy blowout before returning to his colourless home in Sonning. On his way home, he would nip into the kennels and buy some dog food.

Aida the canteen cook was offering *Sloppy Joe and Chips* as that evening's special. Lambert was tucking into her canteen food with some relish, when his mobile phone buzzed. It was a text message from Yuri Vassilev. A very short message, it simply said—*Michael, I have found our man!*

CHAPTER NINE

THURSDAY MORNING was peaceful. Lambert drew the curtains in his bedroom and then opened the window. The smell and sound of an English summer invaded his very being and the sight of his neat and tidy garden filled him with pride.

As he went down the stairs, Mike Lambert could hear a slight scratching noise coming from the kitchen door. He opened the door and let Samanda in. She was unquestionably his dog and the thought of leaving her at some point was quite appalling, if not impossible to contemplate. He would get her chipped by the local vet, so he could take her with him when he took his solo holiday in France later that summer. It was when he planned to abandon Arabella and their ghastly marriage.

Meanwhile, he gave Samanda some of the bone-shaped biscuits that he had bought the night before from the kennels, which she then crunched up on the kitchen doormat. Once more the Braun coffee machine helped to wake up the drowsy police officer, readying him for his surreptitious morning's work.

But first of all he needed to open a new email account with an obscure and unrecognisable prefix.

Whilst he thought of a suitably confusing email address, he watched Samanda chewing up her biscuits. Sipping his strong Arabica coffee he lit up one of his few remaining Victory cigarettes. This morning he would forgo his police canteen breakfast and instead of going to his office in Reading, he would drive to Wokingham where he had noticed a recently opened internet café. It was eight o'clock by the time he was ready to go, so he phoned George his assistant and told him he would be in later.

With the hood down and wearing Kate's Gucci sunglasses, Lambert drove his gleaming Alvis 21 through the morning sun. Travelling along the old London Road towards Reading, he turned left down Butts Hill Road and then into the Wokingham Road, driving on towards the old town itself. When he got there he parked his car in a side road, and then walked back to Denmark Street, where entering a little cul-de-sac he discovered the Rose Internet Café. Choosing a screen at the rear of the café, he went on line and swiftly operating the browser, he entered the Yahoo website.

After various false starts, his new email address was almost but not quite as he had planned. It was *samander2001@yahoo.com* and he immediately sent this address to Yuri Vassilev by *text message* via his mobile phone, and awaited his acknowledgment. After only ten minutes, the Pristina Police Colonel replied—*okay Mike I am ready*—and once again they were in touch.

Lambert then sent a completely meaningless message to Yuri Vassilev's private email address, which he had given to Lambert at their last meeting in Sofia. In it, the Reading policeman thanked the firm of *Icon Printers,* for their quotation to print 10,000 assorted seed catalogues in English and that he would be in touch with them in due course. He signed the email— Richard Hampton, c/o Flanagan's Irish Bar. While he waited for Vassilev's reply, he bought an indifferent cup of cappuccino coffee from the bar and smoked a cigarette. When he left the Rose Internet Café his head was spinning, and his mind was temporarily calcified.

The email he received in reply from Yuri Vassilev propelled the Reading policeman into a world he would hardly have believed existed two weeks before. Not only did it confirm the true identity of the dead man but in it he also informed the Chief Inspector that the Russian woman had recently left Sofia and had flown with her daughter Patricia to Belgium.

A first for the Reading policeman, it now appeared that Liam Side—the alleged murder victim of the Kennet Narrow Boat Mystery—might in fact himself be the murderer. Colonel Vassilev was perfectly clear in his email. The fingerprints belonged to one Vladimiro Ilich Rizotis Pinero and Lambert did not need to be told who this man was, because he already knew. While he was in Sofia Lambert had read all about Vladimiro Pinero in *Newsweek Magazine*. The ex-Interior Minister of Peru had fled his country together with ex-President Takahashi, leaving millions of USD unaccounted for. This was old news.

Lambert also knew that the cat had been let out of

the bag, because at some point the Americans would want to know where the fingerprint enquiry had come from and as a result, ask why they had not been informed about it through the usual channels by the British police authorities. Then again, perhaps they did know. There was no guarantee that his recently found friend Colonel Vassilev was not working for the Americans all along. In fact, that would answer many of the questions the Reading policeman had been asking himself, especially why or how Vassilev was working for KFOR in the first place? Perhaps the Bulgarian had been their man all along.

Lambert decided to create a smokescreen and to buy himself a few extra days, so when he returned to his office he made no mention of his recent revelations and simply told Durant and the rest of his team, that he had gone to Wokingham to track down a spare part for his Alvis. Once more he visited the dyspeptic Superintendent Burrows in his office.

This time he found him contentedly sitting at his desk, reading the *Express* newspaper and smoking his pipe. 'Lovely morning Lambert, and perfect for a nice round of golf. I think I will go to Calcot for lunch today, and see if I can make up a foursome.' His sunny disposition was in total contrast to the previous occasion they had met. 'I took you up on your suggestion by the way Lambert, and gave all that bloody paperwork to Sergeant Burkett; he's only got a year to go before retirement and he said that he would be delighted—so, problem solved! Now how can I help you, Chief Inspector?'

He explained to Burrows that there were problems in finalising the identity of the murder victim, in order for the body to be released by the police to the Coroner's Office, but that it was important to get all the police *ducks in a row* before a proper inquest could be held. He further explained that in the event of a foreigner's death, it was customary to check certain details prior to any inquest. He told Burrows that he would like to double check the man's fingerprints through Interpol, which might take a few more days. They both agreed that by going through the usual channels it would help the Berkshire Coroner to finally draw the whole matter of the cause of death to a close.

Burrows cheerily gave Lambert permission to sign all the necessary documents and blithely left the room whistling. Before he left, Lambert noticed a new addition to the items on display in the Superintendent's glass-fronted office cabinet. Lurking amongst twenty-five years of photographs and awards, he saw that a pink bottle had suddenly appeared in a new place. It was standing next to a sepia photograph of a very young Constable Burrows, who was propping up a large black bicycle and wearing white cycle clips.

After he had attended to Interpol, the Chief Inspector took himself off to a quiet corner of his office to have a concerted think. Having told his crew that he wanted absolutely no interruptions from anybody, he sat in his comfortable club chair and gazed through the office window, absent-mindedly inspecting the car park, his shining Alvis 21 and smoking his very last Victory cigarette. It had been almost three weeks since the discovery of the dead man on the narrow boat, and now it was time to track down the true killer. It was also time to go over his trip to Sofia in minute detail and to consider the sequence of events as they occurred. He was still not sure if he had been deliberately misled at some point and he needed to keep an open mind on events.

The murder was clearly about money and had been very carefully planned. It involved three main players that he knew of, plus the two individuals who for the time being he categorised as Balkan henchmen. Together with Liam Side himself, these men were also the possible killers. Then there was Kwong.

What was Kwong? It seems he was the facilitator and probably the banker who arranged the arms deal. Together with Vladamiro Pinero he must have purchased the MiG 29s on behalf of the Peruvian State with the blessing of President Takahashi, because this would have taken care of the end user's certificate.

Then, what was Side? He was the go-between, who helped to authenticate the deal and who negotiated the actual terms of the purchase. He would have also been their man on the ground in Eastern Europe. If, as the Cavalry and Guards Club Sergeant believed, the South African Liam Side could also be a white Zimbabwean called Leon Szeidovitz, this would go a long way to explain how he was able to travel unchallenged through Serbia—and in and out of Belorussia—without the inconvenience of getting a visa; except for exit visas from Bulgaria which were clearly present in his South African passport.

All three countries had maintained friendly ties with

one another for many years, due to their perceived communist affiliations and the ongoing friendship of Mugabe, Milosevic and Lukashenko who were all in power during this time. The fact that Side was a cultured white man would have made little difference to the programmed minds of various government officials, so he could more or less come and go as he pleased; especially if he had two passports, which he would certainly have had at the very beginning.

What assumptions could Lambert make about the money? Except for the fact that it was a very great amount, the 200 Million USD had to go somewhere secure. And so as not to be noticed, it also had to go into a very deep pocket, and that meant Kwong. As a world trader, he was able to pay for the aircraft with barter goods. With his status as a Confirming House and a Trade Financier, he would only have required a solid Swiss insurance policy to cover the risk of the transaction. As to the barter goods themselves, the post-Soviet era and Gorbachev had virtually closed all the doors to client states in need of Communist largess, which meant that these barter goods could have consisted literally of anything.

The only two motives for murder that the Reading policeman could summon up were firstly, that one of the three main movers wanted more money and was getting rid of an unwanted business partner, or secondly, that the Peruvian had been bumped off because—for some reason or other—he or a colleague had refused to pay someone. So where was the money and who was controlling it? It was now back to Kwong.

To Lambert it was also a practical matter of evidence. He could speculate from now until doomsday on the various combinations of opportunity or even suspicion, but in the end, what stuck in his mind was the mobile phone found on the boat. Why was it so important?

A simple answer would be that it connected the murder directly to Liam Side. Without Constable Adams' find, by now they would have given up the chase or would have been floundering around in the dark, chatting to the corrupt Sofia police force and wasting British police time and money. Therefore, the mobile find was his good luck, which was obviously why so much effort had been put into getting it back. But then again, it might also have been left there by someone on purpose for them to find!

And the two henchmen? He either put them down to a leftover from the Zhivkov Communist era in Bulgaria, or to the even more troublesome remains of President Milosevic's Serbia. There were plenty of hard cases in both these countries who had access to the West and who came equipped with an arsenal of well-established resources and weapons. Hit men were now becoming two a penny in Eastern Europe—since the end of Communism—and thugs had to be paid like everyone else. The only question remaining in Lambert's mind was whether the hit men had been hired as assassins, or whether they were actually a part of the deal? If it was the latter, then there could well be more murders to look forward to in the near future.

Finally, where was Liam Side? The answer to that—according to Mike Lambert at least—was in Belgium. Since Side's passport had been used in the transport of Vladimiro Pinero through Blackbushe Airport from Grimbergen, by now it would have probably been dumped somewhere. He in turn would either have had to use a duplicate passport—if indeed he had one—or, he was openly residing in Belgium somewhere as a white Zimbabwean called Leon Szeidovitz. The latter was Lambert's most likely scenario.

The suspect would also be inclined to remain close to his daughter Patricia, a matter which the Russian woman would surely know absolutely nothing about. She would have been lured to Belgium by a third party with some sort of promise attached. This would probably have involved money or even a job; but it was also far too broad a question to speculate on for the time being.

Perhaps Vera Kolova was involved in some way, because she and Liam Side had known one another in the past and she had openly stated to Lambert that she had once loved him? That part of the puzzle would become clearer, if and when he could track down the Russian woman, which was why the Chief Inspector decided to travel to Brussels by Eurostar the following day. Now that he had her name and National Passport number and possible dates of arrival, the Reading policeman believed that there might be a good chance for additional information to be discovered, regarding this woman's whereabouts, by going to Belgium himself.

It would also be a good opportunity to test the

efficiency of the Belgian police and their immigration authorities. 'I know that my decision to go to Brussels is a bit on the spur of the moment, George,' he said to his bemused assistant, 'but I have a hunch that this is where I will find that Russian woman.' Sergeant Durant no longer believed that he was a part of the case and found it quite difficult to follow his boss's train of thought. 'A little bird told me this morning that she left Sofia last week sometime and had flown to the Belgian capital. So, I thought I would start from there, George. She might be able to tell us something we don't already know about Liam Side, because we still don't have the full picture of his most recent activities and it might be able to help us with our enquiries.' Durant noticed that his boss's ashtray was now full of Marlboro dog ends, meaning his cheap Bulgarian cigarettes had finally run out.

Lambert smiled at his muddled Sergeant. 'By the way, how is your Russian railway watch, George, is it keeping good time?'

Durant loved it and kept it in his jacket key pocket. He liked to listen to the clockwork ticking. 'It's great thanks, Boss. I had to open it up and adjust it a little bit, but apart from that it's absolutely fine!' He didn't tell his Boss about the sepia photograph of a pretty young woman that he discovered inside the case, because that was his secret.

'Can you book me on tomorrow's 8.58 Eurostar from St Pancras please, George? Oh, and if I give you my front door key, would you also pop round home for me and feed Samanda? Arabella is away for the week and that Prothero woman next door won't speak to me!' George Durant was a helpful man and Lambert was a good boss. 'I will also need to be back in the UK by Sunday evening, so if it's possible you had better book me onto the 17.56 from Brussels for the return journey? Being Sunday, I should imagine that all the British MEPs will be going the other way.'

That evening Mike Lambert decided to have an early night because he needed to be up by six the next morning, and on the road by six-thirty. He went to the little Davenport writing desk and wrote a note to Arabella:

Dear Arabella,

I shall be away for three more days on police business and will return on Sunday evening. You probably won't be back by then, but in case you are, I have bought some more dog food for Samanda. But I am afraid that there is little else in the house, so you might need to go shopping.

Mike.

Carefully folding up his note, he inserted it into an envelope, then after writing her name on the front, he left it on the hall table for her to discover on her return. Having fed Samanda he put her into the garden, made himself some buttered toast with Marmite and headed for the shower room. Afterwards he packed his small Samsonite overnight bag, climbed into bed and switched off the light.

His alarm clock went off at six the next morning, and after an electric shave and some strong filter coffee, he was fully dressed by six-thirty and on the road. It was another beautiful day although a little windy. When he opened the front door, his note to Arabella was swept off the table and landed on the floor just behind the umbrella stand.

Although it was fairly early, the London-bound traffic was still quite thick and although moving along steadily, it began to slow down at the Heston Service Area. From there on, the traffic was a little erratic until he got to the Chiswick flyover.

Lambert was feeling relaxed and almost light-hearted as he listened to *McCoy Tyner and Stephan Grappelli*. They were performing at their classic concert in Warsaw. Playing amongst others numbers—*I Didn't Know what Time it Was,* and *How High's the Moon*—it was the first and the last time these two great musicians would play together before Grappelli's death.

When he got to Hammersmith, he found a space in the multi-storey car park just off Glenthorne Road, walked down to the bottom of King Street, jumped on the Piccadilly Metro and made his way to St Pancras. On arrival he went straight to the Eurostar Ticket Office and Travel Centre. Two Standard Class train tickets were waiting for him to collect, which meant that he would not have to hang around in Brussels Midi on the return leg of his journey. With no luggage to speak of except his Samsonite overnight bag, there were no boarding delays.

The train was on time and waiting on the St Pancras platform. After going through Passport Control, Lambert boarded the train, carefully installing his bag in the locker above his seat. Asking his neighbour to keep an eye on his bag, he made for the buffet car in order to supplement his meagre breakfast coffee. Two fresh croissants with a large cappuccino coffee, and the Reading policeman was ready to face the two-hour journey to the Belgian capital. Remembering that he still had last week's copy of *Newsweek* in his bag, he removed it, sat in his allotted seat and relaxed. This time he re-read the article about the missing Peruvians with concentrated interest. Realising that serendipity might well have changed his life forever, it had by chance also landed him in the biggest murder case of his career.

The Eurostar arrived at Brussels Midi at just after 10 o'clock that morning and Lambert walked out of the station into the Rue d'Angleterre and made for the taxi rank. On his way he inserted his bankcard into a nearby ATM machine and got some Belgian Francs in return. Ten minutes later he arrived at the Welcome Hotel in Quai au Bois à Brûler, registered at the reception and then went up to his African themed room. Surrounded by tribal wall masks and with a faux Leopard skin bed cover and carpet, it gave him the impression of living in a large canvas tent nestling somewhere on the African veldt. The only thing missing was the sound of wild animals in the distance.

Jumping into the shower, the piping hot water washed away his tiredness and brought him back to life. By eleven-thirty that morning, he was at the nearby taxi rank and on his way to the World Trade Centre in Boulevard du Roi Albert II. Practically a straight road, he arrived within twenty minutes and walking through the Chaussee d'Avers entrance, he entered the offices of the Belgian Federal Immigration Police.

The receptionist was an attractive Police Sergeant who listened intently to Lambert's story and carefully inspected his Police Warrant Card. 'Why don't you go to Interpol, Chief Inspector?' She gave him a quizzical look. 'This surely is the normal procedure.' Lambert explained to her that it was a matter of time, and that he was in a hurry to track down a particularly callous murderer. He told her that he needed to do this so he could issue a European Arrest Warrant for the Belgian authorities to carry out a proper legal apprehension. He did not mention anything about his views on Interpol or anything about *chocolate teapots*, because he was in Belgium after all, and his observations might easily be misunderstood.

'I will have to discuss this briefly with my Boss, Chief Inspector, so if you don't mind waiting for a moment?' The Sergeant waved Lambert in the direction of some plastic seating and disappeared into a nearby office with a glass partition. He could see from where he was sitting that his request was being taken seriously, by the way in which the Sergeant and her female senior officer were looking at him and pointing. Finally the Sergeant returned and handing back his Warrant Card, she asked the Reading policeman to wait for a few more moments. He could see that her senior officer was on the phone and nodding to somebody on the other end; no doubt an even more senior officer. She put down the receiver and walked through into the reception.

'Good morning Chief Inspector Lambert, my name is Major Hendrickx.' They shook hands, and with a friendly smile she invited him into her office. 'It is not very often we get to meet an English police officer here at our headquarters in Brussels. I'm afraid our work here is normally very dull and repetitive.' She was an attractive woman in her mid-forties; her blonde hair swept back over her head and held by a clasp. Her uniform was immaculate and her beautifully manicured nails hardly seemed to fit into any prescribed view of police work.

'Thank you for meeting me, Major Hendrickx.' Lambert wished that English women police constables might look as pleasing as this Belgian officer. 'I am aware of course, that my coming here in this way is a little unorthodox, but I am investigating a serious murder and time is running out.'

He went on to explain that he was tracking a suspect who he believed was presently living under an assumed name somewhere in Belgium. He told the Major that this man's daughter Patricia had recently flown to Brussels from Sofia, together with her Russian-born mother, which was cause for him to believe that there was some sort of connection. He said that if he could track down the mother, he might be able to pinpoint the father who he believed to be a dangerous killer of South African origin. He also pointed out that his suspect was known to maintain various identities and so by pursuing him directly, it would simply waste police time and money. 'It turns out that he is a very slippery customer Major, and nobody's fool. He would notice any concerted police activity if we were lucky enough to get close to him.'

Lotte Hendrickx complimented the Englishman on his dedication to duty and told him that IBZ would help him to track down the Russian woman and her daughter. She explained that it would take about two hours to attain the information required, and that it would cost him a good lunch at a nearby restaurant, which Lambert agreed to with an enormous grin on his face. But before leaving he gave the Russian woman's Passport coordinates and her approximate time of arrival at Zaventem International Airport, Brussels.

As far as Vassilev was able to find out from his friends on the Bulgarian side, Patricia and her mother had left Sofia airport the previous Wednesday or Thursday, and were both registered in one Russian passport. The arrival time at Brussels International would have been sometime between seven-thirty and eight o'clock in the evening, and travelling under the names of Patricia Side and Natalia Orlova.

There would have to have been an official Bulgarian exit stamp on the passport. But, there should also have been written notarised permission for Patricia to travel abroad, signed by both her parents. Were this not the case, this oversight could be explained in Sofia—due either to a bribe or simply because of total incompetence—but the fact that they were allowed through Belgian Immigration would remain for the present at least, an open question.

It was just a short trip by taxi to Aux Armes de Bruxelles in Rue des Bouchers. A beautiful old Brussels brassiere, it had been owned and run by the same family since 1921. The Brussels police chief and Mike Lambert were made very welcome by the present owners and given a window seat overlooking the crowded street.

'What is it like working in England Mike? Everything is so formal and regimented here in Belgium.' Lotte Hendrickx was on a goodwill mission too, as well as looking forward to some good food. Lambert noticed that she was wearing a ring on the wedding finger of her right hand and an expensive looking gold watch.

'I'm a detective, Lotte, so I am freer than the uniformed police. I also run my own team at the Thames Valley Police Authority, so to some extent I am also my own boss. Next year I expect to be offered the job of Superintendent, which by your present Belgian ranking system would mean promotion to the rank of Lieutenant Colonel.'

It was clear that to Major Hendrickx, all these military rankings were of little interest. 'Next year we are going to change our whole police ranking system in Belgium, Mike. As from next year I will be called an Under Commissioner instead. Rather like the British police, we no longer feel the need to display our authority but to police the country by consent—now that we are all part of this wonderful new Europe!' She laughed at her exaggerated explanation and the simple irony of change.

Lambert approved of her modesty. 'I was a full Major in the British Army before I joined the Police force, Lotte, so all these ranks don't mean much to me either, I'm afraid. I just like my job and the guys I work with, and that's all that really matters to me right now.'

Lotte Hendrickx found the Englishman easy to talk to. 'My husband John is an MEP for the European Ecolo Party. He is also spokesman for the Green Party here in Brussels, Mike, so my job fits in very conveniently with his politics.' The Belgian policewoman seemed very middle class and confident. 'And we have a young son Martin who is presently taking his Baccalaureate at the Sorbonne in Paris who also wants to join the police.'

As she went on, it began to sound more like a family business than a vocation. 'As a politician my husband John can confirm to you the benefit of having a steady job in the family, especially with his unpopular views on saving the planet! And so being in the police service has its financial benefits as well.'

Lotte recommended the lunchtime menu and they both started with a delicious cream fish soup with tiny fried croutons, and Lambert ordered a very dry white wine to go with it. For their main course Lotte ordered a mixed Fish Waterzooi and Lambert went for his favourite Moules Frites. They finished off with Brussels Waffles with Callabout chocolate sauce. With an espresso coffee and a cigarette to follow, the afternoon had finally arrived and it was time to return to the World Trade Centre.

It turned out that Natalia Orlova and Patricia Side had arrived the previous week, on the Thursday evening flight from Sofia. When it came to the point where she handed over her passport, the immigration officer had quite rightly asked for proof that her daughter came with the father's consent. She was unable to comply with that condition, but at her formal interview she explained that she had received an invitation for work in Belgium, that the child's father was waiting for them at the airport lounge and that by now he would be getting worried about them.

Her passport was checked and rechecked, and finally she started to become hysterical and abusive. Shouting at everyone, accusing them of persecution and intimidation, she even threw a chair at one of the officers and had to be restrained. When Patricia started shouting and screaming too, the immigration officers finally gave up and they let them both through into the main airport. As a simple precaution they photocopied the letter she had received offering her a job and included it in their report to IBZ the following day.

Although the Immigration Officers concerned were reprimanded and cautioned, as one of many such incidents at the time, the fault was laid fairly and squarely at the door of senior management and to a poor training programme. A week later the whole matter had been practically forgotten, and hidden amongst the bureaucratic muddle of a modern airport. It was only noticed when Lambert came along.

The address on the official letter offering employment was The Delmar Hotel, Schpuwvegers Straat, Bruges, and the document was duly signed and stamped by the owner, a Mrs Vera K. Vanhecke. From an office map of Bruges he could see that the hotel was situated in the tourist area, was close to the canal and within walking distance of the town centre. It was clearly time for the Reading policeman to move to a new location. Thanking Lotte Hendrickx for her company at lunch and her help in tracking down Side's daughter, he took his leave.

Back once more at the Welcome Hotel, Lambert sat outside in the late afternoon sunshine and smoked a duty free Marlboro cigarette. He felt good about himself for a change, because for once he was not carrying round Arabella's rebukes and unflattering remarks which he habitually did in England. She seemed hell-bent on reducing him to the level of a philistine, whilst elevating herself and her pretentious friends far beyond their true realistic pecking order. As far as he was concerned, most of them were a bunch of thick provincial pseudo intellectuals all trying to be something they were not.

He also felt much freer in Europe, away from the constant UK cult of personality and the twitty TV interviewers and presenters, who talked so much crap on their daytime programmes. Somehow they had contrived to turn the inhabitants of *Middle England* into a tribe of babbling halfwits. Why did people believe that it was how they should actually behave?

Prior to his trip to Bruges, Lambert decided that he would treat himself to a solo gourmet dinner that evening. This would not be too difficult because, from what he could see, Quai au Bois à Brûler was awash with classy restaurants of every description. Close to the European Parliament it was clear from the sea of suits that it was a place for political assignation and discussion. But there were also some pretty girls to be seen, so it could not exclusively be about business.

But first he had to carefully plan the next two remaining days. Now he knew that Vera Kolova was also called Mrs Vanhecke, he decided to go to Bruges the following day to look for his quarry there. Taking Vera Kolova's card from his wallet, he phoned the Delmar Hotel and asked the receptionist if he could talk to her.

'Sir, you want a room, yes? We have only one available tonight.' Lambert explained that he was a friend of Vera Kolova from Sofia, and wondered if she was there in Bruges. 'Oh no Sir, she is in Paris with her husband, it is their wedding anniversary this weekend.'

At first his heart dropped but then his innate English common sense began to take over. He realised at once how little he really knew of Vera Kolova or even if she had told him the truth about anything at all. He reluctantly conceded that this was now probably unlikely and that during his stay in Sofia, he had probably been fed a series of lies and half-truths.

Lambert's problem was that he had found Vera Kolova a very attractive woman. Once again he perfectly understood why he should never become emotionally involved with anyone during the course of an investigation. Turning back once more to basics, it made him even more suspicious about the modus operandi of Yuri Vassilev and his openly friendly assistance. It was clear to the Reading copper, that throughout, he may only have known what *they* wanted him to know and no more. That evening Mike Lambert booked a table for one at La Dolce Vita Restaurant.

The restaurant was situated next door to the Welcome Hotel, and full of wonderful kitchen aromas, it had been difficult to ignore when he had walked past the building earlier. Grilled Moules St Jacques with mushrooms, followed by Escalope of veal flambé in Marcella wine and finally, a thick slice of chocolate Tiramisu—together with half a bottle of French Merlot—Lambert finished his meal with a good sized cup of strong Belgian coffee. Sitting at a pavement table he watched the passing crowds and taking his time, he quietly puffed on a small Cohiba cigar. By eleven o'clock that evening Lambert was ready for bed, having experienced the most delightful and self-indulgent day of his career as an English policeman. He also believed that he was reaching the end of the *Kennet Narrow Boat Mystery*, but that would have to wait until the following day.

The next morning he rose at eight o'clock and wallowed in a hot tub. By nine he was in the breakfast room filling up his plate with a huge assortment of ham and cheese together with some healthy grainy bread. With an unending supply of strong coffee, by ten o'clock Lambert was ready for the road. The jolly lady hotel receptionist was pleased to arrange for a hire car, which as she explained he could drop off at Brussels Midi train station on Sunday afternoon when he was due to return home. Very soon a red Peugeot 206 arrived at the entrance door from Avis Rentals and before he knew it, he was on the road and motoring out of the capital into the Belgian countryside. Practically a straight road, he drove past Ghent through Aalter, arriving in Bruges by eleven thirty and his final destination at the Hotel Montovani.

The hotel was situated a few doors away from the Delmar Hotel which was on the opposite side of the road. The receptionist at the Welcome Hotel had kindly made his reservation for him, insisting on having a room overlooking the street at the front of the hotel. When he arrived, he parked his rental car in the adjoining street, entered the hotel and registered. When he got to his hotel room, although it was not in a perfect position, he could just see the entrance to the Delmar Hotel from his window. This was all he needed to do, and after having informed the hotel receptionist that he was suffering from a bout of flu and therefore staying in his room, he prepared himself—if necessary—for a 24 hour vigil.

It was a quiet street with many small terraced houses as well as the two mid-sized hotels. Parking spaces were at a premium and so cars stayed in their allocated spaces, the inhabitants of the neighbourhood preferring to walk or cycle everywhere. Older people could be seen struggling with heavy shopping bags, but there was very little street corner gossiping, as one might expect in a similar urban British setting.

Perhaps they were far too petty bourgeois to indulge is such friendly banter and were purely preoccupied with maintaining their aplomb in this introspective Belgian society. Lambert also noticed that the lace curtains opposite very often moved, as an inquisitive viewer watched the goings on in the street. This pleased Lambert greatly, because that was exactly what he was intending to do and would therefore probably be ignored.

Ordering a pot of coffee, some water and a sandwich to be brought to his room, the Reading policeman settled himself in the window seat and began to watch the street for signs of Natalia Orlova and her daughter Patricia. Since the hotel maintained a non-smoking policy, the Reading policeman had to ignore his natural inclination to chain smoke when on a stake out.

But the comfort of his room compensated for his isolation, and the presence of BBC Prime on the cable TV service, helped to keep him entertained with old editions of *Dad's Army* and *The Last of the Summer Wine*. By mid-afternoon his patience was rewarded, by the sudden appearance of a blonde woman of some thirty years of age and a little girl of about five or six.

With his window open he could hear the woman loudly telling off the child in Russian. The street had very little traffic and so her voice carried and he was able to hear her constant admonishments with clarity. Suddenly she changed her language, and started her tirade again, but this time in English.

'Stop grizzling Patricia, we have a nice place to live and finally I have a job. You will meet some other children soon, then you can play with them in the park or down by the canal. There are nice long walks by the canal and the trees are very beautiful at this time of the year.' Then back into the Russian language and around the street corner where they disappeared from view.

So he had been right about Vera Kolova and had also been right about following his hunch. Now, all he had to look for were signs of Liam Side and then the story would be complete. But, of course he didn't appear. Later that evening there was another sighting of Natalia Orlova and her daughter and a further one at eleven thirty the following morning, just as Lambert was leaving the hotel and making for his hire car in the adjacent road.

But that evening, Lambert needed a break from his eight-hour vigil and having established that the Orlova woman was in Bruges with her daughter, he conceded that his mission was virtually complete. He would notify Lotte Hendrickx of his findings on his return to Reading, send her a description of the wanted man and a copy of his photograph from his edition of *The Balkan Western News*.

At this point he would not issue a European Arrest Warrant for Liam Side and would keep matters as they were for the time being, at a very low key. If the local police could be inveigled into keeping an eye on the Delmar Hotel and certain of its occupants for a few days—and if Liam Side aka Leon Szeidovitz were to appear on the scene—with the help of Lotte Hendrickx his arrest could be easily achieved in due course. Lighting up the first cigarette of the day, Lambert was pleased to leave the confines of his Bruges hotel.

Walking into the nearby City centre, Lambert could sense the history of this beautiful 16th century provincial capital, enjoying the mild evening, the canals and architecture which had remained virtually unsullied by modern times. He found a pretty street café, ordered some coffee and sat there smoking. With the appearance of a huge chunk of chocolate cream cake, he began to relax, casually looking at the passers-by and what was left of a summer's day.

It was dark when he returned to his hotel and the receptionist asked if he was feeling better from that morning's Flu. 'Yes, thanks for asking, but still I think I will have an early night.' She smiled and wished him goodnight and he made for his room and a long hot shower.

The following day he was back in Brussels by two o'clock and drove directly for the train station. Leaving his car keys at the Avis desk, he was then free to roam the station at his leisure. There were two hours or so before his Eurostar express left for London at 5.56 p.m. that afternoon. In the departure lounge he made for the café, bought himself a sandwich and a beer, and found himself a comfortable seat at a corner table. It had been a busy trip but now it was time to return home to Sonning and his wife's ongoing rant about his apparent shortcomings.

Returning to Hammersmith that evening on the Piccadilly line, it was humid and uncomfortable. Spewed out of the train at Hammersmith Station, he was then caught up in the usual pushing and shoving crowd, finally to be relieved, when he was sprung through the turnstile at journey's end. Walking into the multi-storey car park in Glenthorne Road, he was overjoyed to see the reassuring sight of a gleaming Alvis 21. Climbing behind the steering wheel Lambert inserted his ignition key, pressed the starter button and with the purr of the six cylinder engine, he made his way back to the sticks and his house in Sonning.

The motorway out of London was slow and apart from a few boy racers Mike Lambert thought it best to go with the flow. He relaxed behind the wheel and went over his most recent achievements. If he was right, the whereabouts of Liam Side aka Szeidovitz would be somewhere in Bruges. But Bruges was a very big area— not just a city—because it included the port of Zeebrugge and the urban and provincial areas surrounding the old City.

It was clear that Mrs Vera Kolova Vanhecke had managed to get Natalia Orlova and Side's daughter Patricia to Bruges, by some as yet unexplained ruse and that the Russian woman was probably unaware of any previous relationship between her host and Side.

Typically, she probably believed that she and her daughter were in Belgium due to a stroke of good fortune giving them an opportunity to escape to the West from Sofia. If Yuri Vassilev was to be believed— that Liam Side's only remaining Bulgarian passion was his little daughter Patricia—then he would be holed up somewhere in the vicinity of the Delmar Hotel and would appear at some point. Now, the only logical thing for the Reading policeman to do was to wait.

It seemed that Arabella had also been waiting. She had something to tell him. 'I've decided to leave you, Mike. It has been on the cards for some while and Marcus Smith has asked me to move in with him at his house in Cookham. I've told you about him in the past; he is the painter I met at the Maidenhead Guild of Artists. I think you should know that we have been together in Brighton for the last few days, but then— being a policeman—you probably knew that all along.'

Lambert laughed out loud, which made Arabella look very angry, but surprisingly she said nothing. 'Well Arabella, you could have fooled me! I mean, I have been sleeping in the spare room for over two months now!' He went into the kitchen chuckling, put on the kettle and she followed him in.

'Is that the only thing you have got to say, after all our years of marriage?' It was one of those hackneyed questions which bore no relation to real life, a kind of indictment of the past; as though it was only a trivial matter and life went on normally despite the infidelities.

Lambert had no wish to have an argument. 'I think

that you have had more than your fair share of things to say in the past, Arabella. No doubt at some point I will find out why you have suddenly owned up to your indiscretions. By the way, did you get my note?'

'Yes, I found it on the floor by the hall stand; the wind must have blown it off the table.' She seemed to find it difficult to say any more, and to look him directly in the eye. 'Look, I am sorry things have come to this, but you must have realised that I haven't been happy for some time.'

He was still unconvinced, but realising that there might be some kind of back story, he left it at that. 'When are you off then, and what shall we do about the house?' Lambert thought he might as well hear everything while he was at it.

'I will just take a few things that belong to me for now, and then we can decide what to do later.'

It was very clear that the whole thing had been worked out in minute detail. Someone attached so firmly to their possessions and as materialistic as Arabella would never risk losing the paintings of her acquired relatives, her collection of dolls and dollhouses or her antique collection of Czechoslovakian glass paperweights.

Looking around the room, Lambert realised that much of what he had just imagined would happen, had happened already. There was no sign of any of her stuff in the drawing room, but then he had only been home for about half an hour and had not found time to count the teaspoons. 'When do you intend leaving?' The tears of regret were beginning to cloud his eyes, but not his judgement.

'Oh well, during the course of next week I suppose. If I am gone by Friday, will that be okay with you Mike?' The aggravating and condescending tone was returning to her voice as she attempted to make her obvious treachery seem quite a normal occurrence. How strange it was—after twenty years or more of married life together—that Arabella was becoming a stranger. How thin the veneer of civilized behaviour could be and when it came to it, how fragile the truth.

The following morning Lambert left the house early, not wishing to speak to or even set eyes on Arabella. He fed Samanda and then let her back into the garden, made himself some filter coffee and then headed for the reassuring surroundings of the Reading Police canteen. There was no more to be said.

Sergeant Durant was in the canteen together with one of his team of detective constables. Elly O'Sullivan looked much better in civvies than the usual garb worn by female officers. 'Morning you two, did I miss anything this weekend?'

'Two Herberts did a robbery at the Esso station by the Burghfield turn and they are now sitting in their nice comfortable cells next door. There was a domestic assault up in Tilehurst a few doors away from Sergeant Park in Links Drive and he's in the next door cell to them, and then there are the usual drunks who are due to be *bound over* this morning. Pretty average I'd say Boss, what do you think Elly?'

'What was it like in Brussels Boss?' Constable O'Sullivan was a very jolly girl prone to crack jokes all the time. 'Did you bring us some of those famous chocolates back, the ones full of cherry brandy?' But Lambert was far too pissed off to enjoy their company and finally slunk off to the counter, ordered a Full English with two rounds of toast and sat on his own at a corner table.

'He is in a bit of a mood this morning, Elly, and I think I know why.' George Durant was not about to openly discuss Friday night's embarrassing events with an outsider, nor was he looking forward to talking about it to his Boss either. In fact, he honestly hoped that it would simply go away altogether. It had all happened when he went to Sonning to feed Lambert's dog Samanda.

He had just let himself into the house with the Chief Inspector's key and was on his way to the kitchen when a voice called out, 'Marcus, is that you darling? I'm in the bedroom.' With the sudden appearance of a strange naked man from the kitchen, Sergeant Durant panicked, and then all hell let loose. Grabbing the naked man by the arm, Durant swiftly pinned him onto the floor in a half nelson. As he twisted his arm behind his back the naked man started to scream for help.

At that point Arabella Lambert came flying down the stairs—wearing only her knickers and a bra—and started to thump George Durant on his back with her fists. All he could think of saying was, 'Good evening

Mrs Lambert, I have come round to feed the dog. Sorry about the intrusion'—before releasing the bearded man, apologizing profusely and leaving the house with as much dignity as he could muster, and as quietly as possible. The result was that, whatever had happened in Brussels would remain unknown for the time being, and anything currently happening with the *Kennet Narrow Boat Mystery* would have to wait.

When Mike Lambert returned home that evening he noticed that the dining room chairs were missing and so were his wife's clothes. When he went into the kitchen to make some tea, he discovered that his Braun filter coffee machine had gone together with the electric kettle and most of the saucepans. The next morning he decided to change all the door locks together with the passcode for the security system. From now on Arabella would have a fight on her hands.

CHAPTER TEN

SERGEANT DURANT said nothing to his boss and therefore put Michael Lambert's somewhat sombre mood entirely down to his unfortunate domestic circumstances. It was well known that the marital attrition rate amongst policemen was high, largely caused by the long hours of police work and the constant emotional strain. This was especially so amongst detectives who investigated murder cases. Very often the heightened stress of their work together with an erratic home life, was sufficient for an able policeman to abandon the police force altogether and find an easier job in the private sector.

Lambert did very little that Monday morning and just sat in his office making a few phone calls. His first call was to Lotte Hendrickx informing her of his stay in Bruges. He asked if the local Police might keep an eye on the Delmar Hotel to check if the Russian woman was still living there with her daughter and if possible, to let him know when Mrs Vera Vanhecke was back in residence. He neglected to say that he would like one last opportunity to speak to her and to discover a little more of the truth, concerning her so-called non-functioning marriage.

George Durant was not wrong in his analysis, but he was not to know that the Chief Inspector was also guarding some vital pieces of evidence which he had accrued over the last few days. Lambert understood that if certain facts were to become public, they would create a totally different picture and a furore of speculation in the press. That is why he had kept his most recent findings to himself concerning the *Kennet Narrow Boat Mystery*. But there was one final interview Lambert had to conduct and this was once again with Antony Kwong.

His second phone call was to make an appointment to meet the Taiwanese businessman the following afternoon, but this time it was with the proviso that there would be no one present except for Kwong and the Reading policeman. It should also take place quietly at his London office. The appointment set was for the following Wednesday at three o'clock in the afternoon. After that the Chief Inspector chose to go home telling Durant to hold the fort. He was not in any mood to carry out his duties.

It was now Tuesday morning and he needed time to change the house locks and to make a few adjustments to his home environment. Sergeant Durant was more than pleased to inform Superintendent Burrows that he was taking two further days' leave of absence and that it was for domestic reasons. 'I don't know how that poor sod Lambert has managed to put up with that bitch for so long,' was his withering remark to George Durant, as he sipped his tea and studied the racing results in the sports section of the *Daily Express*. 'We all realise he is a bit of a hero, but you don't get mentioned in Dispatches for staying married to a cow like her Sergeant, well not as far as I know!' It seemed that Burrows was well aware of the situation, and far more observant than he appeared to be.

Lambert decided to change the locks himself and went off to a hardware store at the Cemetery Junction to buy a replacement Chubb lock for the front door, a double rim lock for the main bedroom door and some new security bolts for the French windows and the kitchen door.

No doubt Fiona Prothero would be carefully keeping watch while all this was happening, but this time her role as an informer would exclusively be reserved for the local gossips. Unlikely to have been primed by Arabella, she was still probably seething about her vacuous husband's last trip to Bulgaria and his pathetic infidelities. His menopausal status would have made him very popular amongst the current herd of willing girls found hanging around the bar at Flanagan's Pub in the capital Sofia.

By eleven that morning he had changed the locks and, making sure that he had the only set of keys available, he put the spare set into the glove compartment of his beloved Alvis and locked it up securely. Returning to the kitchen and rustling around in a cupboard, he discovered an old whistling kettle which in the past had been used for camping. Filling it with tap water he put it on the gas stove. With a splash of condensed milk, Lambert made himself a mug of

Nescafe and sat smoking a cigarette at the kitchen table.

Picking up the house phone, he then dialled his Reading Lawyer. 'Chris there please? It's Mike Lambert calling?' The old PBX exchange crackled and buzzed, but soon he was talking to his friend Chris Josephs. He was the Senior Partner of an old Reading firm of Solicitors, had bought into the partnership in the seventies and was now fully integrated into the town. Lambert liked him because he was not self-important, like so many of his contemporaries.

The Chief Inspector was not a man who admired the stuffed shirts who claimed to be local paragons of justice. When he came across them in court he found their way of thinking quite redundant and often pitied their clients. As Masons and Rotarians they might have sounded convincing with a whisky in their hand, but the acid test of their true ability was the *Quarter Sessions* and how they performed there. Lambert sounded quite upset when his lawyer answered his office extension. 'Chris, it's Mike; Arabella has finally left me and I need some advice.'

Chris Josephs had known Lambert for some years. 'My dear chap, I am so sorry, although from what you have told me in the past it has been on the cards for some while now.' It was getting to the point where most of his Reading lawyer's friends were also now divorced. 'Has she actually moved out of the house Mike, I mean, are you now left there on your own?'

'I spoke to her on Sunday evening Chris, and she told me that she will be gone by next Friday, but she didn't appear yesterday evening at all. I think by the rate she is doing her furniture removals, I will be sleeping on the floor by then. So I changed all the locks this morning and the code to the security system. I hope that's perfectly legal, because she has taken my bloody filter coffee machine and the electric kettle!'

'What about the toaster, Mike?' It wasn't that Christopher Josephs did not take Lambert's situation to heart, but as friends they both knew that a divorce had been likely since Kate and Jebb had left home a few years before. Lambert had always said to Josephs that they would stay together until their children had grown up. 'If she wants to take things from the house Mike, it would be better to make an inventory of the contents and agree between you what she can have. The sale of the house is another matter—there are hard and fast rules about that.'

'She said she was moving in with someone called Marcus Smith, Chris, apparently he owns a house somewhere in Cookham. She says they met at the Maidenhead Guild of Artists, although heaven knows why, she can't paint to save her life—bunch of phonies really.'

'Well, don't upset yourself too much, Mike. Deal with it like one of your cases and stick to the facts and rely on your instincts. You know as well I do that UK law is very clear about matters of divorce. And get your bloody house valued by a proper firm of Chartered Surveyors, not some iffy estate agent that tells you the *usual crap*. Remember, when it comes to a court case a professionally qualified valuer can give evidence in court under oath, which usually stops all the mindless speculation and also saves on costs. And by the way, you need to do that sooner rather than later Mike, so don't go moping about feeling sorry for yourself, will you?'

'The trouble is she has already helped herself to many of our better antiques. Hasn't this bloke Marcus Smith got any furniture in his house? I noticed when I got up this morning that not only have the Hepplewhite dining chairs gone, but a birdcage stem side table and the old Davenport desk has also disappeared too. She must have been very busy this weekend. I wonder why?'

Looking around his Sonning home, it seemed to have completely lost its charm. It was grey and rather lifeless. If he was to survive, with the humiliating prospect of a rancorous divorce, he believed he would do well to move out of the house shortly. But first it had to be sold.

That afternoon Lambert went round the house carefully listing every single item. When it came to his own personal possessions he made sure that they remained locked in the main bedroom which he now occupied. That morning he had fitted a double rim lock to the door. At the very least he would have one last bastion from which to protect his privacy when Arabella's magpies finally appeared on the scene. As to the rest, the majority of possessions seemed of little value to him, although he knew that they would occupy a great deal of Arabella's attention in the weeks to come.

He took Samanda from the garden and put her into the car. He then carefully locked up all the doors and windows of the house and made sure that there were no unlocked side gates to the garden. As he left the driveway he could see Fiona Prothero peeping from behind her curtains next door, reminding him of his recent trip to Bruges. Lambert smiled at her as he steered the Alvis towards the Henley Road. Very soon he would leave the village of Sonning to stew in its own juice and start a new life somewhere else. But first he had to complete the case of the *Kennet Narrow Boat Mystery*; only this time it would be for his own peace of mind and personal satisfaction.

That evening Fred Stuckey the Henley vet was pleased to see Samanda and her owner too, although he much preferred animals to people. When the Reading policeman explained that he wanted to have her chipped and certified for the EU, he laughed. 'Going away to France are we Mr Lucas, and taking Samanda too, lucky girl?' The Henley vet remembered dogs' names but often forgot their owners. 'I will have to keep her in overnight Mr Langston, because sometimes there is an adverse reaction to being chipped and it's best to keep an eye on them until the next day.' Samanda didn't seem to notice his leaving; she was too busy jumping up and down, and being petted by Fred the vet.

The next morning was sunny and so Lambert went for a long leisurely swim in his pool. Afterwards as he lay on the grass and while he dried off, he remembered how things used to be. There had been a vital ingredient missing for some time. He knew that, and he tried to imagine what that could possibly have been. He came to the conclusion that it was probably called contentment, but it was also called Samanda and looking at his watch he saw that it was nearly ten o'clock and he was due at Stuckey's clinic at ten thirty. With a quick shower and an electric shave he was in the car, and within fifteen minutes, on the road.

'She's as right as rain Mr Lampton.' Stuckey was from the old school and loved all animals but dogs in particular. 'She was poorly for a bit last night, but she ate up all her biscuits this morning and she's ready to go. Aren't you Samanda?'

When he returned to the house in Sonning there was a furniture van parked in the driveway. Arabella was standing there furiously trying to explain away the futile journey to the van driver and his two helpers. One of them seemed to be shouting at her.

Motoring past the house, Lambert tooted his horn and waved. He knew he would have to make an early start to London, but first of all he would spend a little time in Windsor and take Samanda for a well-deserved walk by the Thames.

On his return to the house at midday, there was no sign of the furniture van or Arabella. He let himself into the house; saw that everything was intact and put Samanda into the garden with some more dog biscuits. Having changed into a lightweight dark blue suit and tie, the Chief Inspector firmly closed the front door and drove to London.

Once again he parked the Alvis in the Glenthorne Road multi-storey car park and made for Hammersmith Underground Station. It had been a very tiring journey. This time he took the Circle Line to Moorgate and then changed onto the Northern Line for one stop, to Old Street. It was about two thirty when he got to the rather inauspicious 1960s' office block in City Road. Lambert walked in and was greeted by a friendly shout. 'Blimey, it's the galloping major isn't it? Is that you Constable Lambert, sorry, I mean Chief Inspector? It's Ron, Ron Trimble; don't you remember me, from Ladbroke Grove?'

'Course I do Ron.' Lambert warmly shook Trimble's hand and smiled. 'Must be fifteen years almost, Ron? Sergeant Durant told me you were here. Not thinking of retiring then, Ron, I see. Still, it looks like you landed on your feet.' Lambert noticed that the retired policeman still had a slight limp from the injury he had suffered in Notting Hill during the infamous riots. Lambert remembered that it was touch and go if he would make it back on the force at all, after the kicking he'd received. But he did, and then served for many more years as their senior Desk Sergeant.

'Spect you have come to see the Chinaman, haven't you, Major? Mr Durant told me that you were interested in him. Funny bloke really; but he looks after us okay as long as we keep our noses clean and him out of trouble!' Ron Trimble and his crew would have been regarded by Kwong as his front line troops in this dreary building.

'I'm afraid you will have to sign his book before I let you go up though Major, it's the rules you see.'

Lambert signed the book making sure that his signature was perfectly legible and then Trimble accompanied him to the lift saying, 'We will have another chat later when you come down Mr Lambert, we can go over old times like. We had some good times down the Ladbroke Grove nick, didn't we?'

There was a mousy looking woman presiding over the reception area of Antony Kwong's office on the 4th floor. She asked the Reading policeman to wait for a minute while her boss finished a meeting with a previous caller. Within a matter of minutes the previous visitor left by a rear door which led straight to the lift. The mousy woman politely asked the Chief Inspector to follow her and once more he sat opposite the portly figure of Antony Kwong. On this occasion the Taiwanese businessman seemed to be much friendlier towards Lambert than before. He briefly stood and gave a short bow, then returned to his office chair. 'How can I help you Chief Inspector?' He lent back in his seat and stared expressionlessly at the policeman.

'I have asked for this private meeting today Mr Kwong because I have reason to believe that your life may be in danger. It turns out that the body we found on the narrow boat in Reading is not that of Mr Liam Side, but a business associate of yours called Mr Vladimiro Pinero. He is the missing Peruvian Minister for the Interior under the Takahashi administration, who with your help purchased a Squadron of fighter jets from the Belorussian Government some five years ago. Is that true Mr Kwong?'

Antony Kwong was unsure of the Reading policeman's reason for being there. If it was for money, then how much, and if it was for justice, what for? He could not work out precisely where he stood and decided to play the innocent. 'I am sorry to hear about the death of my friend, Mr Lambert, because we have done a lot of business together over the years. Trouble is, politics; it always gets in the way, but that the risk.' He continued to stare at Lambert, his face showing no emotion.

'Did you know he was dead, Mr Kwong?'

The Taiwanese businessman looked around the room as if searching for a hidden answer. 'I thought he might be when he stopped sending me faxes from Zurich—that where he was one month ago.'

'Do you know who killed him Mr Kwong, or is there someone you might suspect?'

'Maybe those Bulgarian gangsters killed him, maybe Mr Side is also with them. I think they are ex-MVD. Many Bulgarians have worked for the Russians over the years. They are devious people and very good at espionage. They are good at blackmail too.'

'Are you telling me that you are being blackmailed Mr Kwong?'

'This is secret business between governments involving very important people. My company is the largest in the Far East, with resources you can only dream of Mr Lambert and Taiwan is one of the richest countries in the world. So, tell me what do you want from me?'

Lambert knew that Antony Kwong was getting round to offering him a bribe in order for him to go away, but nonetheless he went on, 'You are of course aware that in the United Kingdom, arms dealing is regarded as a crime unless of course you have a full licence issued by the British Government. Are you also aware that if you are not properly licensed you could go to prison for these activities, Mr Kwong?'

The Chinese man was becoming agitated and his face was becoming visibly pale. 'It not done in London it done in Taipei, I am just a shipping agent.'

Lambert pretended to look at his notes. 'I believe that the profit from this deal would be in the order of some 200 Million USD and that is a lot of money, Mr Kwong. Would that have something to do with your alleged blackmail, Sir?'

'How you know about this money Chief Inspector, this is secret business?'

Lambert removed a photocopy, on which the MiG 29 engine numbers were printed and put them in front of Kwong. 'I have it on good authority that these are engine numbers for a squadron of MiG 29s which you purchased on behalf of your client Mr Pinero from the Byelorussian Government and shipped to Peru. Is that true or not Mr Kwong?' Lambert snatched the photocopy off the desk as if he had lost his temper. Raising his voice, he continued, 'It is also well known Mr Kwong that the Russian Government was not pleased with this deal; but what is more interesting, is that they only put a value of 100 Million USD on the whole purchase, while the actual amount paid was in excess of 350 Million USD. Assuming commissions, transport costs, shipping and insurance of 50 Million USD, what happened to the rest of the money, Mr Kwong?'

Kwong started to blink uncontrollably as though he had something in both eyes, but the Reading policeman understood that it was for another reason. Antony Kwong was losing face. By appearing to become angry Lambert had achieved his purpose, because the Chinese man suddenly began to lose his self-control.

'They were rubbish jet fighters—they couldn't fly because they were so old and the Russians refused to renovate them. Why should I pay anyone for such rubbish?' His eyes were becoming red as his blood pressure rose and angry people say silly things.

'But you have already told me that you were just the shipper, Mr Kwong. Surely it would have been your customer Mr Pinero who would have been the one to refuse any payment due for commission, not you? Not unless you were holding the cash, Mr Kwong, and refusing to help your old friend Vladimiro Pinero.'

'He not matter because everything is now changed. President Takahashi was my client, not bloody Vladimiro. He just a runner and he unimportant Chief Inspector and you can't prove anything because you have no evidence to prosecute me either. So, why you do all this?'

'I know one thing, Mr Kwong, and that is this; if you don't pay the commission and procurement fees that you owe, you will be the next murder victim no matter what you say. The people who you have been dealing with are quite ruthless—something I know from my own experience—and they are frightened of no one. Did you know that Mr Pinero had been extensively tortured?'

The Taiwan businessman now turned even paler while his eyes continued to blink furiously. 'What you mean, tortured?'

'The autopsy report was clear. I have it here; I will read it to you. Dr Singh the pathologist says in his report:—"*Because we found evidence of large amounts of Thiopentone Sodium or Sodium Pentothal in his bloodstream, it would account for the fact that he was easily killed. Other than a number of injection punctures in his left and right arms and a little bruising, he seems not to have put up any kind of fight at all… Whoever killed him must have placed him in his Lloyd Loom chair and just shot him, perhaps from a distance of about ten feet or so, because there were no powder burns or discharges… It was a low velocity .22 bullet, much as you can find anywhere in the UK, which is why there was no exit wound.*" That, Mr Kwong, is the anthology of a professional assassination, of a man who by my reckoning had been interrogated and tortured for at least two weeks prior to his death. These people are sending you a very clear message.'

Antony Kwong could stick or twist, it was up to him. He either had to own up or to deny everything. The cocky Chinese businessman from the Institute of Directors was no longer quite so confident, and despite his featureless oriental face, a very frightened man. Chief Inspector Lambert decided to *Guild the Lilly*.

'A .22 target pistol is the gun of choice for many professional killers because it is not very noisy and does not create any blood splatter. It is very efficient and extremely accurate. Also drugs of this nature are not available to everyone Mr Kwong. These men—and we think there were two of them—knew exactly what they were doing. They were obviously trying to get their hands on some cash and—if they were successful in extracting any information from Mr Pinero—I can assure you Mr Kwong that you will be their next target. As Dick Turpin our famous English Highwayman used to tell his victims—Your money or your life!'

'Can you offer me some protection, Chief Inspector? You sound like a man who knows his way around. I have a wife and children to support.' How many times had Lambert heard that remark before?

Lambert went on: 'You told me when we last met that you know someone who works for MI5. Let me tell you what they will do if they get involved, shall I? First of all they will not believe you until you have given them a lot more information about this arms deal and the various individuals involved. If you can convince them that you have just cause, they will have to get approval at Government level in order to proceed. At which time, the newspapers will get to hear about it and start speculating on all your business activities. MI5 will then want to know all about these other activities and remember—this is all happening before they agree to protect you. They will destroy your business, your reputation and finally, they will send you home in disgrace. My advice to you, Mr Kwong, is to pay up and hope that the people who you have managed to upset decide to leave you alone. You can surround yourself with as many ex-SAS personnel as you like, but if these two guys decide to kill you, now or at some in the future, they will!'

Lambert failed to mention that he was the only policeman in the UK who knew the true identity of the murder victim, but that was partly for his own protection. He also wanted to see if this would inveigle his reluctant host into making payment. Lambert was savvy enough to realise that Kwong was not going to phone up some piffling under manager at UBS, but he might be tempted to get on a plane to Zurich in order to finalise some outstanding business by using one of the many private Swiss banks.

Lambert had one last question: 'How much money do you presently owe Liam Side, Sir? I presume he was acting as your Eastern European agent during the course of these negotiations.'

'He expects me to pay two and half per cent of net amount. He works very hard for his money, Mr Lambert. He was like my friend. But what about his passport, that is very worrying to me.'

'Mr Kwong, I have not said a word to you about a passport, nothing. If you know about Mr Side's passport then you still have a lot more to tell me. My advice to you is to tell me now—if you want my help—and to stop lying and trying to cover things up. This is my country, not yours, and here you are the foreigner. This makes you far more vulnerable than you may think and I could be the only hope you still have left. So stop lying to me, please!'

'I not lying Mr Lambert. When Pinero went missing I tried to contact Mr Side but he had left Sofia. Then I found out that he had been to England through a friend of Mr McNeil my solicitor. I could not work out why he had gone missing. Then the threats started coming from these Bulgarian gangsters. I know this is a very dirty trade, Mr Lambert, and believe me, nice people do not do this kind of business. Mr Side was also not so nice when he was a soldier in Africa, but we needed these two men to make contact with the right people in Belorussia.'

Kwong explained that after the changes, throughout all the old Soviet Republics, soldiers were stealing anything they could get their hands on and selling arms to practically anyone who could pay. Liam Side discovered these two arms dealers in Sofia and trusted them to put the deal together, not quite realising how dangerous the two retired agents were.

'Liam Side had a daughter in Sofia. Did you know that Mr Kwong?'

'I not know Chief Inspector, no. He was a very secretive and lonely man. I knew he had been journalist with news magazine in Sofia, and he told me that he sometimes worked for the South African Government. That why I wanted to use him as my Procurement Agent. He said he occasionally went to Eastern Europe buying plant and equipment for them and understood the banking system.' Kwong thought for a moment – 'You mean that they might have threatened him too?' Lambert left by the rear exit and took the lift to the ground floor.

Ron Trimble recounted nearly every event which had happened at the Ladbroke Grove nick during Lambert's stay as if it had all happened yesterday. 'Remember that famous Shakespearian actor bloke we caught down the bogs in Portobello?' Ron heaved with laughter. 'I had to give evidence in court that day. I remember he did Portia's speech from the *Merchant of Venice*. I couldn't stop giggling and the stipendiary magistrate told me to shut up and fined this bloke ten quid!' At least Ron Trimble looked back on the past with a smile on his face.

Before he left Lambert gave Ron his business card and asked him to phone if he knew when Kwong was leaving for Switzerland. He would probably be able to do that if a courier brought a package for Kwong from a travel agent—his most likely solution. When he returned to Hammersmith on his return journey, he went directly to an electrical shop in King Street. There he bought himself a Gaggia espresso coffee machine and an electric kettle.

That evening on his return to Sonning he sat in the kitchen and drank the first of many homemade cappuccinos and relaxed in the peace and quiet of his home, but not for long. At seven o'clock Arabella phoned: 'I think that it is reprehensible of you to change the locks Mike, I don't know how you have the gall to do it!'

Lambert took a deep breath. 'Look Arabella, I have made out an inventory of all the furnishings, fixtures and fittings in the house, including those items which you have already removed. I am not interested in your things or your various collections, but you can't just come here when you like and take what you want. Remember you have moved out of the house to live at Marcus *what's his name's* place in Cookham? So get it into your head that for the time being I still live here on my own and that I need certain home comforts. My suggestion is that I post you a copy of the inventory— or leave it at Fiona Prothero's if you wish—and we can then discuss what you need, okay?' At this point the phone went dead, and peace returned to the house.

Samanda was allowed into the drawing room that evening as a special guest and Chief Inspector Lambert was also allowed to smoke as they watched TV together. Later that evening Mike Lambert carefully copied out his inventory of house contents, put it into an envelope with Arabella's name on it, and the following morning he dropped it through the Prothero's letterbox. It was Thursday and time to go back to work.

Early that morning, Ron Trimble phoned the station, told Lambert that a package had arrived and that it looked like Kwong was leaving immediately for Switzerland. With this information the Reading policeman then telephoned Heathrow Airport Police and asked them to confirm Kwong's departure and his intended destination.

Taking an early lunch in the canteen, George Durant was there with Elly O'Sullivan. 'You all right Boss, you looked a bit dodgy the other day?' Lambert smiled, replying, 'As a matter of fact George, I haven't felt this good in years!' It was surprising how a plate of Irish stew could cheer the day.

Later that afternoon Heathrow Airport Police reported that a Mr Antony Kwong had left on the midday flight to Zurich and that he had travelled Business Class with a return ticket booked for the following Sunday evening. That was all Lambert needed to know for the time being, and so once more he turned his attention to everyday police matters.

At about 7 o'clock, Arabella turned up with a shortish man with a wispy beard, who suggested that they went for a drink at the Bull. He seemed to Lambert to be a little sycophantic, deferring to Arabella as if she was arbitrating the terms of some major contract. Lambert found it hard to grasp the sudden change of roles, seeing her more as the witness to a crime than participating in it. Marcus Smith was probably a calculating little prig for all Lambert knew, and was trying to play all sides into the middle.

But Lambert was very clear. 'Arabella, just tick the bits you really need now and we can sort the rest out when the house is sold. It is actually very simple, because until we get a divorce I have no intention of furnishing Mr Smith's house for him while I sleep on the floor. I suggest you two have a chat about it and then we can decide what to do tomorrow, okay?'

'Oh, I think he does have a point there Arabella,' the bearded man smiled at Mike Lambert as if looking for some sort of approval for his intervention, 'it is getting a little crowded in Cookham with all the extra things.' Would Marcus Smith spend the rest of his life dealing with her peccadilloes?

Or was the real question, how long would it be until the next one? 'Well, it seems we are all agreed then,' Smith nodded in a schoolmasterly way, as though he was concluding a meeting with some winging parents, 'I think we can go now Arabella, and thank you Michael for your time.'

Perhaps there would be no more stupid arguments either, now the soppy Marcus Smith was acting as a buffer to Arabella's aggression. They both left in her Citroen Deux Chevaux and Mike Lambert wandered home down the lane and for once, he was pleased to be on his own.

For some years he had got into the habit of working long hours when possible and arriving home later in the evening. By then it was a matter of eating if Arabella had cooked that evening, or fixing himself something simple. He wasn't a bad cook, but in common with many men of his generation he had become used to the woman's role in the home. Arabella was no exception; after all she was at home most of the day and took charge of the domestic arrangements. She shopped at Sainsbury's and made daily visits to the local corner shop and the newsagent but then so did most of the women in Sonning village.

Now it was different and he started to look forward to getting back in the evening and enjoying his solitary lifestyle. It was not so much that there were more home comforts on offer to him, as there being considerably less of Arabella. That and the welcome bark by Samanda, was beginning to help him to readjust to his new bachelor existence. The following morning the Gaggia espresso machine made a welcome change to his diet of Nescafe with condensed milk, and the Baguette au Beurre with sour black cherry compote was a marked improvement to the usual police canteen fry-up.

The next few days were uneventful, although there was a friendly cricket match on the Sulhamstead ground between the police team and a visiting team of London lawyers the following Sunday afternoon. The game was fairly slow due to the advancing years of the visitors, but at the same time Lambert felt that—if nothing else—his medium pace bowling was improving his waistline. George Durant's googlies were pretty destructive and Constable Adams showed a fast turn of speed with three out. His batting was even better, but the team felt a little guilty when they declared at tea, with seven wickets to spare.

The roly-poly lawyers enjoyed their day out and complimented the police team on their gamesmanship, by sponsoring a freebie celebration at the Jacks Booth pub that Sunday evening. Everybody went home in high spirits including Michael Lambert who was out for thirty-two runs, including three fours and a six hit out of the ground.

Monday was a different story, especially when the Chief Inspector got a surprise telephone call from a Colonel Coetzee. 'Good morning Chief Inspector, it is Aubrey Coetzee speaking; we met in Sofia with Ambassador Biko at the South African Embassy, do you remember me?' Lambert was amazed to hear his voice although it had only been just over two weeks since they met.

'Of course, how are you Colonel, and how is sunny Sofia?'

'I'm in London now, Mr Lambert; they have moved me here to the South African High Commission in Trafalgar Square. Can you believe all those damned pigeons? I need to have a private chat with you if it is possible, it's about Liam Side. Perhaps we could meet somewhere convenient for us both like Henley-on-Thames; it's quite important.'

'Do you know Henley at all, Colonel Coetzee?' Lambert was astonished to hear from this enigmatic man. 'We can meet at the *Little Angel*, if you would like a good steak in a traditional English pub. I am sure you will enjoy it there. What shall we say, seven o'clock this evening? Shall I book a table?'

'That will be fine Mr Lambert, only I would rather not talk over the phone if you don't mind and anyway its nice weather and it will be good to get out of London for a bit.'

It was also time to have a word with Burrows. It had been over a week since they had spoken, and now that the Superintendent was less bogged down with his depressing paperwork, he had become more aware of his surroundings and the day-to-day running of a modern police station.

'Look Lambert, we are all very sorry to hear about your home life going up in smoke, and well, although we have all been expecting this to happen for a long time—if you pardon my impertinence—I want you to know that we are all on your side, whatever the outcome.' Burrows was embarrassed and shuffled about in his chair. 'And you can have as much time off as you need,' he added as an afterthought.

'That's kind of you to say so, Sir, but right now I think that work is the best remedy for my present state of mind. I might have been expecting it for some while too, but when it happens...' His voice trailed off as he searched for words to describe his otherwise solitary condition, '...there are very few people Mr Burrows who I can actually talk to about it.'

Burrows cleared his throat and fiddled awkwardly with his pipe. Not knowing what to say other than what he already had, he looked awkwardly round his office at nothing in particular.

Lambert let him off the hook. 'I expect you want to know what has been happening recently with the *Kennet Narrow Boat Mystery*, Sir; and the answer is not very much I'm afraid. I am still awaiting the fingerprint report from Interpol on the dead man, but we both know that they are slow, so there is no news there. But what is interesting Sir, is that I have just received a phone call from a Colonel Coetzee and I am meeting him this evening in Henley for a steak at the Little Angel. If you remember, he was the spook at the South African embassy in Sofia. He tells me that he is now working at the South African High Commission in London. He has something he wants to tell me, but apparently not over the phone.'

'You do get around, don't you Lambert. I hear you went to Brussels last weekend, what was all that about?'

'I went to see the Belgian Police Immigration Department at the World Trade Centre, because I wanted to know more about how they operated. I heard that Side's Russian girlfriend Natalia and their little daughter Patricia had flown from Sofia to Brussels the previous week and I wanted to know what had happened. My reason was straightforward enough, because if Side was dead, I needed to know how she gained entrance to bring the child to Belgium without his notarised permission. However, it turned out that she hadn't got this document and in fact had simply blagged her way into the country. You see, Sir, I don't know what to do next, if it turns out that the dead man on the River Kennet is not Liam Side. What if he had given his permission? What are we supposed to believe then?'

'Well, we will have to see, won't we Lambert? But meanwhile, I think you have spent quite enough time and money on this case for now and my advice is to wait until we hear from Interpol and let that be an end to it. Find out what this South African geezer has to say this evening—I expect you could do with a good rib eye stake now you're leading a semi-bachelor existence once more—and then we will go from there.'

At five o'clock the sun was still hot when he returned to Sonning and once more he took to the pool for some overdue exercise. Samanda snuffled around the pool wondering if it was okay to jump in or not. In the end she went to sleep under a laurel bush leaving the garden to hum silently with the sound of insects. In the distance Lambert could hear the buzz of a strimmer and the sound of the occasional door closing in the distance, but it was still the sound of summer, as he lay on the lawn in the sun.

At six o'clock he went into the house and made himself a cup of tea. Carrying it upstairs to his recently repatriated en suite bathroom, he ran a hot tub and relaxed in the bubbles. Within half an hour he was dressed and ready to drive to Henley for his appointment with Aubrey Coetzee.

The gleaming Alvis purred up the Sonning Lane to the Henley Road, and on to the town itself via Wargrave and Shiplake. Turning right at the main cross section he drove along the high street, crossed Henley Bridge and then turned left into the Little Angel car park. Coetzee was sitting on a bench outside the pub drinking a pint of Brakspear's Special Brew.

The grey-haired man was friendly and greeted Lambert with enthusiasm. He waved over one of the waitresses and asked for a menu. 'What are you going to drink Mr Lambert?' He looked very much at home in his jeans and trainers. 'This stuff seems very drinkable.'

Lambert ordered a pint of Brakspear's Best Bitter and offered Aubrey Coetzee one of his Marlboro cigarettes. 'This place used to be my second home once, Colonel, when I was a young man. In those days I used to drive a 1948 MG TC and invite pretty girls to sit on the bonnet in the car park. I had just joined the cavalry and all young officers had to have a red sports car.'

Coetzee smiled amiably. 'Call me Aubrey please, perhaps I might call you Mike?' He looked up at the last of the day's sunshine and closed his eyes. 'I expect you could get a pretty girl to sit on the bonnet of that beautiful Alvis of yours as well, if you wanted to,' he laughed at his own joke. 'It is a very special car Mike, you must be very proud of it?'

'I did a nut and bolt restoration on it five years ago Aubrey and I think it is now almost perfect. Getting it serviced properly used to be a problem, but these days I have a young guy in Henley who looks after it who specialises in classic cars. The main thing is that it is reliable.'

'I expect you were surprised to hear from me so soon Mike, but I have always had a hankering to stay in the old country and my wife Gwen said she desperately wanted to come to the UK. She hated Sofia, but like me she loves Tom Biko. She said that Sofia was a cultural desert; despite what the Bulgarians say about it themselves, but what do they know? So now we occasionally go to the theatre—especially the wonderful fringe theatre—and we even went to Sadler's Wells the other day to see Romeo and Juliet by Prokofiev. My wife told me that it was about time this old soldier became more civilized and Mike, I am enjoying every moment of my overdue education.'

The rib eye was perfect in the Little Angel restaurant and the service was suitably low key. For a while the two men discussed their service careers, Aubrey Coetzee on the plains of Africa and Mike Lambert in Northern Ireland, the Falklands and in the Arab Emirates. He told the Reading policeman how he was originally from Zimbabwe and had served in the same Selous Scout Regiment as Liam Side which was where they had first met.

'Mike, Mr Biko and I have never lied to you about Liam Side, although I admit that I left out various parts of the story which referred to my personal friendship with Liam. What I didn't tell you was that, when everything folded up in Zimbabwe, it was me who convinced Side to go to South Africa. You see, I was by then the Commanding Officer of the Selous Scouts and when we were disbanded and the blacks started to take revenge on individual members, it was time to leave. Liam left some time before me, but we kept in touch.'

'What did you do in South Africa, Aubrey, when you got there?' Lambert could not quite see their job prospects being particularly good.

'I did what I always had done Mike, except I went from being a soldier to being a policeman. It was practically the same occupation but without any of the honour or glory. Even a member of the hard-bitten Selous Scouts knows the difference between soldiering and murder and I got sick of it. It was then that Liam decided to turn his back on his violent past and more or less became a total pacifist. Afterwards, when we had both left the police, I got a job with the Interior Ministry and Liam became a bloody travel agent.'

'Why are you telling me all this, Aubrey?'

'Well Mike, although I believe I am talking to a sort of kindred spirit, there are parts of this story that you cannot possibly understand. For example, after Liam escaped to London in 1980, I was still carrying out my orders in South Africa to the letter. This finally took me through the Reconciliation and Truth Commission mincing machine, where I was forced to admit all the terrible things I had done—things I will never be able to forget—and which I will be forever mortally ashamed of. But we are all trying to move on from our most recent history and it was thanks to Thomas Biko that I was allowed to work with him in Sofia. You see Mike, it simply proves that the ANC is more forgiving than any of us whites.'

'Why did Liam Side go to Sofia then?'

'What can I say? He was going bust in London like many at the time because the property market was collapsing around his ears. He was getting sick of Patsy his girlfriend who was fast turning into a *money freak*. She in turn was getting tired of Liam, because by then she was supporting him financially through her travel firm in Fulham. The arguments began and then this George Panov character persuaded him to move to Sofia to get away from his creditors and from this bloody girl Patsy into the bargain. It seemed the perfect solution.'

'Where did the *Balkan Western News* come from?'

'Well, he'd spent a number of years before writing articles and publishing a travel magazine in South Africa, so he was quite experienced. There was nothing for the foreign community to read in Sofia, so he went to the big western companies, who offered him their advertising support and overnight the *Balkan Western News* appeared on the Streets.'

'Aubrey, please, the suspense is killing me! Just tell me why you are really here; let's get it all out into the open.'

'Liam Side contacted me a few days ago Mike, and before you get angry, you must remember that Side is an old friend of mine. He knows that you were in Bruges last weekend and that you stayed at the Hotel Montovani and he knows why you were there. But you don't know why he is there, and you have no idea the danger his daughter Patricia is in either. Now, I don't know all the ins and outs of this murder case of yours Mike, because neither Liam nor you have told me the whole story; and to be quite honest, I really don't want to know anyway. He just wants me to give you a message.'

'Aubrey, just tell me what it is, please.'

'He wants me to tell you that he was not involved first hand with the man's actual murder. He says that all he did was to rent the narrow boat and purchase the Morris Traveller. He admits that he stayed on the boat for two weeks but left three days before the murder apparently took place, which was when he went back to Belgium. He told me to tell you that his mobile phone was not found on the boat by accident any more than the Cavalry and Guards Club tie.

'When the two killers left Belgium they asked him for a tie for the victim to wear, which he gave them together with his passport. Leaving the old copy of *The Balkan Western News* behind was a genuine mistake by the killers who must have thought it was an English magazine and therefore it didn't matter.'

With a further pint of Brakspear's bitter apiece, Lambert sat and took stock of what had been said. Aubrey Coetzee continued, 'Side freely admits to giving his passport to the two men knowing that they would use it to transport the victim to England, but he claims that they threatened to kill his daughter Patricia in Sofia, if he did not. As for the mobile phone, when they asked him for it, believing it might contain phone numbers which could represent a risk to them, he lied and said that he had lost it. That's all I know Mike, make of it what you will.'

Mike Lambert did not need to be reminded that Aubrey Coetzee was in London on a diplomatic passport and immune to any intervention by the authorities. That meant that he could not be held to account, let alone be cross examined as a witness. So at ten o'clock that night they shook hands and parted on good terms. Coetzee climbed into a large white Mercedes with a black driver, and Lambert into his Dark Red Alvis convertible.

Before he left he asked Coetzee one final question: 'By the way Aubrey, what happened to all those deals you told me about in Sofia; the ones that Liam Side had procured for the South African Government?'

'No problems there at all Mike, everything turned out fine in the end.'

THE EPILOGUE

THE *KEELUNG STAR* made its way through the Gulf of Aqaba having disgorged a cargo of plant and machinery, some manufacturing equipment and finally some expensive European luxury goods. This latter category included about fifty Mercedes and BMW motorcars, which had been stolen from the streets of Hamburg. All fifty were innocuously boxed up in 20-foot containers and described in the ship's manifest as cement mixers. Almost half of the luxury goods were destined for Iraq, together with the majority of the motorcars. By the time these stolen cars arrived in the Middle East, the German insurance companies had paid up, totally lost interest and given up.

Before leaving Jordan, amongst many other things the Taiwan flagged vessel loaded up with a consignment of 20 containers the contents of which were described by the shippers as engine parts. Apparently destined for the Indian Army and their aging T-72 battle tanks, it represented just a fraction of a much larger order for spare parts, assembled from a huge Jordanian stockpile of Russian army surplice. The rest of the containers loaded were packed with fertiliser or chemicals intended for the burgeoning Indian pharmaceuticals industry.

On its way through the Red Sea the container ship called in at Port Sudan terminal, where it dropped off some building materials together with a few more stolen vehicles. In return it collected a consignment of cotton, gum arabic, oilseeds and senna, plus a quantity of sea salt from the nearby Sudanese evaporating pans. The Taiwanese cargo ship then sailed on through the Red Sea at a steady 15 knots until it slowed down to pass through the Strait of Djibouti where it entered the Gulf of Aden.

Being a mid-sized container vessel it was not only able to enter shallow water ports and small harbours, but also to navigate along wide rivers like the Amazon, in order to offload cargo with its on-board crane.

It was a very modern vessel and her captain was proud to be its master. With seven officers and a crew of fourteen men, it came equipped with the most up-to-date navigation equipment and all the security arrangements necessary for such a valuable cargo ship to travel in safety through the Arabian Sea and onwards to Mumbai.

With a totally Chinese crew, this *cellular ship* had been built in the Ouhua Shipyard in China and with its modern design, it was regarded as the quintessence of modern Asian maritime transport. Travelling in an almost straight line towards their destination in India, the only fear that Captain Chaing had was the possibility of being boarded by Somali Pirates. These disgruntled Somali fishermen called Burcad Badeed were now a part of the Al-Shabaab—a radical Islamist organisation—which was hell-bent on capturing valuable ships and holding the crews to ransom.

First officer Tuan was on the bridge when he first noticed a powerful fishing boat approaching and duly alerted the Captain who was resting in his cabin. He also informed the crew about it over the tannoy system. On the horizon he could see another much larger boat, which he took to be some sort of mother ship. Making sure that all the hatches were battened down and locked, with the crew in the safety room, Captain Chaing decided to increase the speed of the *Keelung Star* to its maximum of 19.5 knots and to await the outcome.

Very soon the fishing boat was behind them and the small arms fire began. With bullets bouncing off the bridge and cracking one of the portholes in the adjoining stateroom, the captain realized that their pursuers meant business. Ordering the boson to throttle back, the ship began to gradually slow down. As it did the first pirate climbed over the side of the ship and the rest began to follow, leaving one man behind to steer the fishing boat.

Making his way up to the wheelhouse, the Somali pirate waved his AK47 at the officers inside the wheelhouse and fired a few shots into the air. Huddled together next to the controls, the ship's officers simultaneously raised their hands in surrender. When the First Officer unlocked the door, the pirate leader plus two of his cohorts boldly entered the bridge and demanded that they stop the ship's engines immediately.

Captain Chaing had to speak some English in order

to successfully navigate the oceans of the world, because it was a necessary language for most seafarers who needed to communicate with Pilots and Customs Officials. Although he was not fluent in the language, he understood the orders given by the bearded and sunburnt leader of the pirates. Unquestionably intelligent, the man appeared to be in complete control of the situation. He ordered his men—who by now had become at least ten in number—to round up the crew and to search the ship. 'Where is the safe Captain?' he asked in a quiet reserved voice. 'Don't make me hurt you Captain, you don't get paid enough to be a hero.'

When the safe had been located and the cash removed, the pirate leader demanded the ship's log and the cargo manifest. When he had received these documents he told the ship's Captain to remain in the wheelhouse, then taking the keys to the adjoining stateroom, he locked all the officers inside and put a guard on the door. The ship by this time was some 300 miles from land and wallowing motionless in a deserted sea-lane. It was completely out of sight of anything or anybody and there seemed little hope of rescue. But Captain Chaing knew that there was one possibility.

Secreted on the consul of the bridge there was a panic button. If Captain Chaing could manage to press it without being noticed, it would trigger an alert. Broadcasting on a range of channels it would silently transmit their alarm signal and their present GPS position to any naval gunboats in the area, or the many support vessels which now formed part of the MSPA Combined Taskforce 150.

Based in Bahrain, the British Navy had two Hunt Class minesweepers in the vicinity, both of which had been participating in recent manoeuvres with the Royal Saudi Naval Forces. It was *HMS Kingsclere* that intercepted Chaing's alert and immediately made its way towards the Taiwanese container ship. Two hours later, it came alongside the *Keelung Star*. Over the loudspeaker, the Commanding Officer of *HMS Kingsclere* ordered the pirates to lay down their weapons and to surrender.

HMS Kingsclere was a 750-ton mine hunter from the Second Mine Countermeasures Squadron based in Portsmouth. Armed with a 30 mm rapid fire small calibre gun, and two Mk 44 Gatling guns, it presented quite a formidable opponent to the lightly armed pirates with their AK47s and RPG 6 grenade launchers. With a complement of 6 officers and 39 ratings—including two divers and four marines—this highly manoeuvrable warship was the perfect vessel for dealing with any Al-Shabaab armed pirates.

Lieutenant Commander Charley Loftus gave the order and the crew launched a Zodiac rib boat. Donning their bullet proof vests, pouches, and Sig Sauer P266 Pistols, they picked up their Heckler & Koch 53 Carbines, jumped into the waiting inflatable and made for the stern of the *Keelung Star*. Using grappling hooks to bring the Zodiac alongside, the sailors and marines experienced no resistance at all and were simply confronted by a ragged band of swarthy sunburnt bandits, standing passively in the stern area of the boat with their hands held in the air.

Not a shot had been fired in anger by either side and when the British sailors had searched each of the pirates, there was no sign of any weapons to be found. As soon as the pirates set eyes on the British gunboat, they had apparently thrown all their arms and ammunition overboard.

When Commander Loftus came on board from his dingy, he firstly made sure that the officers and crew of the container ship were unharmed. Leaving his first officer Lt. Phillip Griffith on board, together with two hefty marines, he returned to *HMS Kingsclere* accompanied by his ten Somali prisoners. When these men were properly secured on board he radioed Lt. Griffith and gave him his orders.

'Phillip, the weapons we are looking for are in twenty containers which they picked up from the port of Aqaba. According to our smelly friend here they are all on the foredeck and described in the manifest as spare parts for the Indian Army. Mr Smelly didn't have time to open them all, but the ones he did manage to get into were full of brand new AK47s made in Bulgaria. The 20' containers are packed with approximately 600 rifles apiece with two of the containers full of ammo.'

Lt. Griffith laughed when Commander Loftus referred to Lt. Commander Max Kintbury as 'our smelly friend,' because as far as he was concerned that was a gross understatement.

Captain Chaing was not surprised when the British Navy officer informed him that he had been ordered to inspect the entire ship's cargo. He had been warned by

Commodore Lim, his boss in Taipei, to expect a full search if ever they were boarded by the MSPA taskforce. Moreover, he specifically told Chaing not to try and bribe anyone, especially not the British Navy. He said that they had a habit of sticking to the rules; of prosecuting any prisoners they took into custody and destroying their fishing boats afterwards. 'Don't mess with the British' were his parting words.

'What you want from me Lieutenant?' The Captain seemed unperturbed by his ultimate fate. 'And when do we continue our passage?' he innocently asked.

'Well, Captain Chaing, first of all we have to see if your cargo is as described in your manifest. If it is not then as you know—according to the new maritime protocols—we will have to offload any illegal goods we discover on board your ship at the Customs warehouse in Port Mumbai. Of course if you don't agree with this, your boat will be arrested and held offshore. I don't know how much the people who chartered this vessel are prepared to pay for demurrage—or from whom your owners might expect payment—but I do know one thing Captain Chaing, whatever happens you will lose your ship!'

Captain Chaing thought for a moment and then suggested that they sat down to talk in his office. 'I know why you are here Lieutenant Griffith, and I know what you are probably looking for.' It was the usual story about drugs, illegal immigrants and arms.

Captain Chaing went on, 'I admit that I have one such consignment on board Lieutenant Griffith. I received a firm instruction from Taipei telling me to change the destination and the end user of this consignment—prior to our arrival in Mumbai—which I have already done. I am not a stupid man and I know you British cannot be bought, so I will not insult you by offering you a bribe. I know you are nothing like those bloody Russians. So, tell me what you want?'

In the end the Taiwanese captain agreed to cooperate with the British authorities and willingly showed the young British Naval Officer which of the containers held the illegal arms. Explaining that his instructions were to tranship the whole consignment to somewhere in South America, he said that this was not so unusual and that it often happened when goods were sold in transit whilst at sea.

Lieutenant Griffith went outside onto the deck and radioed his Boss. 'He's taken the bait Sir, and come clean. I think he believes he can keep his job if he cooperates, and why not? I checked the Waybill and it has been clearly changed since Aqaba and the goods are now destined for Port Lima in Peru. It is very clearly what we thought it would be. The question is what to do next?'

Once more the young naval officer sat opposite the Chinese Captain and smiled at him. 'Well Captain Chaing, I think that there may be a solution if you are prepared to help us. I can see that this consignment was declared *Free On Board* in Aqaba and it is now clearly registered as part of your deck cargo.'

He stood up and looked out of the window of the

charthouse. 'We also know Captain, at this time of the year there are often some terrible squalls in the Arabian Sea, and that it is not unusual for deck cargo to be lost in a gale. If we can find a nice deep spot somewhere close by, Captain Chaing, we could simply drop these containers overboard and forget we ever met one another. What do you say?'

'What about pirates Lieutenant, what you do with them?'

'They were unarmed when we got on board the *Keelung Star* and there is only a slim chance that we could convict them under those circumstances. We videoed the whole event and there were no guns to be seen at any time and so there is very little evidence to prosecute them for armed piracy. We will probably put them back in their boat and send them home.'

'Where is the money they stole from me?'

'If you dump the containers as I suggest, I will immediately return your cash and anything else they might have stolen from you which we are holding as evidence. Then perhaps, we can forget that anything happened at all. Is that all right with you Captain Chaing?'

The 45-ton deck crane dropped the twenty containers into the wide and deep Arabian Sea. By evening all the containers had disappeared from the deck and were residing in the deep—well away from the FARC drug lords of Colombia or the prying eyes of the authorities—and were never to be seen again. 'What can I do with the crew; how I keep their mouth shut?' Captain Chaing seemed to have realised the consequences of his actions a little late in the day.

'Why don't you bribe them Captain?' Lt. Griffith handed the Chinese captain a canvas bag containing the contents of the safe which had been removed prior to the Royal Navy incursion. 'There should be plenty of cash in here to shut their mouths.'

After the three British sailors had left the container ship and returned to *HMS Kingsclere*, the *Keelung Star* got under way once more and finally disappeared over the horizon. Remarkably the pirates had now changed into navy issue fatigues and had even shaved off their beards. This seemed to reveal a strange white stripe around their faces as their very British countenances became exposed to the razor.

Despite the heat, the corned beef and Branston pickle sandwiches were undoubtedly an improvement to the SBS's recent Somali diet and the milky English tea, a reminder of home. It would be the last jaunt for this undercover marine team who were shortly returning to their home base in Portsmouth, their tour of duty now complete.

Max Kintbury was almost through his third pink gin by the time the officers assembled in the mess room. They said it was to congratulate him for becoming an Englishman again. 'Bloody hell Max,' Commander Loftus was in a jovial mood, 'didn't the fuzzy wuzzies ever twig who you were, I mean, you don't exactly look like a Somali do you?' Lt. Griffith giggled, 'They probably like dressing up Sir!'

Despite all the teasing, Max Kintbury was looking forward to returning to his desk at Vauxhall Bridge—

especially now he had a proper window to look through—and MI6 would seem a very relaxing place to be for some time to come.

Antony Kwong was a vindictive man and he had lost face over the purchase of the squadron of MiG 29 fighter jets. He knew that they were very cheap when he bought them, but he had no idea that they had been out of service for years. Both he and his Peruvian accomplices had been fooled by the two Bulgarian arms dealers and had unwisely taken their word that the aircraft were perfectly airworthy and in operational condition. It seemed that the amount that the Peruvian Government had agreed to pay had clouded their judgement, making the deal quite irresistible. Antony Kwong was a very greedy man, but then, so were the Peruvians.

Having lost his accomplice Vladimiro Pinero along the way, and with ex-President Takahashi hiding away in Japan, Kwong was now sitting on a sizable amount of cash. This was held in his current account at Dubrulle & Fils, a private bank in Zurich. On his recent visit to Switzerland and at the suggestion of Chief Inspector Lambert of the Thames Valley Police Authority, he had decided to pay off some of the outstanding commissions due, in order to protect himself from future harm.

Firstly, in order to finally obliterate the presence on earth of one Liam Side, he paid the sum of 5 Million USD into the numbered account at Dubrulle & Fils of a certain Leon Szeidovitz.

Secondly, in order to placate the Bulgarian arms dealers who had caused so much mischief with their lies, he decided to only pay half of the 50 Million USD they claimed he owed them, and so he transferred 25 Million USD into the numbered account of one George Panov at the same bank.

Kwong did not consider that the Bulgarians had fulfilled their commercial obligations concerning the purchase of these MiG jet fighters, and had intentionally misled him. That is why he had lost face.

The following Sunday he returned to London feeling much more confident and secure. The next morning he was back in his City Road office. Gazing at the battery of fax machines before him, he considered his immediate future. One of his more distressing faxes that morning was from his head office in Taipei.

It informed him that a consignment of spare parts destined for the Indian Army in Mumbai had been lost overboard during a squall, from the container ship *Keelung Star* and that he would have to make a claim for their loss, from his Lloyds insurers. The fax also included details of the consignment, a copy of the Waybill and a photocopy of the relevant page from the ship's manifest.

Antony Kwong knew he would now have to claim for a much lesser amount from his Lloyds insurance policy. But in so doing, he would also negate any involvement in the illegal traffic of arms to the FARC by his Peruvian counterpart Pinero, who was now well and truly dead. It seemed that he would remain unaffected although slightly out of pocket.

With this thought in mind, he started to feel a bit peckish and decided to take a taxi to the Fook Lam Sun Restaurant in Gerrard Street for his favourite dim sum breakfast.

Getting out of the taxi in Shaftsbury Avenue, he walked around the corner into Wardour Street and then into Gerrard Street itself. Still fascinated by the sights and sounds of Chinatown, he liked to be there amongst the London Chinese and looked into the different shops and grocery stores along his route. As he gazed through the window of a shop selling delicate almost transparent porcelain, Antony Kwong felt a slight sting in the calf muscle of his right leg.

Absentmindedly rubbing it, he continued to look through the window at all the beautiful eastern artefacts. It made him think about his home in Taiwan and the family he hadn't seen for so long. Then casually wandering along to his preferred restaurant, he sat at his private table and ordered his usual dim sum and his much-loved jasmine tea. Two days later Antony Kwong was in hospital and two days after that, he was dead.

The autopsy carried out by an experienced Home Office forensic pathologist confirmed that his death was caused by poisoning. The pathologist had found a platinum pellet embedded in Antony Kwong's right calf muscle containing the poison ricin. It was presumed that this pellet had been fired from an air-gun of some description, most probably a hand held pistol.

The hospital specialist confirmed that when he arrived at St Thomas's Antony Kwong was suffering from a very high fever which then developed into a coma. At the inquest the Coroner established that there was no known antidote to ricin poisoning and recorded a verdict of murder by a person or persons unknown. In the end Lambert's prediction that Antony Kwong would be sent home in disgrace had almost come about, apart that is, from him being encased in an airtight lead-lined coffin.

Max Kintbury had one last duty to perform—now he had got over his Somali adventure. His features had recovered from the excessive sunburn which he had experienced and his face was no longer striped like a Zebra. He'd been told by Sir Hilton Cotteslow his bureau chief at MI6 that he needed to have a natter with a certain Chief Inspector Lambert from Thames Valley Police Authority in Reading.

For this purpose he was advised to go and see him under the ruse of a possible house purchase in Sonning Village in Berkshire, where the Reading Policeman was selling his house due to a pending divorce. The following Saturday morning he knocked on the front door. It was answered by Michael Lambert who invited Max Kintbury into the house to look around. The appointment had been made through the office of the local estate agent, and seemed quite authentic.

'Saw the board outside and thought we should have a chat, Mr Lambert.' The suntanned spook spread himself out on Lambert's sofa and began his explanation. 'Sorry, but I'm not here to buy your house,

Chief Inspector, but to talk about our friend Mr Kwong and his buddy Vladimiro Pinero. By the way, did you know Mr Kwong is dead? He was murdered by a poisoned pellet in Gerrard Street in the West End two weeks ago, and in broad daylight too! There are not many who will mourn his passing I'm afraid, or that shit Pinero, but I have also come here to talk to you about the somewhat enigmatic Liam Side. Because, you see Chief Inspector, what you may not know is that he is one of us.'

Commander Kintbury explained that the Americans up until quite recently had regarded Peru as a pariah state, despite there being a right-wing government in power. What the US didn't want was a squadron of MiG 29s flying around causing havoc in Ecuador, where there had only recently been a bloody border conflict. By encouraging the purchase of some duff jet fighters, it had turned out to be the equivalent of stopping them altogether. With this, and tying up their resources to block any future arms purchases, it seemed a perfect solution to the menace of an escalating South American war.

'What you also don't know, Chief Inspector, is that there was also the little matter of some 10,000 AK47s which were due to be delivered to the FARC in Colombia by our dear departed Mr Pinero.' Without a need for an end user certificate and once inside Peru, they were to be sent by road to the north of Peru and then shipped to the FARC *drug lords* in Colombia by river.

He stretched himself out on the sofa. 'It turns out that

these FARC gangsters were due to make Pinero's payment, with a large shipment of cocaine. This would have ultimately found its way onto the American streets in no time at all, and they would have probably enjoyed using these guns against the Yanks as well at some point! I am sure that you will be pleased to know that these unhealthy sweets and toys now reside at the bottom of the Arabian Sea; I know, because I helped to put them there.'

Lambert looked quizzically at the action man before him. 'What you are saying, Commander, is that without Liam Side, your chums in the US would have remained in the dark over an event that was taking place in their back yard. How interesting! So, what would you prefer me to do, Commander Kintbury—stick or twist? The Thames Valley Police Authority is always at the disposal of MI6.'

'My people are in favour of burying someone called Liam Side somewhere nice and quiet in Reading, and forgetting the whole thing, Mr Lambert?' Max Kintbury looked tired and needed some time off. Whatever they said about being a secret agent, he found it practically impossible to find any totty, let alone have any private life. What he needed was to go sailing for a few weeks; that would do the trick.

He went on: 'We think that you should let Liam Side and his daughter Patricia quietly disappear and start a new life somewhere, Chief Inspector; after all, he isn't exactly Ronnie Biggs, is he?'

'They have both disappeared, Mike,' Major Lotte

Hendrickx kept her word, and as agreed the local Bruges Federal Police had kept an eye on the Delmar Hotel. 'Apparently Mrs Vanhecke is back from her trip to Paris and again managing the hotel, but there is no sign of the Russian woman or her daughter. They have both vanished.'

It seemed that Lambert had been right about Kwong. At the very least he had managed to inveigle him into paying Liam Side what he owed him. It was now obvious that he hadn't paid the others because it seemed the Bulgarian gangsters—who were good at settling scores—had bumped him off.

'Lotte, can you check one other thing for me and see if either of them has been through an airport recently; it might be that the Russian woman has left the country?' Lambert was sure that she had, but because he didn't like messy loose ends, he needed to know where she had gone.

'I'll let you know later Mike; as you already know it takes a good two hours to check through all the Belgian airports.'

The following morning the Belgian policewoman phoned him at his Reading office. 'She's flown to Moscow, Mike. She left yesterday morning from Brussels Zaventem, and there was no sign of her daughter Patricia, so she must have left her behind.'

Clearly, Liam Side had finally been paid by Kwong and the Russian woman in turn, had also been paid off. 'That's much as I expected Lotte, and thanks. I promise to catch up with you soon.'

Later that morning Sergeant Durant knocked on the Chief Inspector's door and entered clasping a bunch of faxes. 'We've just received the fingerprint report back from Interpol Boss, and it seems that our murder victim really is Liam Side. They said they were sorry about taking so long in getting back to us, but they had to get confirmation from the South African authorities in Pretoria. They told Interpol that they had lost contact with Side as far back as 1980, so we were lucky to track him down at all.'

Lambert yawned and stubbed out his fifth Marlboro of the morning and leaned back in his office chair. 'You had better go and show this report to the Super, George; I'm sure that he will be pleased to hear about the result. Oh, and tell him that I will write up my report to him later today and drop in sometime tomorrow for a chat, that is, if he has got the time. I heard him whistling this morning, so he must be in a fairly good mood and that usually means a round of golf.'

The road trip down to Portsmouth didn't take long, and the Alvis 21 effortlessly purred all the way. Lambert arrived at the ferry port and went to customs to declare Samanda's ISO microchip, her Pet Passport, vaccination and rabies certificates and then joined the queue of cars crossing by Brittany Ferries to the Ouistrehan ferry port near Caen.

He made sure that Samanda had a good long walk around the port area before the trip, because the rules of the ferry company were that dogs had to be muzzled and kept in the car during the journey. The ferryboat to Caen did not have kennels on board, unlike on other routes. Lambert made sure that Samanda had received no food for 24 hours, which made him feel a little cruel, but it would diminish the possibility of any unwanted messages being left in the car during the trip. The problem was the six-hour journey, which although good for him, was not so good for his dog.

To Lambert the sea journey had always seemed like part of the holiday, but this time it was more a break from the past. The house in Sonning was under offer and for the sake of peace and quiet, he had walked away from his marriage with considerably less than Arabella. She had convened so many meetings to discuss the house contents—together with her sycophantic and accommodating boyfriend Marcus Smith—that his conjugal replacement was beginning to feel more like an old family friend.

In the end he agreed that most of his things could go to Kate and Jebb. They were both in the process of buying flats in London, having now got good jobs, so all he took with him in his Alvis motor car that day were his personal possessions and anything he could fit in which he might need in France.

There was an opening for a senior Police Officer *on secondment* in the newly formed Europol, a European police group situated in The Hague in Holland. They seemed intent on employing a large number of British bobbies to fill their ranks and he was to become one of them. It would not mean that he had given up the

Thames Valley Police for good but it would give him a necessary breather. The move would give him a few quiet months to himself in Calvados, where his little village house was situated.

Luckily his house was of no interest at all to his acquisitive ex-wife Arabella, who hated provincial France and its inhabitants and so there was very little chance of them meeting there by accident.

Taking the ring road around Caen, Lambert soon found his way onto the Rue National 158, a dead straight Roman road which took him through the green fields and quaint villages of Central Normandy. When he got to St. Pierre-Canivet he turned right, driving swiftly until he arrived at the village of Treprel and his pretty townhouse.

Parking the Alvis in front of the integral garage door, he finally released Samanda, removed her muzzle and making his way up the steps, opened the front door and let the excited Labrador into the house and then into the back garden; finally they were home.

Later that week a letter arrived. It was postmarked Havana, Cuba. Lambert opened it to find a photograph of a man quite similar to Liam Side. He was standing in front of an old American 1950s' Studebaker Starlight and next to a little blonde girl of about six years of age. On the reverse side of the photograph someone had written:

Wish you were here, the jazz is fantastic, the weather is great, and the people are kind. Come and visit us sometime—Leon and Patricia Szeidovitz.

BV - #0184 - 220426 - C0 - 203/127/27 - PB - 9781861510006 - Matt Lamination